BONE DRY

BONE DRY

BETTE GOLDEN LAMB
& J. J. LAMB

Five Star • Waterville, Maine

This novel is a work of fiction. Names, characters, places and incidents are either the product of the author's imagination, or, if real, used fictitiously.

First Edition
First Printing: January 2003

Published in 2003 in conjunction with Tekno Books and Ed Gorman.

Set in 11 pt. Plantin by Myrna S. Raven.

Printed in the United States on permanent paper.

Library of Congress Cataloging-in-Publication Data

Lamb, Bette Golden.
    Bone dry / by Bette Golden Lamb & J.J. Lamb.
        p. cm.—(Five Star first edition mystery series)
    ISBN 0-7862-4912-9 (hc : alk. paper)
    1. Cancer—Patients—Fiction. 2. California—Fiction.
3. Extortion—Fiction. 4. Nurses—Fiction. I. Lamb, J. J.
II. Title. III. Series.
    PS3612.A544 B6 2003
    813'.6—dc21
                                            2002190702

To our sons, Clifford and Michael, with love.

We gratefully acknowledge all those who provided us with information, guidance, and encouragement: "The Group"—Theo Kuhlman, Margaret Lucke, Laurel Trivelpiece, Mary Walker, and Judith Yamamoto; for the technical details—Melody Childs, RN, and the University of California Oncology Department; and for unselfishly giving of their time—Marcia Muller, Bill Pronzini, and Marilyn Wallace.

PROLOGUE

Waiting for the right moment was making her nuts.

Ghent was everywhere today, everywhere except in his office. Twice she'd tried to get to the cold storage units, but each time the lab chief had been roaming the work area.

Did he know?

Was he watching her?

God, if she didn't do it soon, it wasn't going to get done, and Frankie would beat her again.

She used her toe to nudge an insulated, oversized lunch box on the floor. Everyone was used to seeing it; made ratty remarks about how fat she was, and why. But they never turned down the cookies she baked for them.

Well, no goodies in the box today. It was empty except for frozen Super Ice to protect the packets . . . if she could ever get her hands on them.

"Faye!"

She spun around on the stool. Ghent was hovering over her.

"Where are the hematology printouts for Urology?"

"Just a sec," she said.

"I don't know where the hell your head is, Faye, but it sure hasn't been here."

"Sorry."

It was the second time she'd been yelled at this morning and it still wasn't noon. If she didn't get to the packets soon, she'd . . . she'd what?

A few minutes later, the ER called for ten units of plasma. Some kid had been shot and was bleeding like a

7

stuck pig. Suddenly the room was a frenzy of working technicians, Ghent in the middle of everything.

She grabbed a lab cart, put the lunch box on the lower shelf, and walked quickly to the rear of the lab. Her stomach cramped as she moved into the freezer repository area, then dry heaves wracked her.

What if someone was watching her? She refused to look back into the lab.

She snatched up a pair of insulated gloves and a pair of tongs, grabbed Carl Chapman's supply of marrow from the freezer, and tossed the packets into the lunch box.

Cold sweat layered her skin. She clutched the cart handle, unable to move, unable to breathe. Trembling, she finally forced one foot in front of the other, made it back through the lab.

As she slipped the box under her station, Ghent walked up to her.

"Fucking kids," he said to no one in particular. "Imagine, shooting your own brother in the gut over a stupid pair of sneakers."

CHAPTER 1

Gina Mazzio hunched over the engine of the Fiat roadster, ran her fingers along the black wires that sprang from the distributor cap and snaked their way to the spark plugs and coil. They looked okay.

"So why doesn't the damn thing turn over?" Gina muttered.

She conceded that she should have listened to Harry, who had warned her about Italian electrics. She'd gotten pretty pissed at him—boyfriend or no boyfriend, that was going too far. She was Italian and she didn't like either his attitude or his comments. Maybe she'd even bought the damn car just to show him she knew what she was doing. So much for that.

A glance at her watch made her edgy: she'd be late for the morning report if she couldn't fix this mess, and soon. She lifted the distributor cap, grimaced. Green crud covered the ignition points, preventing any meaningful contact.

"Stupid, stupid!" She pulled a nail file out of her purse and scraped and filed away the corrosion. When she was satisfied with the results, she capped the distributor and wiped her hands on a grungy rag and tossed it into the trunk. She looked down at her nursing scrubs. At least she hadn't picked up any grease smudges.

This time when she turned the key, the car started with a satisfying purr. Maybe she wouldn't be late after all. And she sure as hell wasn't going to tell Harry about this.

Following the morning report, Gina escorted a group of

9

volunteers around the Oncology Unit, fielding their questions about bone marrow and autologous infusion. One woman turned particularly pale when Gina described the needle process of having marrow removed from your own bones to save for future autologous replacement following chemotherapy. After that, most of them couldn't wait to get off the unit, the specter of mortality chasing them to the safety of their cars. She couldn't blame them—she felt the same way whenever she really thought about it.

After the volunteers departed, Gina called down to the lab; was put on hold. She sat at the edge of the nursing station desk, tapping one finger staccato-like until someone finally picked up.

"What's the hold-up with Chapman's bone marrow? We're twenty minutes off schedule for his engraftment."

"We're still looking," the voice said at the other end.

"Looking? What do you mean, you're still looking? Let me speak to Ghent," she said. Maybe the Lab chief would avoid his usual sarcasm and clear up this mess.

While she waited, she opened Chapman's chart, flipped immediately to the physician's order sheet: "Autologous bone marrow transplant in AM—Mark Kessler, MD." "Goddamn it!" she muttered, her finger underlining the order. Kessler was overdue, but he'd arrive any minute, demanding answers about his patient's missing bone marrow.

Helen leaned out of the medication room, syringe and vial in hand, questioning Gina with a frown and a tilt of her head.

Gina's eyes widened. She started to say something to her coworker, then held up a hand when she heard the lab chief pick up.

"Bob, what's going on down there? We need to get Chapman set up now. We're almost thirty minutes behind

10

schedule and Kessler's going to be here any second."

"Someone misplaced the goddam marrow," he said. "It's got to be down here somewhere . . . can you hold on a few minutes longer?"

"Jesus! How do you misplace someone's marrow? Chapman can't wait for anything." Once again she scanned his blood work on her terminal. "His white cells are gone. He's neutropenic, for God's sake!"

"Don't tell me what I already know . . . I've got his blood work right here on the screen in front of me."

"Then you can see the problem. If we don't replace those cells immediately, we'll lose him."

"I can't send you what I don't have," Ghent said. He launched into a useless discourse on lab routine and why the marrow shouldn't be missing.

Gina listened, forcing a smile as a patient approached. The woman waved pleasantly in return as she walked her IV pole ahead of her down the hall. Gina offered an encouraging "thumb's up" and sat down, abruptly interrupting Ghent.

"Did you check the computer? Maybe someone moved Chapman's marrow to another repository . . . maybe it's mixed in with the blood units?"

"Listen, Mazzio, where in hell do you think we looked first?" Ghent snapped. "And I don't need some nurse telling me how to do my job."

Covering the mouthpiece, she turned to Helen: "That supercilious SOB is doing his nurses-don't-know-shit routine again."

She received a nod in response, along with a worried look.

"You're not the one who has to give the patient some song and dance about why we're going to postpone his marrow transfusion," she told Ghent.

"I'm sure Kessler will come up with something."

She waved a hand impatiently in the air. "What do you expect him to do? He's not a magician . . . there's no viable marrow match in the Chapman family, and it's too late to go national. The point is," she continued, "he donated his own marrow and if you can't find it, he's dead!"

CHAPTER 2

Frankie was still gone. She knew that.

Faye Lindstrom stared at the clock with dull gray eyes: 10:00 p.m.

He'd left about this same time four days ago, swearing he wouldn't be back until she'd done what he'd asked her to do. She repeatedly searched the apartment with her eyes, hoping somehow he would magically reappear now that she'd finally done it.

Fingering the bones around her eye, pushing at the pain, she visualized the dark purple bruise that was just beginning to turn yellow around the edges. She'd never seen him so angry. He'd not only taunted her, he'd laughed at her, told her how ugly, how stupid she was.

Do it again, he'd told her. Do it again. Over and over he'd said it. And each time that she'd said no, he'd smashed her in the face.

But she'd continued to refuse, insisting she couldn't, wouldn't do it again.

Faye poked at the bruise once more.

The beating was nothing; nothing compared to the deafening slam of the apartment door as he left. That tore her to pieces.

Four days!

Her features screwed into a grimace, her head fell forward. Back and forth, back and forth she moved her head, her long unkempt hair sweeping across her lap, creating its own rhythm, like a silent metronome.

"How could you leave?" she whispered.

Flinging her arms over her head, she lay back onto the cool leather sofa, stared at the fireplace. It was small, of painted white brick, its brass screen almost hidden by a bushy schefflera that had spread beyond its planned limits. On the mantle was a photograph: Frankie staring arrogantly at the camera while she looked up adoringly at him.

Only at him.

Above the photograph hung one of her watercolors. Tears sprang to her eyes when she remembered how she and Frankie had laughed together at her having the balls to think she could ever be a real artist. The tentative piece mocked her, with its weak colors and timid brushstrokes. Still, she was able to smile for a moment as she took in the safe, bland world she'd created.

Faye closed her eyes and rubbed them, a weariness overcoming her. Ninety-six hours without Frankie; ninety-six hours with virtually no sleep.

She stretched her neck from side-to-side, looked around the small, conservatively decorated rooms that were only a few blocks from the hospital. Her breathing became short, ragged as she stared intently at the rigid lines of the hostile gray leather sofa where she was sprawled.

Just like him: masculine, distant.

Although it was her apartment, all her furnishings, except a few of her paintings, had disappeared into the back of a Goodwill truck—floral-printed drapes; fat, floppy cushions on overstuffed sofas; and, worst of all, the shiny brass bed with its draped canopy. "Frou frou!" Frankie had sneered.

Now there was only his furniture, his things. Him! Him! Him, with his turquoise eyes. Him, with his long, lanky body. Him, who penetrated her soul—triggered her heat.

She felt like a stranger in this room.

Faye jumped to her feet and tore off his robe, flung it across the room, rubbed at her skin as though it were on fire. Perspiration erupted on her chest and ran down her body as she stared at Frankie's picture; his knowing eyes aroused her. Her hands rode smoothly across her flesh, caressed her wide hips, cupped under pendulous breasts, brushed back and forth across her nipples—eyes glazed as she caressed the roundness of her thighs, probed her wet inner lips.

Then she remembered; pain slashed through her like a knife. She bunched her hands into fists and drove them knuckle-first into the soft flesh of her abdomen.

"I did it, Frankie," she cried out, pounding at herself over and over. "I did it, just like you wanted."

Exhausted, she drifted aimlessly into the small, spotless kitchen. The appliances shone back at her as she opened a milk container, then stood and simply stared at it. Finally, she shoved the milk back into the refrigerator and snatched up a couple of candy bars from the huge pile that covered most of the bottom shelf. She stuffed her mouth with one, then the other. For the briefest moment she was satisfied, in control again. She grinned mischievously and returned to the sofa, deliberately smearing her chocolaty fingers on the slick leather as she sat down. But she couldn't hold the mood.

"Shouldn't have pissed him off," she confessed to the room. Her eyes focused on the candy stains as she lay back, reaching for the television remote control. "Should have done it right away," she muttered, closing her eyes. Gradually, she increased the TV volume and surfed from one channel to another, her fingers moving on the tiny buttons as though playing a miniature musical instrument. Sound became a roar of music, voices, and blares that vibrated through the apartment, resounding off the walls.

The control was snatched from her hand; her scream replaced the noise that was catapulted into silence.

"How many times have I told you not to do that, darlin'?" Frankie whispered into her ear.

"Frankie!" She twisted around and looked up into his face.

He smiled down at her, his white, even teeth contrasting with dark curly hair. "The neighbors are gonna run us out of here and we're not ready to leave." He rubbed her shoulders; his hands drifted down to fondle her bare breasts. "Miss me, baby?"

"God, yes! Where have you been?"

He slowly unbuttoned his shirt, undid his belt, then shucked off the rest of his clothes. As he stood looking down at her, he stretched his long body and rolled his shoulders.

"I know what you missed," he said, moving around to the front of the couch. He grabbed her wrists and pulled her upright, crushing her body against his.

Spikes of pleasure penetrated her groin; she was enveloped by soft clouds of lavender and purple, then plunged into electrical fires of orange and red. She clung stubbornly to the edge of the abyss.

"I can't do it anymore, Frankie," she whispered hoarsely. "This has to be the last one . . . please don't make me hurt anyone else."

Then his fingers raked across her skin; his body melded into hers. It was no use: she knew that she couldn't resist him; he could make her do whatever he wanted.

Again and again and again.

CHAPTER 3

Gina slowly replaced the telephone receiver.

In the three years she'd been on staff, there'd never been a foul-up like this. They'd actually lost Chapman's marrow.

She'd carefully chosen Ridgewood when she'd migrated to San Francisco from New York. The hospital not only paid the best salaries, it had a reputation as a leading teaching-research facility.

Now this. It shook her faith in the system.

She glanced up to see the hospital administrator walking in her direction. She almost didn't recognize him, having seen him only a few times since her original orientation.

"Good morning, Ms. Mazzio," he said, after straining to read the identification tag clipped to her shirt. "Alan Vasquez!"

He reached over the nursing station counter and offered her a hand damp with perspiration. She sensed that the quick, winning smile crinkling around his eyes was a deliberate distraction.

"Would you please locate Mr. Chapman's primary care nurse for me?"

"That's me . . . Chapman's my patient."

Vasquez started to speak, then turned and looked up and down the busy hospital corridor. Seeing there was no break in the steady flow of personnel and patients, he stepped around into the nursing station. He paused for a moment, seemingly disconcerted that when Gina stood, their equal heights brought her immediately eye-to-eye with him.

"I assume you're aware that we're having some difficulty

locating the patient's bone marrow," Vasquez said, continuing to look around, obviously worried someone might overhear them.

"Yes," she said, running her fingers roughly through her tight curls. "I just got off the phone with Bob Ghent." She took in Vasquez' silk tie and finely tailored suit, then self-consciously wiggled her toes in worn cross-trainers that were long overdue for a good polishing. If Vasquez was visiting the unit, they definitely were in serious trouble—administrators usually avoided the war zone, preferring the safety of their air-conditioned offices.

"We're depending on your cooperation, Ms. Mazzio."

"What do you mean?"

"We want this situation . . . contained."

"Fine. I'm not in the habit of discussing patients or department problems outside the unit."

"Good!"

"Now, if you'll excuse me, I need to let Mr. Chapman know what's going on. He's been expecting his transfusion—" she checked her watch "—for close to an hour."

"I'd prefer you didn't do that."

"Why?"

"Don't tell him his packets are . . . unavailable!"

She narrowed her eyes and tapped out a soft beat on the counter with her nails. "What do you expect me to tell him?"

"Stall him. Tell him anything!"

She snatched up Chapman's chart with shaking hands, flipped it open to his lab values, and held it in front of Vasquez. "Look at his granulocytes . . . they're almost flat."

Vasquez nodded, but never looked at the page.

"And look at his hemoglobin!" She challenged him with her eyes. He stood there, erect, motionless, blank-eyed.

"Mr. Vasquez, at the risk of being rude, I don't think you fully understand the danger Carl Chapman's in."

He stared back at her, only a hint of his ever-ready smile still visible at the corners of his mouth.

"This man's bone marrow is totally suppressed."

Vasquez' eyes dropped to watch Gina's fingers tap insistently on the lab reports. He remained silent.

"Look!" she said, poking repeatedly at the results of the damning blood tests. "Can't you understand? He doesn't have enough reds . . . his cells are becoming hypoxic . . . they lack oxygen . . . without his whites he can't fight off the simplest infection." She knew she was losing control, but couldn't stop. "He needs that bone marrow. Now!"

"I know all of that, Ms. Mazzio."

"Well, so does Chapman." Gina closed the chart with a loud clack. "I won't lie to him."

"And if Dr. Kessler insists you withhold the information?"

"I doubt he would do that. He doesn't make a habit of deceiving his patients."

"What if he orders you not to?"

Gina looked at the administrator; her chin lifted, her eyes cut through him.

"Mr. Vasquez, that man is my patient, too. We've been through terrible times together." She lowered the chart and rested it decisively against her hip. "I've watched him vomit . . . no, puke . . . puke his brains out . . . puke until I thought there couldn't possibly be anything left in him. And guess what? I was wrong."

The administrator winced at her words, but said nothing.

"I've watched him struggle, bully himself to find that extra bit of energy just to get to the bathroom . . . and end up failing. For God's sake, we've cried together—"

"Ms. Mazzio!"

Gina held up a hand. "Please . . . I will not lie to that man."

The air swirled around Gina, blowing contaminants away from her body and clothing, pushing them forcefully back through the door as it swooshed closed behind her.

The dramatic entry into the reverse isolation unit usually reminded her of just how much she enjoyed her chosen specialty. She'd been a Med/Surg nurse until Ridgewood's Oncology Department expanded its treatments to include an autologous bone marrow transplant program. The procedure fascinated her—it allowed patients to donate their own marrow for future use, countering the marrow-destroying effects of high dosage, cancer-killing chemo. She'd never been uncomfortable with her decision to change specialties until today.

As she entered the positive-pressure room, her skin began to itch under the roughness of her face mask. She twitched her nose and mouth back and forth.

"Sorry I took so long, Carl."

Chapman smiled at her. "Thought you blasted off to Mexico without me."

She shook her head, sat down heavily on the edge of the bed. Avoiding his eyes, she reached over and gently took his hand—it was abnormally cold. She ran a thumb over the back of his hand, noting that his skin was paler today, the nail beds drained bloodless.

"What's the matter, Gina?"

She looked at his gaunt face, then into his sunken eyes.

"My bone marrow's gone, isn't it?" He said it calmly, fatalistically.

Her heart raced in response, thumping so loudly it boomed in her ears. She clutched his hand. "Who told you that?"

He gave her a weak shrug.

"Look, it's misplaced, not gone." She stared intently at him. "They'll find it soon."

He shook his head slowly back and forth. A sad smile formed as he stared at a picture of his parents on the bedside table. There was no doubt about the familial relationship between father and son—the same soft blue eyes, fair skin.

"You know, I was totally devastated when they told me I had testicular cancer," he said. "It was so damn unexpected . . . it hit me like a bomb."

Gina gently touched his arm, squeezed his hand.

"But Dr. Kessler has been so encouraging," he continued. "He said the statistics were in my favor—the bone marrow was just supposed to be a backup." He swallowed hard and wiped at his eyes. "There's no way he could have known the chemo would knock me down quicker than most people . . ."

"Carl, they'll find the marrow."

"Everything's changed . . . so different."

"You've got to have faith. They will find it!"

"God, how I regret the way I indulged myself before this happened, and I do mean indulged—going to all the right places, hanging out with all the right people, wearing all the right clothes, having all the right jobs." He laughed quietly. "Pretty damn stupid, don't you think?"

"Carl, please!" Gina stroked his cheek with the back of her fingers.

"Have you ever really looked at the sky, Gina?"

She tried to smile, was sure she failed.

"Right . . . I never did either until this monster landed between my legs." He squeezed her hand tightly, his eyes glinted. "Did you know the sky isn't really blue or pink? It's almost like crystal . . . you can see through it, enter it; if you let your mind take the leap, you're free . . . free of our atmosphere . . . free of our world . . . free in the universe."

"Carl, you're not listening: we'll find your bone marrow."

"Poor little Gina. You just don't understand that there are worse things than death—personal humiliation, family destitution . . ." He shifted and adjusted the bed so he sat up even taller.

"Stop it, Carl! We will find—"

"Goddamn it, Gina, will you stop saying that? You're not going to find it. It's gone!"

"How can you be so sure?"

His voice now fell to a whisper: "I can't tell you. I would if I could, but . . ." He began to cough.

She poured water into a glass. When she handed it to him, his frail hand shook and was barely able to hold the weight. He took a sip and gave it back to her.

"I know you want to be helpful, but I'd like to be alone for a while . . . I need time to think."

"Talk to me, Carl. What's going on in that head of yours?"

A ragged sigh escaped his lips. "I'm just so tired." He reached out to touch her cheek. "I suppose all of your patients fall desperately in love with those beautiful brown eyes."

"Every one of them."

"We would have been perfect together . . . even the same age . . ." His chin dropped to his chest.

She pressed the button to lower the bed and puffed up

his pillows. "I'll come back in a little while. You know where the buzzer is if you need me before then."

As she headed for the door, he said: "I wish I'd met you ten years ago."

"You say that to all the nurses." She blew him a kiss and stepped into the corridor.

As Gina headed for the nursing station, still looking back at Carl Chapman's room, she collided with Kessler.

"You didn't tell Carl about his marrow, did you?"

"I didn't have to. He already knew."

He leaned heavily against the wall, closed his eyes. "God, this is awful."

"What are we going to do with him?"

"I don't know. I can only hope the marrow will turn up in time." He glanced down at the chart in his hand. "Had this gut feeling about Chapman right from the beginning. Didn't even blast him as hard as I normally do. Something told me his kidneys wouldn't hold up to the chemo. And when his hearing started to go . . . ."

"It's not your fault the marrow's missing."

"You know I always stick with the protocol, Gina. Got to stick with the protocols. Too easy to play God with these people, especially when you're pushing poisons. Dammit, I even backed off on the chemo."

"Mark, it's been a tough one to call right from the beginning. Seems anything that could go wrong, has."

"That's why I insisted on the autologous bone marrow. That little voice inside kept warning he was going to need it. Dammit! Only thirty-five years old . . . the guy's as good as dead."

"That's what's so strange," she said. "He seems to know that. I'm telling you, Mark, he knew his marrow was missing before I ever said a word."

Kessler shook his head and straightened his thin frame as if trying to realign all the parts. He looked more like a poet than an oncologist. "I've just been down to the lab," he said. "Checked their logs; checked their specimens. Everything's in perfect order. All the paper work says Chapman's marrow is there. But it isn't. The slot's empty. It really is gone."

They walked slowly over to the lounge behind the nursing station. Gina poured them black coffee. Kessler collapsed into a worn, vinyl-upholstered chair.

"I still say, there's no way Chapman could have known his marrow was missing," Gina said, handing Kessler a steaming cup before sitting down next to him.

"Damn it, Gina, forget that. The point is, if the lab doesn't find his marrow, we're going to lose him."

CHAPTER 4

Gina had just slipped into a new beige skirt when the apartment doorbell rang. She pirouetted in front of the mirror, straightened the collar of the contrasting blue silk blouse, and cinched her belt an extra notch. Only then did she respond to the insistent buzzing.

Covering her ears and shaking her head, she hurried down the hallway and did a rapid toe dance of impatience as she opened the door a crack and peeked out: Harry Lucke tousled his bushy black hair, crossed his blue eyes and stuck out his tongue at her. He stuck a long-stemmed red rose between his teeth and grinned, finger poised over the button.

"Harry, if you touch that bell one more time, you're a dead man."

As she unchained the door he pushed through, grabbed her in his arms.

"You're so lucky, Gina Mazzio . . . luckiest woman in the world." He twirled her around.

"I am?"

"I just signed an extended twelve-week contract for ICU," he said, dragging her toward the kitchen. He snagged a chrome-legged footstool with one toe, stepped up on it so he was now a couple of inches taller than she. He bowed and presented the rose with a flourish.

"Will you get down from there? You make me feel like some kind of giant."

"Aren't you surprised?"

"So who was worried?" She smelled the rose and carried

it across the messy kitchen; onion and garlic skins danced across the counter with the sudden rush of her movements. As water bubbled to the top of a crystal bud vase, she softly whistled a Mozart rondo and sniffed the rose again. After setting the flower in the center of the dining room table, she said, "Besides, maybe I was looking forward to some peace and quiet." When she turned back to him, the humor and sparkle had faded from his eyes.

"Light-footed, as always, Mazzio," he said, sitting down dejectedly on the sofa. "No commitments, right?"

"Don't rattle my chain, Nurse Lucke. I've had a rough day."

"And don't give me that Nurse Lucke crap. You only do it to neuter me, especially when you feel trapped." His eyes burned into hers. "You know damn well how I feel about nursing—I love it almost as much as I love you. What I don't love are the idiotic games we play."

She spun around and dashed back to the kitchen, her teeth digging into the soft flesh of her lower lip. She wished he would leave their relationship alone. Why all this emphasis on commitment? She was already familiar with that game. It doesn't work unless both sides are involved, which Dominick, her ex-husband, hadn't been.

She stirred the marinara sauce in the heavy iron skillet with short, rapid strokes. Why wouldn't Harry stop prodding her, backing her into a corner? As the steam from the roiling pasta drifted around the kitchen and the aroma of the Italian sauce soothed her, she forced herself to turn back to Harry, talking with exaggerated hand motions: "We gonna fighta before we eatta my home-made tortellini?" She poured two glasses of Chianti with a trembling hand.

"Why is it whenever we get into it, you give me your New York Italian act?"

"Thatsa my home."

"Well, what the hell are you doing here then?"

"You know goddamn well why I'm here, Harry Lucke."

She followed as he moved to the window and gazed four stories below at the late evening pedestrians. One moment they were highlighted by the streetlights, next they were plunged into wavy umber shadows.

"Yeah, I know. You're here running away from your bastard of an ex—." He continued to look out the window.

Gina slumped against him. "I put up with his insane rages and physical cruelty for a long time. I'm not going to risk making that kind of mistake again."

Harry turned away from the window and took her into his arms, gave her a sad smile.

"Gina, it's so hard to tell you exactly how I feel . . . I just want you to love me . . . that's all. When you push me away, I go crazy." He ran his fingers through her soft curly hair, outlined the fullness of her lips with a fingertip. "You know, in the unit they call me the miracle man: I can work wonders with collapsing veins, clogged ventilators. Dying patients cross back over the line just because I'm there. But with you . . . I feel like a small, silly man."

She kissed him on the cheek. "Harry, it's not you. There's nothing silly about you. I'm just not ready yet. It's hard to make the kind of commitment you deserve when I'm always looking over my shoulder. Remember, he said he'd kill me if I divorced him . . . and I did."

"But it's been two years, Mazzio. It's time to get on with your life. That part of it is really over."

Gina looked pensively at the other end of the table. Candlelight flickered across Harry's face, softening the array of scars he'd collected in street fights as a kid. She knew much of their attraction was sparked by their similar backgrounds. They'd both grown up in tough neighborhoods, developing rough edges that often needed smoothing. While Harry had survived to become a gentle creature, sweet and loving, her marriage had left her hardened with even more hurt and anger.

Their plates overflowed with homemade pasta; fresh parmesan complemented the hot marinara sauce; and a basket of fresh sourdough sat in the middle of the table.

"I've had one of the worst days of my life, Harry, and I shouldn't take it out on you," she said, shaking her head. Then she told him about Carl Chapman.

"Poor bastard!"

"I know. I can't stop thinking about him." She toyed with the circles of cheese tortellini.

"They might find the marrow yet." He tore his bread into smaller and smaller pieces.

"I keep telling myself that, but I don't really believe it."

"How's Kessler taking it?"

"Pretty badly. Blames himself for letting Chapman's marrow dry up."

"It's not his fault, is it? And from what you've told me, he seems to be a very conscientious person."

"He is. He's just never been able to detach himself like most of the other docs; never learned to distance himself."

"Sounds like that's your problem, too."

She nodded slowly. "Maybe so. But, Harry, you've got to understand, here's this young guy . . . thirty-five years old . . . not a prayer . . . finished."

"They can stall it with transfusions. Maybe it'll buy some time, enough time to find his marrow."

They both picked at their food.

"It was crazy," she said finally, jabbing the tines of her

folk harshly into the tablecloth.

"It goes with the territory. It's part of what we do."

"I don't mean that." She took a large sip of wine and topped off the glass from the bottle. "Chapman knew his marrow was gone before I even told him. In fact, *he* told *me*."

Harry pierced a fragment of pasta with his fork, chewed it slowly. "Intuition, probably."

"Bullshit!" She pushed her chair away from the table in disgust and stared at a diminutive version of Michelangelo's "David." The milky marble piece rested on a pedestal next to her secondhand love seat. Her eyes slid across the swelling of muscles—arms, chest, thighs. "Harry, he just didn't act normal."

"What do you expect from the guy? He isn't normal."

She planted both palms on the table and leaned toward him. "Damn it, Lucke, I'll tell you what I expect!" Her face was scarlet, the corners of her eyes teared. "I expect rage, Goddamn it! I might even settle for disbelief . . . but not stoicism. Carl Chapman's been a fighter; why the sudden change?"

Harry's craggy face drooped in sadness as he rounded the table to encircle Gina in his arms. She pounded her fists gently on his shoulders as rush after rush of salty tears stained his shirt.

CHAPTER 5

Frank Nellis scrutinized the woman: sallow skin, hunched shoulders, arms crossed over her boobs. Nothing but a lifeless, droopy, used up bimbo. A bimbo with frightened rabbit eyes. *There's something going on in that pea brain of yours, isn't there, little girl?*

He willed her eyes to meet his, demanded she look at him. There was no response.

"Darlin', you're awful quiet," he accused. "Haven't said a word since I came home."

She responded with a watery smile, bit off a chunk of a large Snickers bar, and chewed mechanically. She half turned and focused on him, eyes narrowed. She probed him in a speculative way, setting off a string of firecrackers in his brain.

Cunt's going to back out on me!

"Why don't I run a nice warm bath for you, darlin' . . . help you relax," he said sweetly.

She straightened, fluffed her hair, ran her fingertips tentatively across the delicate skin around her right eye. The shiner had yellowed except for one dark spot over the eyelid, like a clown with only half her makeup on. She touched the eye again, winced, and nodded.

When the tub was filled, he poured a capful of her favorite scented bath oil into the water and called to her. The room was warm and steamy when she entered. He was in the tub, waiting. She stood by the sink, looking timidly at him.

"Come on in, baby. Frankie will make all your worries go away."

She tilted her head, hesitated, then slowly removed her robe and draped it across the toilet seat. Stepping into the tub, she lowered herself between his long legs.

"If I keep gaining weight," she mumbled, "we won't be able to squeeze in here together . . . got to dump the candy bars . . . never used to gain weight." She pressed back against his chest, fingering the long strands of hair that floated on the perfumed water.

"Always fussin'," he said, cupping his hands under her breasts. "Don't you know I love you the way you are, darlin'?" He slid one hand down and circled her round tummy. "You shouldn't fret about the candy . . . it just makes you sweeter."

They soaked in silence, the only sound coming from the water lapping against the tub. He waited; she would have to tell him.

"It finally happened today," she whispered. "They found out Chapman's marrow is missing."

"So?"

"Everybody was terribly upset."

"Yeah, well, we knew it wasn't going to make anybody's day . . . especially Chapman's."

"But Frankie, they keep talking about how horrible it's going to be for him. You don't know what it's like . . . you're not there. I had to help look for it . . . go through the files . . . search the storage area, all the time pretending I didn't know what happened to it." She twisted around to look at him. "I almost screamed it out a couple of times."

He gave her a forced smile and moved his hands up and down her body, palms pausing to circle lightly over her nipples.

"Scream out what, darlin'?"

He watched her bite into her lip, turn away from him.

"I wanted to tell them I knew where it was . . . that I could save him."

He smashed his fist down into the water, splattering the surrounding walls.

"And were you also going to tell them that you're the one who stole it?" He squeezed both of her breasts in his large, rough hands, punctuating the pain by digging his nails into her flesh.

"No, no!" she cried out. "I wouldn't, couldn't tell." She tried to squirm out of his grasp.

"Then what is it you want, bitch?"

"I want to put it back where it belongs," she whispered.

"What?" He moved his hands to her shoulders, twisted her around, and pressed his forehead hard against hers. "Say that again, Goddamn it! I don't believe what I just heard."

"I want to put it back," she pleaded, her face a mask of pain.

"Put it back?" he spat. He leaned over and bit into her neck, then her shoulder.

"Frankie!" she screamed, pushing at his head.

He unclamped his jaws and watched rivulets of blood run down her back and into the water. He licked the wounds once, twice before whispering into her ear, "He can only have the marrow if he pays the lousy fifty grand!"

"Frankie . . . he doesn't have the money. He's going to die!"

"Listen to me, you little cunt: That's his problem, not mine." He clapped his hands hard against the sides of her head, wrapping his fingers across her face. "We've stashed one hundred grand from those other two jerks . . . but it's not enough. Do you hear me, it's not enough!" He swung her head back and forth so violently, water flew out of the tub, drenching the floor.

"Do you hear me, you bitch! Not enough!"

She screamed his name again, tried to brace her arms against the sides of the tub to keep from toppling over, but ended up clutching desperately at his thighs.

"That's the first real money I've ever had," he shouted. "I ain't about to quit now because Chapman doesn't want to pay."

"But Frankie, there are others. They'll pay."

He wasn't interested in her protests. He listened as her breathing deteriorated into ragged gulps of air and grunted exhalations. He forced her head around. Bubbles of saliva gathered at the corners of her mouth; she looked at him with widened eyes, the whites enlarging in spasms of desperation.

"Please, Frankie. Can't we let him live?"

He pushed her head into the water, dunking her over and over until she stopped struggling. Then he leaned back and let her lie on his chest, looking like a fish sucking for air.

"Let's tell it like it is, baby: This whole scam was your idea in the first place. Shit! The only thing I knew about marrow was that dogs sucked it, clawed it, lapped it up from bones. 'Bone dry,' my drunk old granddaddy used to call it." He snorted a laugh. "And that old bastard was right: that's just what Chapman is, bone dry."

"Frankie!" she gasped.

He caressed her head and whispered in a soft, loving tone, "Don't give me any more shit, darlin', or I'll throw your bones to the dogs."

At 10:45 p.m. Frank Nellis entered Ridgewood Hospital, mingling with the employees about to start the graveyard shift; the security guards never looked twice at him.

He took the elevator to the oncology unit and followed a group into the employee locker room. Nothing appeared to have changed in the six months since he'd quit his job there as an orderly. Coming in at the change of shifts kept him from being conspicuous, put him in step with the ebb and flow of hospital life—a distinctive rhythm as compelling as a beating heart.

He went directly to a large laundry cart filled with fresh burgundy scrubs, the color for third floor personnel. Once he changed into a set, he shoved his street clothes into a vacant locker. No one paid any attention to him, which he'd counted on—turnover was high among the nonmedical staff.

He went down the hall to the utility room and selected a cleaning cart. He filled a bucket with fresh water and placed it in its designed slot on the end of the cart; a mop with a retractable handle fit conveniently into the bucket. He toyed with the inventory of supplies, stalling until he was the last one left in the room. Then he went to the far corner where the bright red "sharps" containers were stacked, filled with used, contaminated needles and scalpel blades.

He untaped, then removed the thick plastic top to one of the containers. Carefully, he lifted out a used 10cc syringe with a 16-gauge needle still attached. He pulled the plunger out of the cylinder and filled it with water, patiently working with it until he was able to force the dried contaminants from the needle tip. He hid the empty syringe among the paper supplies and started down the hall toward the reverse isolation rooms.

Nellis looked through the glass partition of Room 318— a bedside lamp spilled its dim light onto a sleeping patient. He double-checked the name on the plaque beside the door: Carl Chapman.

The area was quiet, unlike the beehive of activity during the day shift. Still, a few seconds earlier he'd almost collided carts with another orderly coming around a corner. The man had looked inquisitively at him, but Nellis had given him a pleasant nod and continued on his way. *The bastard probably thinks he's going to be replaced,* he'd mused.

He continued to stand outside Chapman's room, listening for anything unusual among the normal night sounds of the hospital. From the nurses' station just around the corner, there was an occasional rise of laughter, followed by a quick slide into silence as they chided themselves for making too much noise. He listened again: coughing; the sound of a call button; silence.

Removing a small aspirin bottle from his pants pocket, he held it up to the light and viewed its liquefied contents. Smiling, whistling under his breath, he uncovered the purloined syringe and drew up the smelly, viscous solution from the bottle.

Nellis entered 318.

The released air flowed through his hair, whooshed over him; he jumped slightly at the sound, which seemed much louder than he remembered. He stood still, poised to run. *Fuckin' bitch! I shouldn't even have to be here. Can't take a chance on her spilling her guts.* When Chapman didn't move, Nellis silently approached the bed.

The dim light cast distorted shadows of blacks and grays across the bed. Chapman's eyes melded into the darkness, leaving two large holes that stared blankly in an eerie gape.

Shit! He looks like a corpse already.

Nellis stopped at the IV pole at the side of the bed: a bag of dextrose 5% solution dripped into a well, then flowed down a tube into Chapman's wrist. He examined the tubing and selected one of the ports for his injection.

He raised the syringe, inserted the needle, and plunged the solution into the tubing. Then he watched as a dark mixture of tap water and feces flowed into Carl Chapman's vein.

CHAPTER 6

Tracy Bernstein stared dispassionately as the med tech wrapped a tourniquet around the bulge of her arm muscle and inserted a large needle into a distended vein in the crook of her arm; fifteen seconds later her blood had filled four large tubes and the procedure was over.

All that carrying on, she thought, remembering past hysterics whenever she'd had blood drawn: clenched fists, swallowed screams, fainting. Now, she barely noticed it—it was the least of her worries.

The tech pressed a cotton ball to the punctured area.

"I'm always glad when you do it. You're good," Tracy said. "For a vampire, that is."

The tech smiled, her face flushed.

"How'd you get hurt?" Tracy asked, pointing at the woman's eye.

"You know, the same old story . . . ran into a door." They both laughed, but Tracy was vaguely aware that her question hadn't been answered. The tech now seemed distracted, avoiding her eyes as she turned to her IV tray on the bedside table and labeled the color-coded tubes of blood.

Tracy mentally opened a file and pulled up profile specs for the medical technician: thirtyish, ordinary, medium height, overweight; insecure, timid, feels safe with dark colors, cutesie designs.

Still at it, you dodo. She forcibly withdrew her eyes from the lab tech.

One of the reasons her husband had divorced her was for

37

this very thing—called it her type/class/black-and-white act—automatically typing people. He hated it. Accused her of doing it to him, violating him. He never could accept that it was just a tool, an aid in her work. But then Gary wasn't savvy about a lot of things, especially having a middle-aged, self-sufficient woman at his side, particularly one who owned the hottest fashion house on the West Coast.

Poor Gary and his weak ego.

Oh hell, stop making excuses for poor Gary. Poor Gary's heart is black as coal. If it wasn't one thing with him, it was another. She rubbed her arms as if a sudden chill had pierced her. Couldn't wait to run. Take off with his thirty-year-old, face-perfect, body-perfect secretary. Slender tentacles of loneliness laced through her chest, curled upwards to encircle her throat.

The lab tech stood with her back to Tracy and pretended to straighten her tray. At the same time, she eased an envelope from her pocket and slipped it into the top drawer of the bedside table.

"Bye, Mrs. Bernstein," she said over her shoulder as she picked up the tray and moved toward the door.

Tracy waved distractedly. I like people, she thought defensively. Why else would I want to dress them in beautiful clothes? She wasn't a pervert just because she instinctively visualized people and wrapped them in her own creative designs. Have I ever hurt anyone by studying a face, gestures, nationality, body shape?

She shook her head. I've got to stop beating myself up about this. Forcing her legs over the side of the bed, she took a deep breath, and muttered, "To hell with you, Gary Bernstein!"

★ ★ ★ ★ ★

In the small bathroom, Tracy unwrapped the multicolored scarf of abstract design that she'd pirate-tied around her head, laying the silky square on the sink. As she stood in front of the shower, she allowed her hospital gown to drop to the floor. She stared at the crumpled material.

When she'd arrived two weeks earlier, she'd insisted on wearing her own nightgowns. But one-by-one the satin, lace-trimmed, pastel garments had been washed and put away. Chemotherapy had caused her body to erupt from every orifice, staining everything with vomit, bloody urine, and diarrhea. Within a short time, the need to wear her elegant lingerie became unimportant.

It had been two months since they'd yanked out her ovaries, along with everything else. But she still felt like a stranger within her own body—her skin was different, everything seemed wrong—and no matter how hard she tried, she couldn't settle into her mutilated anatomy.

Running her hands over her body, she explored the blotchy skin. When her fingertips rode over the irregular incisions, she burst into tears. Moaning, she tentatively pulled at the few tufts of dull red hair on her head. It was all that remained of her luxuriant tresses. She wiped at her face with the back of her hand, swallowed hard, and grimaced from the pain of a large ulceration in her mouth.

"It's not me anymore!" she cried out to her mirror image.

There was a knock at the bathroom door, but she didn't respond.

"Tracy?"

She turned as the door opened and looked into the worried eyes of Gina Mazzio.

"I had a hunch you were in here crying," Gina said, stepping into the room. She reached into a stack of fresh patient gowns and put one on over her uniform. "Let me help you."

Tracy said nothing, simply allowed the nurse to help her into the shower. Inside the narrow stall, she kept her back toward the spray to protect the Hickman catheter in her chest.

Gina gently soaped her back.

"How could I have been such a fool, Gina, ignoring the twinges of pain, the bloating?"

"Tracy, sooner or later you're going to have to forgive yourself, stop hating yourself . . . hating your body . . . for having cancer."

"How on earth can I? And if it wasn't for my ex-husband noticing my gut hanging out, I probably never would have found it. Imagine having to be grateful to that son-of-a-bitch."

"Hey, from what you've told me, you're lucky to find any redeeming feature. My ex doesn't even have that."

Tracy smiled and reached up for the handheld showerhead to rinse herself. "You know, Gina, it's the strangest feeling when the water hits my belly. I feel like they've eviscerated me." She stopped rinsing and fingered the scars again, wishing for the hundredth time that it was all just a ghoulish nightmare.

They were interrupted by a voice calling Gina's name from outside the bathroom. When the door opened, Helen asked Gina to step outside for a moment.

"Will you be all right?" Gina asked Tracy.

Tracy nodded, but once alone, she realized she barely had the energy to dry herself with the towel.

During the past week, she'd progressively become more exhausted—walking to the bathroom, taking a shower, even eating, had sapped her strength and tested her willpower. Although she knew the massive doses of chemo were her only hope, she also knew they were killing her.

This morning her doctor had answered her complaints with a warning: her bone marrow suppression was approaching its lowest point from the aggressive treatment; he was talking about transfusing her in the next few days with the marrow samples they'd taken a month earlier. His comments made her think of her sister Veronica, who had taken her to the hospital that day for the marrow withdrawal. They'd immediately gotten into a heated argument:

"Damn it! You have to tell Mom and Dad," Veronica had said in the car. "They're going to have to know sooner or later."

"I don't want to deal with that now," she'd argued. "When they learn the cancer has spread to my bones, they'll go off the deep end. I need some time . . . please!"

Her sister hadn't changed her mind, but stayed with her at the hospital while the doctor once again explained the marrow retrieval and storage procedure. She would be given general anesthesia, then four incisions would be made for access to the iliac crests of her hip bones. A sharp stylet would be introduced through an aspiration needle at each site directly into the bone. A total of one liter of marrow would be collected by syringe from the four locations. The marrow would be treated, purged of any cancer cells with 30 minutes of chemotherapy, then mixed with a medium and DSMO preservative prior to being frozen.

It had all gone exactly as the doctor had described; she'd been released to go home. Two weeks later, after the incisions had healed, she'd been admitted to the oncology unit for treatment.

Veronica had been sworn to a reluctant secrecy, and

Tracy still had not worked up the courage to tell the truth to her mother and father.

She retied the scarf on her head and hobbled toward the bed, gauging each step carefully. She sat down and rested on the edge of the mattress, taking up her hand mirror from the bedside stand. Her face was ashen and her usually vibrant green eyes had turned to a watery olive-drab.

"God, you look terrible." She moaned and pulled open the drawer to get her makeup. Balanced atop the brocade case was a white envelope with her name printed in block letters:

Tracy Bernstein
Room 312

Puzzled, she opened the envelope and found a typed note inside:

We have your bone marrow. This is not a hoax.
Do not discuss this with anyone. ANYONE!
Talk and we'll flush your marrow—and others'—down the toilet.
The price is $50,000. TOMORROW!

The letter slipped from her hand as she clawed at her chest. Everything was separating into polka-dot lightness and darkness; a scream surged upward, but jammed in her throat; the room accelerated into a mind-crunching spin.

CHAPTER 7

Helen squeezed Gina's arm sympathetically. "I'm sorry, but it looks like Chapman is dying. He's been asking for you."

Gina nodded. "He barely responded when I saw him earlier this morning . . . vitals signs were sinking . . . spitting up blood. Just kept hoping. Talk about denial."

"It's horrible, but you've got to face it, Gina: he's septic . . . Bactec shows he's flooded with E. coli; damn endotoxins are destroying him right in front of our eyes." Her voice lowered. "There's not much time."

Gina hurried down the corridor; as she came to the nurses' station, she stopped when she saw Kessler, surrounded by the other staff oncologists, a couple of hematologists, and a critical care specialist. Alan Vasquez stood on the periphery, his face ashen and strained. It had to be about Carl Chapman.

As the doctors milled around Kessler, everyone trying to see one chart, the nurses struggled to move in and out of the station. The medication room entrance was so blocked, one nurse had to elbow her way through, calling out angrily, "Hey, move it! I've got patients who need their meds."

A pathway slowly opened for her. "I don't know why they ever called this a nurses' station in the first place," she grumbled.

This time there were no lighthearted responses.

"Face it, Mark, there's not much you can do," said the critical care specialist. "He's already moribund. And I don't think we'd gain anything by—"

"Don't say it, Joan. I know, Goddamn it! I know . . ." Kessler said, covering his eyes. "I just can't understand how he soured so quickly." He turned to one of the other oncologists and beat a fist into an open palm. "Chapman should have come through this. He had a curable cancer, and we had his marrow for backup." He looked at the ceiling. "How did everything get so fucked up?"

"I could tube him, if you want," Joan Edwards said softly, backing away from her previous stance. "We could also start some blood expanders—"

Kessler looked at her, shook his head, and turned away. "No, he not only put it in writing, he made me promise that if there was no hope . . . to let him go. Without his marrow, he's finished. We all know that."

"I thought we agreed not to discuss Chapman's missing marrow, Dr. Kessler," Vasquez interrupted in a shaky voice.

He flew at Vasquez, clutched his jacket. "If you say one more fucking word to me, I'm going to deck you, you son-of-a-bitch!"

One of the hematologists grabbed Kessler's arm and gently pulled him back. "Cool it, Mark," he whispered in his ear. "He's just an asshole."

Gina turned away, not wanting to hear more. She'd taken a special liking to Chapman; his dying was affecting her much too deeply. She stopped at the entrance to his room, took a deep breath, and entered.

Chapman's eyes were open, but he didn't immediately respond to her presence. She watched the rapid rise and fall of his bony chest—he was having great difficulty breathing and his skin had a cyanotic cast. She swallowed hard, then reluctantly looked at the bedside monitor—his blood pressure had dropped dramatically, his heart was now accelerating wildly.

Chapman's faded blue eyes sparked for an instant as he recognized her. He gasped, "You'll have . . . to take . . . that trip . . . to Mexico . . . for me . . . Florence Night . . . ingale."

Gina reached for his hand, was chilled by its coolness.

"Eh! Who ever said Mexico was so great?" She bent over and kissed his forehead; tears ran down her cheeks. "All my friends say it's not what it's cracked up to be."

"Thought I'd have . . . more time . . . didn't think it would happen so fast."

"None of us did, Carl."

"Started last night . . . didn't it?" he wheezed.

"I don't know . . . it's difficult to say."

"He didn't tell me . . . but I knew . . . something had to be . . . wrong."

"Dr. Kessler?"

"No . . . the nurse . . . thought I was asleep . . . injected something . . . my IV . . ." He couldn't continue.

Gina held his hand, stroked his forehead. What's he talking about? Who injected what? She mentally reviewed his overnight medication orders. "I don't think there was anything ordered for last night," she said. "Maybe it was this morning."

"No . . . dark . . . darkness everywhere." His eyes opened wider. "Dark . . . Gina, it's getting so dark."

Before she could respond, they were interrupted by the arrival of his parents.

"Is he—" the mother asked, tears streaming down her cheeks. When Gina shook her head, Mrs. Chapman came over and gave her a quick hug. Chapman's father started to take her hand, then changed his mind and bent over to kiss her forehead.

"I'm so sorry," Gina said softly.

They moved to the head of the bed, the parents on one side, Gina on the other. The corners of Chapman's mouth turned up slightly to form a faint smile; his eyes lost their focus.

Chapman looked from Gina to his mother and father. They were all so sad. There was so much he wanted to say to them, but he was too tired.

He stopped fighting to hold his eyes open.

Don't want to die . . . should have told them about the money . . . no . . . better this way . . . mom and dad . . . not enough money . . . too old to start over. There was something else, something important. But he felt himself dropping away. He grabbed the side of the bed and held on. Then he remembered.

"Gina . . . the others . . . should have told you . . . must help them."

"Help who?" Her voice came from so far away.

He forced his eyes open and tried to speak again, but his mouth was frozen. He couldn't even feel his lips with his tongue.

Someone had to stop him. Got to do it. Can't go yet.

Slowly, he raised an arm and pointed at his IV, then his hand dropped heavily back onto the bed. Tears welled in his eyes.

Too late . . . too late . . . too late.

He was caught in a great rush that tore him away from them. Icy pain bored into his head as he fought to repel a crushing pressure. Suddenly, he was released. He floated up where he could look down on his parents, holding each other, crying.

Don't be sad, Dad . . . Mom . . . I'm here.

He saw Gina bend over him, gently close his eyes. She moved slowly around to his parents, wrapped her arms around their shoulders.

Don't be sad, Gina.

He tried to return, to stand in the room with them. Each time he was held back, becoming more and more disconnected.

He curled into a ball, caught in a cocoon of sadness.

Extending a hand downward, he tried to hold on. But now they were gone, shadowy forms melding into a vast darkness.

CHAPTER 8

Gina sprawled on the living room floor next to the coffee table and rested her cards on the table, waiting for Harry to discard. They were into their fourth game of 500 rummy. She pulled at her tattered jeans, twisting and untwisting loose threads until little knots of cotton interlaced with the shredded material over her knees.

The table had been cleared of everything except a large bottle of chardonnay, a basket of crackers, and a ball of provolone. She impatiently reached for a knife and cut them each a large chunk of cheese, then tore off the surrounding wax.

"Harry, this isn't chess. Just throw out a card . . . any card."

"Oh, no you don't, Mazzio. I'm through playing just any old way." He rubbed his bare chest. "You've already won everything except my jeans and Jockey shorts. You've only lost your blouse. So I'm not going to give you just any card."

An hour later, when they were down to only panties and shorts, Harry cried out, "Aha! Rummy!" He spread his cards on the table and checked her hand. "Looks like you literally lost your pants on that one."

"I should have known it. You always win in the end." She lay back and slipped out of her panties and threw them at him.

"Somewhat of an exaggeration, my dear. But I do have years of experience at this game." He rubbed her panties against his cheek. "Nice." Sipping from his wine glass, he

48

looked wickedly at her. Her hair was disheveled from pulling absentmindedly at her curls and her eyes were red-rimmed.

"And what game is that?"

"Get Naked Rummy, of course . . . been playing it since nursing school."

"Part of the official curriculum, no doubt. I can see the course description now: Nursing 101. 'Getting Down and Dirty.' Bet there was a run on enrollment."

"Mazzio, sometimes you're too cynical." He scooted around the table next to her and took his underwear off with a flourish. "How about, 'The Dynamics of Being Human'?"

"Harry, you're a flake, and you didn't need to take off anything else. The game's over."

Ignoring her, he said, "Nakedness is part of it. People aren't really equal with their clothes on."

"Did you say this is something you did with your class-mates?"

"There was a group of us, three guys and ten gals. We were in the same college dorm, all nursing students." He reached for the wedge of cheese Gina offered and took a large bite. "It started out as fun and games, then turned into something very serious."

"Thirteen naked serious people?"

"Yes, thirteen naked serious people," he said, gently pinching her cheek. "It became a problem-solving forum. It's strangely soothing being surrounded by naked people holding your hands, hugging you."

"I'll bet!"

"It certainly wasn't what you're thinking, Mazzio. It was very asexual."

"And you were all student nurses?"

He nodded. "In our final year. Not exactly a time of wine and roses. When things got too difficult . . . well, anyone in the group could call a sit-in. And we had a lot of them."

"But why naked?" she asked, filling her glass with more wine.

"Clothes encourage pretensions. They cover up how we really feel, mask who we really are."

"What did you talk about, personal problems?"

"Rarely. The group was more into gut-wrenching issues, things we still talk about today: death and dying, AIDS, euthanasia—"

"—cancer, losing patients, losing hope." She burst into tears, squeezed her eyes shut, wrapped her arms around his waist, and burrowed her head into his chest.

"Yeah," he said, gently gliding his fingers lightly over the fine hairs of her arms. "It's all part of the same thing."

"God, does it ever get easier?" She lifted her head to look into his eyes.

He smiled, his sapphire eyes looking very ancient. "Only if you don't give a rat's ass, love."

They held each other for a long time, rocking gently back and forth.

She broke the mood by reaching for the wine, emptying the bottle into her glass.

"This stuff's getting to me," she said after taking a sip. She stared speculatively up from the floor at her sculpture of Michelangelo's David. "Did I ever tell you about the first time I saw the real thing?"

"I don't remember."

"Caught you, Harry Lucke. And you say you hang on my every word."

"Oh, I do. Particularly when you call me things like sensational, sexy, sensitive. Things that point to just some of my admirable qualities."

She sat up, reached for the sculpture and brought it to the floor.

" 'Yet shall not vauntful Death enjoy the prize,' " she said.

"Interesting. Your very own?"

"I should be so lucky. Michelangelo wrote it; one of his sonnets." She ran her fingers over the David. "Isn't he beautiful?"

Harry nodded, then ran his fingertips across her cheek. "No, he's interesting. You're beautiful."

"When I saw him at the Accademia in Florence, he took my breath away."

"Something you continually do to me."

"I don't know why I identified with him. I mean, he's obviously quite male."

"Something you're obviously not," he said, nuzzling her neck.

"No, but I knew standing before that sixteen-foot sculpture just what David must have felt. Strong, noble . . . sure of what had to be done . . . yet, exposed and vulnerable." She put the sculpture down, turned to him. "I don't feel strong or noble anymore, Harry. Only vulnerable."

He held her eyes as he finished his cheese, reached for her wine glass and stole a sip. "Welcome to the grown-up world, beautiful," he finally said.

She gave him a perplexed look.

"How old were you when you first saw your sling-toting friend?"

"Nineteen."

"Yeah, well . . . behold the arrogance of youth," Harry said.

"What do you mean?"

"What is death to some healthy, snot-nosed kid? They don't feel vulnerable or afraid."

"What are you talking about?"

"You think David was noble for putting his life on the line?"

"Maybe. I'm not sure."

"You watched Carl die. You knew there was nothing noble about it. So what's the difference whether it's from cancer, a bullet, or a slingshot?"

"And you call me a cynic?"

He bent over and gave her a long, lingering kiss. "I'm not a cynic. I'm a realist. We give the best we can to every patient, but they still die. And their deaths make us feel vulnerable. That feeling is never going to go away, Gina. Not if you have a healthy respect for death."

She lay silent for a long time, her fingers caressing the sculpture. Finally, she set it aside and wrapped her arms around him, squeezing him to her while she covered his face with loud smacking kisses. "Someday I think I might have to admit I love you."

"Someday, my beautiful Italian princess, you'll not only admit it, you'll scream it from the rooftops."

Gina awakened with a jolt, her thoughts filled with Carl Chapman. She glanced at the clock, then at Harry, who had decided to spend the night. It had been only three hours since they'd curled up for sleep. She lay there tossing and turning until she finally gave up and crawled out of bed. She stood at the bedroom window, bathed in moonlight, looking out at the bright night sky.

It reminded her of when she was a little girl and her father would waken her on hot summer nights. They would sneak up to the roof of their apartment house and he would tell her about the magic of the different constellations spread throughout the endless universe.

Tonight, Orion's belt blinked back at her and she smiled at her remembrances before she turned away.

Padding through the dark apartment into the kitchen, she stood before the open door of the refrigerator, the escaping cold making her shiver. She reached in and retrieved a container of milk.

Light from the range clock barely penetrated the darkness as she felt her way into the living room. She collapsed on the sofa, milk container in hand. Almost immediately, she heard Harry's footsteps scuffing down the hallway.

"What's the matter, doll?" he asked, plopping down next to her. "Can't sleep?"

"It keeps niggling at me."

"What?"

"It's just not right, you know? It keeps running through my head, plaguing me."

"What?"

"Carl, how he knew his marrow was missing." She tipped up the carton and took a gulp of milk. When she finished, Harry reached over and wiped away a trickle from her chin. "I just can't accept it," she said, ignoring him. "I don't even understand it."

"Gina! You've got to let this go, once and for all."

"I can't."

"You've got to, for your own peace of mind."

"All right, I will. I promise. But only if you can explain how a huge hospital with all its grants and complicated research, checks and double checks, can lose a patient's bone marrow."

"You've just explained how. It's a complicated system. Things go wrong."

"No, Harry. There's something else going on here. I feel it." She set the milk carton down on the coffee table and washed her face with her hands. "I can still see the look in Carl's eyes when he told me that his marrow was missing. He knew. But how? When I asked him, he wouldn't say."

"Wouldn't or couldn't? And is it any different than someone saying, 'If anything had to go wrong, it would naturally happen to me'?"

"That's a cop-out, Harry. Carl wasn't like that. He'd gone through a lot of pain and suffering, but he was still an optimist—at least until the day his marrow disappeared. That was the day he gave up."

"I think you're reading too much into it."

"That isn't all . . . today, just before he died, he tried to tell me something."

"What?"

"It had to do with his IV . . . he even pointed to it just before he died."

Harry pulled her to him. "Gina, it's all over. There's nothing you can do about it now."

"I'm not so sure about that."

CHAPTER 9

Gary Bernstein was more than an hour late as he strode past his newly hired secretary, barely nodding hello. She trailed behind him into his office, watched as he took off his corduroy jacket, threw it haphazardly across a chair, then unrolled a large sheaf of naval architectural drawings. As she waited for him to acknowledge her, she looked out the wall of windows that provided a spectacular view of the bay and the Port of San Francisco. When he finally finished weighing down the curled papers with large Lucite blocks, she said, "There's a Tracy Bernstein who's been calling every five minutes. A relative of yours?" She looked at him expectantly, but when she received no reply, she continued, frowning. "Look, Mr. Bernstein. I don't want to hound you . . . but I just started this job two days ago. I'm going to need some kind of input from you for a while."

He looked at her with gray stormy eyes underlined with dark circles.

"I'm sorry, Dotti," he finally said with a weak smile. "I don't mean to be distant." He collapsed into his desk chair, leaned back, and ran a trembling hand through his unkempt hair. "I'm just so behind." He pointed to the blueprint of a ship propulsion system atop the pile of drawings. "That little baby should have been ready a week ago."

"Is there anything I can do to help?"

"There will be. But for now, I'd appreciate it if you would just bring some coffee."

"How do you like it?" she asked.

"Cream and plenty of sugar." Before she could leave, he

said, "By the way, Tracy Bernstein's my ex-wife."

Dotti nodded. "I thought so. She seemed very upset. The last time she called, she asked me to tell you that everything is in tiny black boxes . . . does that make sense?"

He compressed his face with the palms of both hands and whispered, "Yes, it makes sense. Thank you."

After she left for the coffee, he stared long and hard at the telephone. He was totally exhausted, not remotely up to talking to anyone, particularly Tracy. But her using that phrase left him no choice . . . neither of them had ever failed to respond to that private signal, no matter how angry, no matter what the situation. Now, the longer he waited to return the call, the more stymied, the more helpless he felt.

"Hope this is okay," Dotti said, setting a steaming mug in front of him.

Gary nodded his thanks, indicated she should sit down.

She slipped into the sculptured leather chair directly across from him, and sipped from her own cup of coffee. "I've been known to be a good listener, if you need one," she said.

Gary stared at her speculatively. She didn't look anything like Shelly, whose job she'd taken. This woman was middle-aged, ordinary looking, probably would never turn a head. Shelly? She was another matter. You couldn't ignore her if you wanted to: voluptuous curves, shapely long legs, corn-colored hair that draped around her face like finely woven silk. You had to resist the urge to touch her to see if she was real. Now, he truly saw his new assistant for the first time since he'd hired her. No glitter, no flash, but she had disarming warmth.

"Since my divorce," he said, "everything has been a little out of whack. No . . . a lot out of whack."

She waited for him to continue. When he didn't, she asked: "How long has it been?"

He picked up one of the Lucite blocks, turned it from one side to the other, held it up to the light. "Three months and four days," he said.

"Was it a long relationship?" she asked, adding more sugar to her coffee.

"Nineteen big ones." He stood abruptly and drifted over to the window, coffee mug in hand. It was a foggy day on the bay, filled with various shades of gray—moody, like a monochromatic Turner painting. "Know why it ended?" he asked, turning his head toward her.

She shook her head, straightened the lapel of her checked jacket, and pressed further back into the chair.

"I suddenly found myself the center of someone else's world for the first time in my life. I counted more than anything else. Anything!"

"Sounds like a pretty compelling reason."

He retreated from the window and slipped back into his desk chair, put his feet up on the edge of the desk. "Yeah, well, if that had been the real reason, maybe it would have made sense. The truth of it is, I just plain got . . . entangled."

"I'm not sure I understand."

"I got involved with the excitement of being with a new, young, beautiful woman." He ran his fingertips along the stubble of his beard. "She made me feel so incredibly talented, intelligent, witty . . . didn't second-guess every decision I made. There were so many differences between her and Tracy . . ." His voice trailed off, leaving his face in a deep frown.

Dotti looked at him noncommittally and set her coffee cup on the edge of his desk. "If you found the right person, what's the problem?"

"I'm not sure I did," he said. "It all happened while I was still married to Tracy. The two of us—Shelly and I—spent most of our time either sneaking around or—" He stopped, washed his face back-and-forth with one hand, then continued in a soft voice, "—in the sack."

"But you're divorced now, Mr. Bernstein," she said, raising her hands, palms up. "You're free to see whoever you want."

"You're right, I am divorced. Divorced . . . and miserable." He looked intently at his assistant, whose eyebrows were raised questioningly. "Shelly dotes on me . . . hangs on my every word . . . and bores me to tears!" He crashed his hand down on the desk. "Damn it! It's not Shelly. I can't sleep . . . I can't work. All I do is worry about Tracy . . . worry about whether she's going to live or die."

"Die?"

"She has cancer." He spun his chair around and looked out at the fog shrouded bay. "I feel so Goddamned guilty leaving her all alone at a time like this . . . it's all my fault . . . if I'd been there for her . . ." Loud, choking sobs suddenly shook his body.

Dotti rose slowly from her chair and walked around his desk to place her hands tentatively on his shoulders.

"Damn it, Trace," he whispered. "How could I have fucked things up so badly?"

The phone was picked up on the first ring. Tracy, in a tremulous voice, asked, "Gary? Is that you?"

"Trace?" he queried, barely recognizing her voice. "What's the matter . . . what's going on—"

"You've got to help me, Gary," she interrupted. "Promise me you will." Anguished wails exploded in the phone; she continued in gulps: "You've got to help me . . . help me—"

"Tracy, stop a minute! Tell me—"

"Don't have anyone I can turn to, but you . . . know I wouldn't ask—"

"Tracy! Whatever it is, I'll do it. For God's sake, don't cry . . . please! Don't cry anymore."

"Okay, okay!" There was a long moment of muted sobs. "I'm trying. Give me a minute."

"Tracy? I'll come down. We can talk."

"No! Don't do that, Gary. Don't do it! I don't have much time."

CHAPTER 10

A heavy sigh escaped Faye's lips as she exited Ridgewood Hospital. Dazed by a sudden sense of freedom and the cool fresh air, she looked around aimlessly at the people walking down the hospital pathways. Mostly, she was among weary nurses in white, sagging uniforms. But interspersed in the crowd were other staff, some technicians like herself. She nodded automatically, pasting a pleasant smile on her face for several people she knew.

She stared up at the sun and when she looked away, green dots danced before her dazzled eyes. For just a moment she allowed herself to drift, to forget about Frankie, the day's smart-ass comments about her black eye, and Bob Ghent's constant nit-picking. Then she blended seamlessly with the pedestrian flow that pulled her away from the hospital grounds.

It was an eternity since the start of the day when she had donned her own crisp lab coat. She visualized it now as she had left it behind in a heap, buried in a laundry cart, grimy, heavily coated with blood.

Her mind bounced from one isolated thought to another, trying to find a focus.

Then she remembered: Chapman died!

She swallowed a bubbling, metallic taste and reached to soothe the pain that stabbed her head. The realization finally penetrated her consciousness.

There's no turning back.

On hearing of Carl Chapman's death, a numbness had overcome her, allowing three tubes of blood to slip through her fingers; some of the dangerous fluid had splashed into her eyes as the vials shattered on a work counter. Most of the rest of the day had been a mess of getting medical treatment and filling out the necessary paperwork for documenting the accident—just in case she turned up HIV positive.

Her mind probed the horrible thought once more:

Chapman's dead!

An icy chill made her shiver inside her thick, gray sweater.

Nothing will ever be right again.

She forced one leg in front of the other—visions of Chapman accompanied her on the route back to her apartment:

She'd been called to help collect blood from the dying man. That ghastly face with the haunted eyes seemed to blame her; she'd bitten her tongue to keep from crying out, from bolting out of the room. Even now, she could see that ghostly face searching for her, accusing her.

She jumped as someone touched her shoulder. "Are you all right, miss?" a kindly old man asked. "You don't look well."

She mumbled a reply and staggered away with her head down.

The raucous beeping of a car horn jolted her, made her look up. She turned and saw one of the oncology nurses waving at her from a red Fiat.

"Hey! Want a lift?"

She shook her head. "I just have a short way to go."

The nurse laughed. "So what. Hop in!"

She hesitated, shrugged her shoulders.

The woman leaned over and opened the passenger door. "I see you up on the floor a lot, but I'm afraid I don't know your name." She held out a hand: "I'm Gina Mazzio."

"Faye Lindstrom," she said with a tentative smile, then stared straight ahead.

A car pulled up behind them; the driver lightly sounded his horn. Mazzio gave him a winning smile and waved him around.

"You can tell me to butt out, Faye," Mazzio said, gently touching her arm, "but you look like you could use a lift. That's why I stopped."

"That's nice of you." Her bruised eye throbbed in a stabbing rhythm with each word she uttered. She fingered the bones around it; a comfort habit she'd fallen into in the last couple of days. "But I'm all right. It's just been a horrible day."

"One of the worst," Gina agreed.

Faye pointed down the street. "That's my building, over there."

"So, hop in anyway."

After she slid into the seat, the nurse touched her arm again. "Are you sure you're all right?"

She looked into Gina's concerned eyes and tried to remember the last time she'd had a heart-to-heart with anyone—her friends just seemed to melt away when Frankie moved in. She hadn't realized until this moment just how alone and afraid she was.

"I'm fine. I just need some rest."

Gina found a parking place in front of Faye's apartment building, cut the ignition, and reached into her purse. "Here. Take my card. Call me if you need any help."

Faye fingered the card, smiled when she saw the plunger of a large syringe pushing Gina's name, address, and telephone number toward the needle end of the cylinder.

Faye hesitated only for a second, but then the words just

seemed to fly from her mouth: "Would you like to come in for a cup of coffee?"

Gina looked as though she would make some excuse to get out of it, then quickly smiled. "Yeah, sure." Her hand swept out. "Can't waste a good parking place, can we?"

The lab tech reached out with her key, but the apartment door was jerked open before she could insert it in the lock. A tall, lanky man in his late twenties, dressed in jeans and a sweat shirt declaring, THEY'RE ALL BIMBOS, stood at the entry. He'd obviously been waiting, listening for Faye.

"It's about time, darlin'. I'd begun to worry about you."

Gina watched the woman cringe, automatically finger her eye before he turned his attention to her.

"Come on in," he said, "I'm Frank Nellis."

"Gina Mazzio," she said without offering her hand.

Studying his biting gaze, her mind was flooded with images of green glacial waters. She'd been aware of the speculative gossip involving the lab tech's black eye, and she had to admit it had been curiosity more than kindness that had caused her to offer Faye a ride. Now, having met the bastard who must have hurt Faye, she felt a sense of kinship with the lab tech. Gina sucked in her stomach, pulled herself up to her full height.

"Thanks." She turned away. "Faye, I'd love that cup of coffee you offered."

She sat on the leather sofa while the couple went into the kitchen. Looking around, she noted everything was orderly, tasteful, and strangely empty. When she looked toward the kitchen, Frank Nellis' eyes were invading her—examining, probing with the same calculating scrutiny she'd last seen in her ex-husband's hate-filled gaze.

★ ★ ★ ★ ★

"How many times have I told you I don't want your stupid friends here," Frank hissed in Faye's ear as she fixed the coffee.

"I'll bring home anyone I want. This is my place," she said in a rare flash of anger. "Remember?"

The pig is going to foul up everything.

He gently took her arm and pressed his nails into the soft flesh. She tried to shuck him off, but he curled the nails deeper.

"Gina?" she called out in a quivering voice. He quickly released his grip. "How do you take your coffee?"

"Black is fine," came the answer.

Faye slipped by him with the coffee tray, her shoulders squared.

In the living room, he sat with them and half-listened to their silly conversation, nodding at appropriate moments. Mainly, he watched Gina, taking her inventory.

Not bad looking, if you liked the grease-ball type; thirties; tall, maybe 5-10, or more; sturdy; solid. Too bad. He liked his women soft, compliant.

This one held her chin up. Alert. Ready to spring. The bitch would fight, if she had to, quick and dirty. He wanted her out of the apartment. And she'd better never come back.

Faye closed the door behind Gina. It took her a moment to find the courage to turn around to face him. All the defiance she'd felt minutes earlier had evaporated.

"Why did you bring that bimbo here?" Frankie asked, tugging gently at her hand, pulling her away from the apartment door back toward the living room.

"She's just one of the nurses at the hospital."

"I could see that, darlin'."

"She offered me a ride, Frankie. Don't be mad."

"But baby, I'm not mad," he said, unbuttoning her skirt, pulling her out of her sweater. "We practically live on top of the hospital, darlin', why did you need a ride?" His arms drew her to him; he kissed her neck, murmured soft sounds into her hair with a husky, swollen voice.

This was the Frankie she'd fallen in love with months before all this bone marrow stuff started. Tears filled her eyes. "Frankie, the Chapman man died today," she whispered.

"Served the son-of-a-bitch right," he said, entwining her hair around his fingers. "All he had to do was pay. It's not our fault he was so stupid."

"But Frankie—"

"Pull my clothes off, baby." He yanked gently at her hair as she undid his pants. "Put your hands in there . . . yeah . . . that's good . . . that's great!"

"Frankie, I'm scared." His lips moved over her body, his fingers probed all her tender parts. "I'm . . . just . . . so . . ."

He laid her on the floor and began to tongue her nipples. "Did you get the note to the Bernstein broad today?"

She nodded her head over and over. She would be a good girl; she couldn't allow him to go away again; she couldn't stand being alone. "Help me, Frankie . . . please."

"Oh, I'll help you, baby. Yes I will."

He entered her with an explosive thrust. Her hips lifted and jammed into his.

Everything was going to be all right again.

CHAPTER 11

Gina pressed the heels of her hands tightly against her temples, but the throbbing continued.

Drowning her sorrows in alcohol the night before hadn't helped relieve the peculiar emptiness that gnawed at her. She'd been through this type of depression before, and knew her feelings were directly related to the loss of Carl Chapman. She also knew that no matter how much Chapman had meant to her as a person, her memories of him as an individual would fade from her mind. Soon, he would become part of the mass of now anonymous patients whom she had seen die.

There was a coldness in that, and it bothered her.

She was a fighter, and she'd chosen this type of nursing because there was a combativeness involved. She and the patients could join together to defeat the common enemy.

Today, she had her doubts.

Today, she felt defeated.

Only her private time—time away from work, time with Harry and his offbeat humor—seemed to make any sense at all.

Harry make sense? That seemed like a tall order, certainly not one she was ready to consider at the moment. Instead, she sat at the nurses' station, head in hand, and meticulously charted her 8:00 a.m. meds.

She didn't hear her name called until Helen tugged at her sleeve and almost shouted in her ear. "It's him again, Gina. You'd better go, thank God he's yours."

"Not the brat?" Gina asked.

"Yeah," Helen said, shaking her head, "the brat!"

"Damn it!" she muttered, hurrying down the corridor. It would be nice to have one day without Vinnie Capello behaving like an idiot. He acted more like a ten-year-old than eighteen. Outside his door, she slowed herself, took a deep breath, and casually strolled into the room.

Two male nurse assistants were trying to keep the skinny teenager from yanking out the IV line in his chest.

"That's enough, Vinnie," Gina said calmly.

The patient pulled his arms free, glaring first at her, then at the aides.

"Thanks a lot for taking care of things, guys," Gina said, "but I need some time alone with Mr. Capello."

"Are you sure you won't need some help with this . . . brat?" one of the aides growled.

"I'll call if I do. Thanks again."

She circled around the room, rubbing the back of her neck, still trying to relieve the nagging headache. "So, Vinnie," she said as soon as they were alone, "do you suppose it's just because I'm Italian I get the privilege of being shafted by you all the time?"

"Whadda you mean?"

"You know exactly what I mean—having to baby-sit 'the brat' just because he's Italian, too."

He sneered at her.

"You can drop the tough guy act, kid. After four weeks we know each other pretty well." She sat down on the edge of the bed. "And we both know you're a straight A student, with perfect diction."

He continued to glare at her, but she could see he was fighting back tears as he swiped at beads of perspiration on his forehead with the back of his hand.

"You know, the staff would love to shuffle you off to Pediatrics . . . that's where they all think you belong."

"I don't care what they think." The boy's already pale face turned a chalky white. His hands shook.

Gina gently took his hand in hers. She could feel him start to pull away, then give up any resistance. "You've got to stop making things so hard for yourself, Vinnie. Look at you. You're a mess."

He fought with his tears, then began to pant. Ragged breaths tore at his chest, and a muscle in his cheek quivered uncontrollably. Finally, he gave up, fell back, and cried.

Gina silently massaged his thin, bony back, soothed his hairless head.

"How can you stand to touch me," he muttered, blinking away the tears from his large black, sunken eyes. "Look at me: I've become one of those people in the World War Two concentration camps."

"No you haven't."

"What do I look like then?"

She thought for a moment, then said softly, "You look like a sick, scared kid, fighting for his life."

Tracy Bernstein sat in a chair with a book in her lap. She loved mysteries, had looked forward to reading Marilyn Wallace's *The Seduction*; it just lay there, unopened, unread.

Why hasn't Gary called? She picked at one of the purple blotches on her arm.

He said he would call as soon as he had the money. She looked toward the open doorway of her room, hoping he would suddenly appear, money in hand. What if he can't get it?

Her lower lip was caught between her teeth as she picked at her arm again, then picked harder. Dark blood welled and spread under the skin.

I have to have it today, Gary. Her heart jumped, pounded loudly in her ears. *I need it today.* She reached with trembling fingers for the water glass on her bedside stand. As she sipped the water, she winced and gently tongued the ulcer in her mouth—the water's rush, instead of cooling, seemed to sear the delicate tissue.

The phone rang.

Her entire body erupted in cold sweat; she sat in stunned inertia.

Then, she couldn't move fast enough. She tried to grab for the phone, spilled the water, let the glass slip from her grasp. When she finally encircled the receiver with her fingers, it almost slipped from her wet hand. She held the phone tightly against her ear with both hands.

"Trace? Are you there?"

"I'm here."

"Listen—"

"Just say you have it, Gary . . . please say you have it."

There was a long silence. "I will, Tracy. I promise. Tomorrow."

"But Gary, I need it now, not tomorrow."

"I tried, Tracy . . . I tried very hard." His voice caught, the next words came out in a croak. "I couldn't manage it in only one day."

"Don't you understand?"

"Tracy! Listen to me—"

"You're all I have, Gary, the only one who can help me!" She yanked the decorative silk scarf from her head, revealing the sparse tufts of red hair. She mopped frantically at a mixture of perspiration and tears that ran down her face. "You promised you wouldn't let me down. Damn it, Gary, I'm going to die for certain if I don't get that marrow transfusion."

"I know, Trace, I know. But will you please listen to what I have to say?"

She couldn't respond. The silence grew long, longer. Finally, in a dull, flat voice, she said, "I'm listening."

"I'll have the money when the bank opens tomorrow."

Again, she couldn't bring herself to speak. Her mind tried to comprehend what he was saying, but all she could focus on was the huge pool of blood that had collected under the skin of her arm. She heard him breathe: short puffs, in and out, in and out.

"Guess we were pretty dumb to keep sinking all of our money into the businesses," he offered lamely.

She was suddenly very sad. "Gary? I'm . . . I'm sorry things—"

"I still think we should call the police," he interrupted.

"—fell apart between you and me."

"Trace," he said softly, "I feel so helpless. I swear, I did everything I could to get the money today. I just couldn't make it work."

"I know you tried your best, Gary, but going to the police isn't an option." She lowered her voice to just above a whisper. "I can't take that chance. If we don't get my marrow back . . . I'll die."

Gina was headed back to the nurses' station, her thoughts filled with Vinnie Capello. She glanced in at Tracy Bernstein as she passed her room. It wasn't until she was almost to the station that she stopped and turned around.

Why isn't she wearing the scarf? She always wears it.

Gina's head continued to pound as she dashed back down the corridor. She paused to study Tracy through the glass partition before entering the room. Her body language was all wrong—shoulders hunched, robe gaping, legs splayed, arms dangling.

Tracy, obviously lost in thought, didn't seem to be aware of Gina's arrival. When Gina placed a hand on her shoulder, she jumped.

"I'm sorry, I didn't mean to frighten you." She looked into Tracy's darting green eyes.

"I . . . I don't feel too well."

"Here, give me your arm. Let me help you back into . . ." She reached out, then stopped short. "For God's sake! What happened to you?"

Tracy looked down. "I don't know . . . I wasn't really—"

Gina quickly raised the arm, studied it, and pressed her palms down over the pool of blood that had oozed under the skin of the entire forearm. "Hit the call button. You can reach it from there."

"What can we do for you?" a voice on the intercom responded.

"Helen! This is Gina. We need an ice collar right away!"

"You got it."

Gina checked her watch. "We'll have to hold this under pressure for a while, Tracy. That should stop the bleeding."

She looked up at Gina. "I wasn't paying attention. I think I . . . bruised it."

"You've got to tell us when things like this happen."

"I know. I know," Tracy said. "You've told me so many times I've memorized it: My suppressed marrow isn't putting out enough platelets to clot the blood." She looked up and smiled weakly.

The door swung open and Helen came in with a chemical freeze bag. "Maybe this will do it," she said to Tracy. "A little bleeding?"

" 'Fraid so," Gina said. "I'm hoping the pressure and ice will take care of it."

Helen set the bag on the bedside table. "Okay now?"

"Thanks."

"Here to please," Helen said, exiting the room.

Continuing to apply steady pressure to the oozing subdermal blood, Gina couldn't help but wonder why Tracy hadn't reported the damage to her arm. Something's not right, and it didn't start with this arm. Something else is wrong.

"Did you fall, Tracy?"

"I don't know," she responded brusquely, turning her head away.

Gina studied Tracy's profile: pale and drawn, skin dry, covered with dots of purpura. She knew that the stomatitis resulting from her intensive chemotherapy was making it difficult for her to eat or drink. It was a grueling course of treatment, but even with her difficulties, Tracy had done well up until today.

So why was she sitting here without her scarf? She'd been so proud, almost vain about her once long, beautiful hair. She'd never been without something to cover its loss—until today.

For a meticulous woman, she's looking pretty damn grungy. It was obvious she hadn't taken a shower; her patient gown was used, dirty under a coffee splattered robe.

Something's happened and I'm not catching it, something that's flipped her around 180 degrees. What the hell is it?

"Bad day, huh," she prodded gently.

Tracy's lips tightened. She stared straight ahead.

"It might help if you told me what's bothering you."

Tracy's eyes pierced her with green daggers. "Help? Help who? Me?" She spat out the words. "Gina, you're full of shit!"

"Full of shit?" Gina bent over to stare directly into her eyes.

"That's right!" Red dots of anger spotted her forehead. "Full of shit!"

"Tracy! What is it? Tell me!"

Her face altered into a mask of disgust. "What I need, Florence Nightingale, is fifty thousand dollars . . . and I need it today." She tried to yank her arm free. "Damn it! Let go of me!"

"Come on, Tracy, just give me a few more minutes and I think you'll be okay."

"I'll never be okay. And without that money I'm never going to leave this hospital, except in a box."

CHAPTER 12

Gina was stunned. Never had she seen a patient turn hostile so rapidly without an obvious reason. As she stood there holding Tracy's arm, the tension between them mushroomed to a palpable level. She had transformed from a optimistic individual into an angry, withdrawn patient, refusing to even talk.

When Gina finally stemmed the subdermal bleeding, she made one more attempt to get through to Tracy: "If you want to talk, I'm never too far away. You know I care . . ."

Tracy merely stared at the far wall.

"How's Bernstein's arm?" Helen asked back at the nurses' station.

"Better. Ten minutes on, ten off the freezebag. Talked to Kessler. We've got our fingers crossed."

"How did it happen?"

"I don't know."

"Wouldn't tell you, huh?" Helen asked.

"Nope."

"Maybe she doesn't know."

Gina thought for a moment. "Or she won't say. She seems so angry. It's just not like her to be—"

The call bell interrupted. Helen stepped away to answer it.

Gina reached for Tracy's chart, slowly flipped through the pages. Leafing through several days of doctor's orders, her index finger moved through the pink pages, on to the progress notes, nurses' notes, medication sheets, and lab reports.

What am I looking for?

She put the chart down and tried to find a connection between the written information and Tracy's unexpected change in behavior. There was no explaining it. Then she picked up the chart again, flipping back to the order sheet, she read, *Marrow in AM.*

Tracy was being engrafted tomorrow. Could she be upset over that? They'd discussed the procedure before and she'd never shown this kind of reaction.

Maybe this is about her ex-husband. She closed the chart with a slam. *Damn it, what the hell is the matter with her?*

"Helen, how about changing lunch breaks," she asked, watching the other nurse complete her charting. "I'd really like to go at eleven-thirty, if that's okay with you."

"Fantastic! I hate when it's my turn to go early, makes the day go on forever." She paused, looked at Gina, and cocked her head. "Are you okay?

Gina ran a hand through her hair. "I don't know."

Helen put an arm around Gina's waist and looked up at her. "It's still Chapman, isn't it?"

Gina nodded. "I just need some time to think . . . straighten out my thoughts."

"Go, mine darlink," Helen said, shooing her out of the station. "Leaf everyting to me."

The normally hectic hospital cafeteria was unexpectedly quiet when Gina arrived for her break. She took a deep breath and enjoyed the solitude, wondering if she should take the early lunch more often.

The fiery incident with Tracy Bernstein had left her shaken. She thought they'd established something more than just a nurse-patient relationship since Tracy had been

on the floor. Her behavior now, however, was not just unusual, it was bordering on the bizarre.

Why was she into the money thing, and why fifty thousand dollars?

Gina knew the cost of the treatment, and it wasn't fifty
thousand. Besides, it had already been taken care of. True,
there'd been a big hassle with her insurance company. But
there almost always was. But Tracy had told her they were
going to pay.

So what's making her so angry?

The situation had a familiar ring to it, but she couldn't
isolate it. It just kept nagging at her, trying to push through.

She lifted a red tray from the multicolored stack at the
start of the food line.

Give it a rest!

While she moved along the line, she deliberately distracted herself by examining the high-ceilinged room. Stark
walls alone would have made the huge place an austere
cavern, but the white walls had become a background for a
spray of arrows dancing across the panels like electrical
lightning.

A local artist had been commissioned to do the work.
Most people were enthusiastic about the results. Others,
more vocal, hated it. Even after a year, coming into the cafeteria still could start an endless argument about what art
is, or should be. She'd been the center of many heated dis-
cussions on the subject. Harry laughed at her intensity on
the issue—said she was turning into a crazy Californian.
Maybe he was right.

As she stopped in front of a tray of cheese enchiladas,
she studied the artwork again. Yes, she really did like the
fluidity of the pastel-colored design. The New York hospi-
tals where she'd worked would have painted the same area a

bile green, never giving it an aesthetic thought.

Although she tried to stay with the distraction, she couldn't. Tracy Bernstein was right there in the middle of all those crazy arrows.

Why would a stable person like her suddenly fly apart?

She bypassed the Mexican food and picked up a carton of nonfat milk and a dish of fresh fruit. After paying, she looked around for a seat, spotted Faye Lindstrom sitting alone at one of the picture window tables, and walked in that direction.

"Mind if I join you?" she asked the med tech.

Faye looked tired, but she smiled up at Gina. "Of course not."

Gina slipped into the opposite chair and looked out the window at the mass of flowers in the carefully manicured hospital grounds. They ate in silence; the med tech finished a dish of chocolate pudding, then bit into a candy bar. Gina nibbled indifferently at her fruit and sipped her milk.

"Sometimes I feel like running away, hiding in a garden just like that one out there—"

"—and never coming back," the med tech completed for her.

Gina nodded, then took another small bite. "I suppose it sounds silly for a thirty-five-year-old, but I wish there was a special place I could run away to. A place where there were only happy endings . . . like in the stories my father used to tell me."

Faye laughed bitterly. "At least you had a father to tell you stories. Mine was almost never around. When he did show up, he was drunk and beat the hell out of me." Her eyes narrowed to slits. "I'm . . . I'm glad he's dead." The bitter words contrasted with the delicacy of her fingers as she touched the bones around her eye. "Anyway, those are just fairy tales. If that kind of place ever did exist, it doesn't anymore."

"I suppose you're right," Gina sighed. She reached across the small table and tilted Faye's head towards the light streaming in the window. "Your eye's looking better."

"It doesn't hurt much now."

"Did Frank do that to you?" she blurted, almost instantly regretting the uninvited intrusion.

Faye took a mouth-stuffing bite of another chocolate bar and chewed it deliberately for several seconds before responding. "It's no big deal," she finally said. "Besides, it was my own fault. I deserved it."

"Come on, Faye, no one deserves to be hit like that."

Faye shoved the last piece of chocolate into her mouth, gave a fleeting glance at the garden. "I don't want to talk about it." She quickly looked at her watch. "Anyway, I've got to go back now." She scooped up her tray, causing several empty candy wrappers to fly off into the air.

Gina placed a hand on her arm. "You have my number, Faye. Call me if you need to talk."

The med tech gave her a noncommittal look and turned away.

Gina stared thoughtfully at the back of the retreating figure. Faye's reactions to the beating were all too familiar.

My God! Everyone seems to be flipping out lately. First Carl, then Tracy, now Faye. What in hell's going on?

She sat there, tearing her paper napkin into thin strips that she wove into a basket design. Was there a possible connection? At least between Carl's and Tracy's strange behavior?

She realized both of them had begun acting out of character the day before they were to receive their bone marrow engraftments.

But why?

CHAPTER 13

Frank Nellis checked his watch, then opened the hallway closet door and stared hard at the small freezer on the floor. He resisted the temptation to open it and peek inside. He wasn't supposed to do that.

It was no bigger than an oversized bread box, fit neatly into Faye's hall closet. The stainless steel unit was fed by an exterior liquid nitrogen tank that kept the temperature at minus 90 degrees centigrade.

Inside the cryogenic chamber was biological gold—ten plastic bags, each filled with a combination of 40cc of marrow and 40cc of glucose medium mixed with DSMO preservative. The marrow had been harvested six weeks earlier, then frozen inside the bags.

Once, when Faye had caught him with the freezer door open, she threatened to end the whole business. He poked, prodded, coaxed, pleaded, punched her around. But the cow had her limits. She said he would have to learn the process so there'd be no mistakes. When he finally convinced her he was serious about saving the marrow specimens, she agreed to do her part.

Little darlin's a real humanitarian.

But at the moment, he was alone and the compulsion to look inside the freezer was as great as ever. He thoughtfully scratched his nose, then quickly opened the door, allowing a blast of icy air to engulf his face, almost taking his breath away. "Couldn't resist!" he gasped, catching a glimpse of the frozen marrow. He slammed the door shut, threw a loud kiss at the freezer. "Mrs. Bernstein, I love you."

They'd had that batch since yesterday. He'd watched Faye place it in there while the nurse—the one who'd given her a ride home—sat in the living room waiting for her coffee. The bimbo didn't know that she'd actually helped Faye bring the marrow home.

Would've peed her pants if she'd known.

The vision was so funny it doubled him over. Holding on to the top of the freezer, his mirth swelled to a hysterical pitch. When his body stopped shaking, he wiped at the tears sliding down his face.

"Faye better not tell her. That nurse bitch might want to claim a piece of the action." That idea started him laughing all over again. "Sure, like I'm about to give her anything except a good fuck."

Finally calming himself, he glanced at his watch again.

Fuckin' broads are all so stupid! His eyes narrowed. And that fuckin' Faye is the stupidest of them all.

She'd even refused to dump Chapman's marrow after he was dead. He'd stood in the kitchen, throwing the dead guy's thawing bags of cells at her—at her face, her stomach, her head. Disgusted, he'd stabbed one of the plastic bags with a butcher knife and split it open. The gunk fell to the floor in icy globs, finally defrosting into a bloody mess.

She had stared at him, white-faced, a pathetic look twisting her features. He'd thought at the time that she really did look like a stupid cow, her big, brown, wet eyes watching him while she bawled over a dead man's bag of useless sludge.

What the hell was she moaning about anyway? Chapman was nothing to her, just some dumb shit.

In the end, he'd been the one to throw the slop away. No matter how much fun he'd try to have with her, no matter how much he teased about helping him, he had to cut all the bags open and wash the melting squish down the drain to make room in the freezer for the Bernstein broad's stuff.

He glanced at the temperature gauge—the cow said it was critical that the temperature remain constant. If the stuff started to thaw even a little bit, it could deteriorate.

Technical bullshit!

She'd explained how it was saving lives, talking to him as if he were a little kid. Said how the marrow cells only had to be retransfused into the body so that after two to three weeks they found their way back to where they belonged and started reproducing on their own. She'd insisted that the two of them had a responsibility to handle it just right or else the marrow would be useless.

"So what!" he'd told her. "Just one less asshole in the world!" Besides, once he got the money he'd just as soon dump the marrow as give it back—less trouble, and much less risk.

Faye wouldn't go for it. Didn't want those weaklings to die. Said the hospital would get suspicious if any more marrow disappeared without a trace. If that happened, she wouldn't be able to get any more because of security.

The bitch had a point.

Fuckin' Frankensteins. He closed the closet door.

Or maybe my little girl is lying through her teeth just to get her own way.

He turned and stared thoughtfully in the direction of the bedroom.

It was the first time in his life he'd scored with the right bimbo. He'd been lucky enough to meet her when he was still working for the hospital. Just one look at her and he knew what she needed, smelled her hunger. Yet, she'd not only been smart enough to think of the whole scam, she took most of the chances—stole the junk, put it back when the money was paid.

Shouldn't really fuss with her. Better to leave well enough alone, especially when all she ever wants out of it is a good fuck. And he knew how to take care of that.

Besides, he got the best part. He got the money.

Checking his watch again, he started moving; he couldn't miss the change of shifts at the hospital. It was the best time to slip in, with little chance of being noticed. He knew they were so short of staff at night they had to rely on outside agency personnel to cover, so there were always a lot of unfamiliar faces floating about.

At the front door, he held his arms out, stretched his neck from side to side, then shook his head wildly. Jeeze, he was high. High on the action. High on the thought of getting the money.

He flipped off the living room light, plunging the apartment into darkness. The cow had gone to bed early, just as she did every time he went out for a collection.

Good little girl. Sleep well! You've done your thing. Now it's my turn.

A flash of pleasure tightened his sphincter; a sexual rush tingled in his groin. He moved catlike down the stairs and out of the building, impatient for the confrontation with his prey.

Tracy's mouth had become so painful they'd had to start the morphine drip again. When they'd first given it to her, it had worked well. But as the doses climbed higher, its effectiveness lessened.

She studied the IV fluid. It gave her something to focus on. She watched each drop fall, then studied the array of connections for all the other medications and solutions hanging on the IV pole.

In the past—was it just the day before yesterday?—the rhythm of the drops, along with her nighttime sedation, not only made her feel safe, it hypnotically put her to sleep. But tonight, it all seemed to emphasize her vulnerability—the survival diet, the never-ending medications, the noxious but vital chemotherapy, and the approaching crucial marrow engraftment.

She tore her eyes away; checked the bedside clock.

11:30 p.m.

Twelve hours earlier she'd received the call from that disgusting person, with his vile voice. The conversation had been brief: Had she received his note? Yes! Good! He would come for the money. Tonight.

She remembered the exchange verbatim; it had etched itself in her brain like a living nightmare. She hadn't dared to tell him there'd be no money until tomorrow. What if he wouldn't listen? What if he destroyed her marrow?

She'd been virtually paralyzed the entire day. Every possible fear crowded into the room with her—loss of bodily functions, inability to communicate, suffocation.

Now she stared at her shaking hand as she reached to switch off the bedside lamp. She peered into the semi-darkness until she could see almost as well as when the light had been on.

She thought about Gary's afternoon visit.

He'd been concerned about her condition, apologetic about the ransom money. He seemed different, not the cold, ex-husband, but the warm, caring person she'd originally fallen in love with so many years ago.

What had caused it all to change for them? How had she lost him? Could it be he was gone from her life because of her own stupidity, her unbending ambition? Just thinking about Gary created a huge emptiness in her stomach.

She caught herself drifting off. Did she dare sleep? It was so late, maybe it would be all right. Maybe he wouldn't come until tomorrow, after Gary brought the money.

"Did you think I wasn't coming, Mrs. Bernstein?"

Her eyes snapped open. She tried to rise. A hand pressed down roughly against her chest. She stared at the face looming over the bed.

"I . . . I knew . . ." Her voice drifted off, swallowed by the silence of the room. A metallic taste coated her mouth. She tried to hold her breath. Forced to release the pent-up air, she quickly sucked in more through clamped teeth.

"Where is it?" He crushed down harder, smashing her back down into the mattress.

She stared blankly at him.

He slapped the other hand down onto her chest.

"Where is it?" he hissed.

"There wasn't enough time," she said, struggling to lift up. "I . . . the bank . . . tomorrow!"

His fingers curled, nails squeezing into her breast.

"Listen to me . . . please!" Her hands clenched into claws, then rounded fists. "Please don't hurt me. I'll do anything you want, but please don't hurt me."

His lip arched into a sneer. "What the hell do you think you could do for me? All I need from you is money." He straightened, wiped his hands on his pants.

She bit down hard on her lip to keep from screaming, twisted her head from side to side.

He flung off the covers, pulled up her gown, allowing the cool air to wash across her naked skin.

"Look at you!" he ordered. "Go ahead, look!" He forced her head down into her chest. "You're not even human anymore. Look like a turkey that's been plucked and carved."

He wrapped a finger around the silastic tube in her chest and pulled at the IVs that were attached to it. The plastic bags bobbed up and down.

She tried to blink him away. Her mouth was frozen; only her eyes seemed to function. In the dim light, he'd become a ferocious animal, toying with its catch, waiting to consume her.

Suddenly, he yanked off her silk head scarf, rubbed his hand across her bald scalp. "Bet you used to be a real looker." She reached out, tried to snatch back the scarf. But he pulled it away from her and stuffed it into his pocket. "Now you look like turkey shit." He threw his head back and laughed. "Just what granddaddy used to call women: 'Goddamned turkey shit!' "

"Please," she begged, not daring to move.

"Where's the fucking money?"

"My husband . . . ex-husband . . . will have it as soon as the bank opens . . . tomorrow." She pushed up onto her elbows. "I swear. First thing tomorrow."

His eyes flashed; he slapped her viciously across the face. She fell back onto the bed.

"Please! I don't want to die."

"You don't, huh?" He turned abruptly away from the bed and started pacing around the room, his hands locked behind his back.

"Please . . . trust me . . . I'll have it tomorrow . . . every dollar." Tears welled up, spilled down her cheeks.

He stopped and stood next to her bed stand, staring at a sealed box of syringes awaiting the next day's engraftment procedure. His index finger worried the pull tab until it stuck out from the box. With a sudden motion, he yanked it open. Tracy jumped as the tearing sound slashed through the room.

"Trust you? Oh, I trust you all right, baby." He smiled coldly, his body a tightly coiled spring. "All I lose is money. But you? You lose the wh-o-o-ole crap shoot." He poked at her scars and she winced. "You're already only half a woman."

She tried to crush herself flatter into the mattress. Ripples of shivers made her teeth chatter, and she felt a line of spittle dribble down her chin. "I promise I'll have the money tomorrow," she whispered.

"Promise?" he mocked, tweaking her nipple. "Well, if you want me to trust you, Mrs. B . . . you'll have to trust me, too."

She nodded.

"Noooo, it's not that easy. We're going to play a little game first."

"Game?"

"Well, yeah. It's a little like Russian roulette, but we'll call it Trust." His eyes glinted with pleasure as he removed three syringes from the bedside box.

Watching his every movement, not even daring to blink, her hand inched along the bed toward the call button.

"Mmmm, these are big mothers," he said, reading the side of the syringe. "Fifty ccs. This will hold a lot of air, Mrs. B."

He pulled the plunger until the syringe was filled with air. Two syringes were left unchanged. Slipping her scarf from his pocket, he wrapped it around the three plastic cylinders so they were hidden from her view. "Turn your head. No fun if you cheat."

She turned her head away. Her hand encircled the call button.

"You can look now." When she turned back, he held out the scarf. "Pick one!"

She groped in the silk scarf and pulled out one of the offered syringes.

"Bang! You're dead!" he laughed. He quickly tossed the other two syringes back into the box, pocketed the scarf, then reached for the IV line.

The room started to spin in large swimming circles as she mashed down on the call button. It went off with a raucous buzz.

His eyes widened, then narrowed to dark slits. "You bitch!" He dropped the syringe and bolted for the door. "Fuckin' bitch!"

He stood there for a moment, backlighted in the doorway.

"Have the fuckin' money tomorrow or you can kiss your ass good-bye."

CHAPTER 14

Her sweat-covered body was wrapped around him; his fingers trailed over her back, across her shoulders, down her arms, around her hips.

"When will the beautiful Italian princess marry the stubby, brilliant prince?" Harry asked.

Gina smiled at him, pulling his head down so she could kiss each questioning eye. "This is one princess who's never going to marry again."

He nuzzled her neck, rubbed his cheek against her breasts. "In fairy tales, never is just a long time."

"Exactly."

He turned away with a solemn face, eyed the clock. 11:30 p.m.

"Wait and see," he said, crossing his eyes, running his fingers through his bushy hair until it was a mess of clumps and tangles. "One day you'll realize just how irresistible I am."

"Mmmmm."

He studied her in the soft glow from the bedside lamp. Her face was flushed with a rosy sheen from their lovemaking, but her eyes were focused on something far away.

"The body's present, but the mind's adrift." He fingered her cheek until she looked directly at him. "Where'd you go?"

"I'm sorry."

"What's the matter, doll?"

She arose from the bed, her body a study of soft curves, the long smooth muscles of her arms and legs adding subtle angles. She shrugged herself into a terry cloth robe that had been carelessly flung across the end of the bed.

"I keep thinking about Tracy Bernstein."

Harry shook his head, irritation lining his face as he grabbed his jeans from the mixed pile of clothing on the floor.

"First Chapman, now Bernstein." Zipping his pants, he untangled his shirt from her bra. "If you're not careful, Gina, you're going to burn out, be useless to your patients, useless to yourself."

"Harry, that's not it at all."

"Listen, kid, don't tell me that's not it. I'm the ICU nurse, remember? I've seen this kind of thing over and over. So have you."

Gina stomped into the living room, Harry hard on her heels.

"It's not burnout, Harry. You're way off base."

"I say, when your off time is spent worrying, thinking only about your patients, you're in deep shit, whether you're willing to admit it or not." He grabbed her by the elbow. "You've got to have a life of your own."

She yanked her arm away, padded into the kitchen, and began stacking dinner dishes. Soon she had the sink filled with suds.

"You listen to me, Harry Lucke," she said, washing and standing the dishes in the drain rack, "this is not burnout we're talking about."

He grabbed a towel, started drying the dishes. "It's what I'm talking about."

"That, my dear prince, is because you haven't let me finish what I have to say before jumping to a bunch of erroneous conclusions. And what's this ICU crap you're handing me? Working in ICU doesn't make you an all-seeing guru."

"That isn't exactly what I meant."

"Sure sounded like an ego trip to me."

"Okay, okay," he said, raising his hands high in the air, the towel hanging limply from his hand like a flag of surrender. "I give up. You're right. I'm just an egotistical clod."

The room was still for several moments before she turned to look at him. "What am I going to do with you, Harry?"

They silently searched each other's faces, each other's eyes.

"You could try loving me," he finally said.

"I do love you!"

"Then marry me, for God's sake!"

She wrapped her arms around him. "Give me time, Harry . . . time to trust you . . . to let you in." She squeezed him, squeezed tighter. "Can't you understand?"

He kissed her softly on one cheek, then the other. "Oh, I do understand, Gina. Remember, I'm the all-seeing guru."

"Sorry. That was kind of a cheap shot."

They held onto each other, barely breathing. Harry took her chin in his hand, kissed her lips, and said, "We've been together for six months . . . and in that time I've never seen you so totally preoccupied with your patients."

"That's not quite true. I mean, it's not really the patients . . . it's something else."

"Then what is it?"

She thought for a moment. "Things just don't feel right."

"Like how?"

"Well, number one, losing Chapman's marrow." She slipped out of his arms, grabbed a memo pad, and jotted down some notes. "I suppose I've got to believe it's possible that the lab could lose it . . . but how did Chapman know it was missing? That keeps running through my mind, Harry, over and over. I mean, no one told him about it before me—I checked that out."

"Are you sure Kessler didn't mention it to him?"

"No way! He didn't find out himself until it was time to transfuse. I was the one who told him."

"Gina, I can't see anything hidden or sinister in this."

"What about Chapman's death? I've studied all his lab values; the ones before he turned sour."

"Yeah?"

"They weren't good, but I wouldn't expect him to sink with such an overwhelming infection so rapidly." She added, "And who was he talking about when he told me someone had injected meds into his line the night before he died? There were no IV orders."

"Look, Gina, the man was shot up with chemo . . . cells were badly chewed up. He was probably half out of his head, or dreaming. The whole business is tragic, but I still don't see the mystery."

She threw the memo pad across the counter, began washing the dishes again. He played with the towel, ready to dry.

"It doesn't make sense to me," Gina said.

"So maybe the guy just gave up, stopped fighting. He'd been through one helluva lot. Maybe you're just reading more into this than is actually there."

She shook her head stubbornly, ignoring his comments. "Not Carl Chapman. I don't care what you say, Harry. If Carl gave up, it wasn't because of his disease."

She finished the dishes and started scrubbing the counters. "I admit that up until now my suspicions were rather tenuous. But now it's also happening with Tracy Bernstein."

"What about her?"

"She had a minor sub-q bleed today. She freaked out. Started yelling, screaming at me."

Harry rubbed his chin with one hand, looking at her with concern. "Now I'm really worried about you." He meticulously folded the dishtowel and hung it up. "I don't think you heard what you just said."

"What are you talking about?"

"There is no such thing as a minor bleed with these patients. Everything has the potential of turning into a calamity . . . and don't think Tracy didn't know it."

"Yeah, but she was acting out before the bleed."

"In what way?"

"She was actually screaming that she needed fifty grand right away . . . talked about being carried out in a box."

"Did she say what she needed the money for?"

"All I know is her insurance has already agreed to pay for her care, so it couldn't be that. But that woman was petrified about something."

"Isn't she due for her engraftment soon?"

"Tomorrow. Noon."

"Well," he said shrugging, "that could explain it."

"Harry, don't you think I've been through that whole scenario?"

"I don't know what to think, Gina. Maybe you're too close, too involved to be objective about any of it."

"Damn it, Harry! It's true I have rapport with the woman. It's also true that I like her very much, feel a great deal of empathy for her. But give me credit for some professionalism. She's still my patient, and I haven't lost track of that for one minute."

He studied her. "I don't know. Maybe you're clear about all of this, maybe you're not. But I still think Bernstein's behavior is probably erratic because of her transfusion tomorrow."

"And I disagree."

"Be fair, Gina. Wouldn't it scare you? It sure would scare the hell out of me." He poked her gently in the ribs. "And I'm fearless."

She jumped away, shook her fist at him. "Don't play around with this, Harry." She hunched over, set an elbow on the kitchen counter, and rested her head in her hand. "Both Chapman and Bernstein have reacted inappropriately. No, that doesn't quite describe it. They've acted . . . weird."

"So? What about other patients in the unit? Don't they all go through some kind of crisis just before engraftment?"

"Oh, there's apprehension, all right, but not terror. They know those cells are going to save their lives. Maybe there's some fear, but mostly, there's hope."

"You never told me Chapman was terrified."

"No, because I don't think he was, more resigned than anything." She turned, looked sharply at him. "Harry, are you playing devil's advocate with me?"

He stared silently back at her.

"Look," she said, "Tracy is a vibrant, cocky, professional woman. Chapman was a laid-back, but strong-willed man. Yet both acted totally out of character the day before engraftment. They—" She thought a moment. "They both clammed up. Wouldn't talk, wouldn't confide in me anymore."

"Maybe that's at the heart of this—you feel alienated from your patients."

"Come on, Harry, you can't really believe I'd let my personal hang-ups get in the way. I'm telling you there's some weird shit going on here. Just because I can't pin it down doesn't mean it isn't happening."

"I don't know, Gina—"

"You just don't get it, do you?"

He shrugged.

"Isn't it rotten enough that these people are going through hell, not only from their disease, but from their medical treatment?"

Harry nodded. "It's not an easy way to go."

"Well, what if there's something else threatening them, something that—"

"Something that what?"

Gina padded up to him, pushed her forehead hard against his chest. "I don't know . . . I don't know . . . I don't know."

CHAPTER 15

NEUTROPENIC PRECAUTIONS
Upon entering:
Wash your hands immediately. See the nurse if:
You have a cold.
You have any sign of infection.

Gina's eyes flitted automatically across the warning plaque that had been placed on the wall outside Tracy Bernstein's room. She hardly read it anymore, but it was an affirmation of what she already knew: Tracy was fighting for her life.

Once inside, she went to the sink to wash her hands and study Tracy, who was lying on her side facing the window. Gina stared thoughtfully at the drab scarf that covered her baldness—it was half-on, half-off. What had happened to the colorful scarf that was Tracy's signature?

Gina walked around to the other side of the rumpled bed; the blanket was on the floor, the sheets wadded into clumps.

"So how are you? How's your arm?"

There was no answer; Tracy's fingers clutched harder at a photograph she held against her chest. Unfocused eyes were a tired, watery green.

"I wish you'd tell me what's troubling you," Gina said, gently straightening the scarf.

Raising her head, Tracy looked directly at Gina. Her face had faded to an ashen-gray; her full lips were bloodless and pinched together.

Gina checked her watch. "Why don't I help you up, get

ready for your marrow transfusion?" She laughed thinly. "Think we can do that in four hours?"

Tracy looked through, then past Gina. "Leave me alone," she whispered.

"Look, Tracy, if it's something I've said or done . . . well, I wish you'd tell me. I'm sure—"

"Go away, Gina. I don't want to talk to you."

"Maybe if another nurse took care of you—"

"I don't want another nurse. I don't want any nurse. None of you can help me." Her lower lip quivered. "I just want you to go now. Go and leave me alone."

"Please, let me help you freshen up," Gina said softly.

Tracy's nostrils flared. "Are all nurses so dense? Don't you understand, I want you to leave! Get out! Is that plain enough?"

Gina swallowed an angry response and turned away. As she exited the room, she heard Tracy sobbing.

Now she was not only puzzled, she was fuming. It wasn't the first time she'd been put down as a nurse, but she hadn't expected it from Tracy Bernstein.

"You look like you swallowed a firecracker," Helen said as Gina stormed into the nurses' station.

"I can't believe it! Bernstein, of all people, calling me stupid. That's a curve ball I never expected."

"What happened in there?"

Gina told her about the scene with Tracy.

Helen laughed, shrugging it off. "She's obviously right. Only a dummy would choose to clean up piss, pus, and putridity as a career. It's so . . . so colorful . . . so exciting."

Gina just glared at her.

"Come on. Don't tell me you wouldn't trade all of this for a red power-blouse and an executive office where you could order a bunch of 'those other people' around." She smiled at Gina over her shoulder, her nose tilted upward: "Have that report on my desk in five minutes, Mazzio, or you're fired!" She flicked an imaginary mote of dust off her uniform and giggled. "Can you picture that?"

Gina frowned, then burst out laughing. "As a matter of fact, I can't."

"See? You are a dummy."

Helen sneered at a digital salute from Gina as she walked out of the station, but not before she flipped one back.

Gina stood motionless at the desk, her eyes skimming back and forth across the array of requisitions, charts, phones, and computer terminals. After several seconds of indecision, she tuned into everyone else hustling and bustling, just like any other day. She knew she should get moving—Vinnie Capello had been acting up again and no one wanted any part of him; she had IVs, meds, treatments to get ready; and then there was Tracy's marrow engraftment at noon.

She stepped out of the nurses' station, started down the hall, spun around and went back to the computer. She stared at the CRT for a moment, cleared the screen, and hit the keys to bring up Carl Chapman's lab work.

INVALID ENTRY FOR ACCESS.

She tried again.

THIS CODE WILL NOT ACCESS INFORMATION.

Maybe you *are* a dummy, Mazzio. Why check up on a dead guy?

She punched another series of keys.

97

GUARDIAN VIOLATION

Uh-oh! Any more messing around and the damn thing will shut down. She studied the warning on the screen. Why won't it give me the data on Chapman? Why all this security?

Gina entered the elevator and pressed "B" decisively. It had been a long time since she'd been to the basement in Ridgewood Hospital. And the only complete tour had been three years earlier during orientation. She thought about that original visit and tried to recall the basement layout: There was an auditorium conference room, dubbed "The Hole", the Laundry, the Lab, Pathology, and the Morgue.

As the elevator moved downward, she rubbed her neck and wondered if she was doing the right thing; maybe she should just leave things alone. Helen had ragged her for leaving the floor with so many student nurses interning. But Helen was a buddy and agreed to cover for her. She still felt guilty. Oncology, especially in a teaching hospital with oncologists, hematologists, residents, and interns milling about, could be a zoo under the best of circumstances. Working shorthanded made it a madhouse.

Leaving the elevator, she collided with the lab chief.

"Sorry, Bob."

"No problem." He squeezed her arm. "Not still miffed, are you?" His warm hands held on to her arm just a little too long.

"No, off course not."

His smile widened. "What brings you down to my dungeon?"

"Picking up some blood," she laughed nervously. "Haven't run out, have you?"

He stepped into the elevator, arched an eyebrow as he

gave her a wicked smile before waving through the closing doors.

The corridors were well lighted, but quiet—traffic was minimal compared to the rest of the hospital. She glanced up quickly as she came to each of the bubble mirrors that preceded every turn in the corridor. Yet despite the illumination and overhead mirrors, she kept looking back over her shoulder to see if anyone was following her—a habit she'd picked up in the dimly lighted, underground passageways of the New York hospital where she had trained. When she passed the double doors of the Morgue, she swallowed hard and picked up her pace.

At the Lab, she breathed a sigh of relief and pushed open one of the metal-clad swinging doors; suddenly she was in a different world, a stark contrast to the one where she worked four floors above.

The air was alien, permeated with pungent aromas of unfamiliar chemical compounds. Clicks and clacks, whirrs and buzzes echoed from every corner.

This was a world of theory and resolution, far removed from the anguish and pain of those who provided the fodder for its existence.

Blood analyzers rhythmically probed, while computers swallowed, digested and excreted digital readouts. Calculations were made continuously, unemotionally. Life and death were just empty words here.

No one paid attention to her as she traipsed through the maze of white-coated technicians. Most were standing before counters filled with racks of tubes, pipettes, and flasks. She stopped short; Faye Lindstrom was working at one of the stations. Gina hadn't expected to run into anyone she knew. She watched Faye work for a moment; the woman's hands moved in birdlike flutters as she readied sera from recently spun blood samples for computer analysis.

Gina was about to say hello when a nearby telephone rang. Faye scurried to answer the call, knocking over a rack of blood in the process. A chorus of epithets was directed at her. From the tone of the remarks, it apparently wasn't the first time Faye had made this kind of mess. The lab tech's terrified eyes skittered from one jeerer to another.

It had to be a personal call—Faye listened, then whispered urgently before hanging up the receiver. Only then did she notice Gina.

"So this is your home away from home," Gina said, pretending she'd just arrived.

Faye nodded, grabbed a protective head visor and double-gloved herself, the latex making squishing, snapping noises. "Quite a mess, isn't it?" she said, reaching under the counter for a box of chemical absorbent for the spilled blood.

"Hey, your day seems to be shaping up just about like mine."

Faye looked at her quizzically. "Why, what happened to you?"

Gina waved a hand. "No time now." She started to move on. "Meet me after work and I'll give you a ride home. We can talk about it then."

"Uh, no, I don't think so."

"Oh, come on. I'll wait for you near the fountain." Before Faye could turn her down again she waved good-bye and moved on.

Gina passed the Blood Bank, paused for a moment to get her bearings, and then went on to where the marrow was stored. A technician, busy packing tubes into a large centrifuge, looked up when she entered.

"Hi! I'm Gina Mazzio from Oncology. I wanted to see

how much marrow we have for Tracy Bernstein. Uh, I'm her primary care nurse and she's being engrafted today. Anyway, I was downstairs, thought I'd just pop in and, uh, check it out, okay?"

"Sure, sure! No problem," the tech said, interrupting her work. "God, I haven't heard a New York accent like that in years. Did you take a wrong turn somewhere?"

Gina laughed, felt the tension ease away. "California's just a jump away from the Bronx, as the crow flies."

"Uh huh," the tech agreed with a wry smile. "What's the patient's name and ID number?" She went to a tabletop terminal and keyed in the information Gina gave her. "Looks like there's eight-hundred ccs . . . that's probably about ten packages."

Gina hesitated. "May I see it?"

"The packets?"

"Yes."

"Why?"

"After losing Chapman's . . . well, it's just that I'd feel better if I saw them with my own eyes."

The tech leaned forward and scanned the identification card clipped to Gina's blouse. "Okay, but let's not get administration's bowels in an uproar by even mentioning Chapman's name." The tech stepped over to a stainless steel refrigerator. "The samples were probably moved to this fridge several days ago. Let's see . . ." She pointed to the computer. ". . . oh, yes, my HAL says they're in Section B, Slot six."

Gina watched her open the unit and search the designated area. Instead of coming up with the marrow, she went back to the terminal and rechecked the computer coordinates, then donned a large pair of gloves and searched inside the refrigerator more thoroughly.

"What's the problem?" Gina asked, having also read the information on the terminal screen.

"I'm going to have to check the main storage vat to see if the packets are still there. Maybe they haven't been transferred yet."

"I thought you said they would be here; isn't that what the computer says?"

"Should be here," the tech said, shaking her head, "but they're not." She frowned and bit her lower lip. "I'm going to have to run this down myself," she added, hurrying out the door.

As soon as she left, Gina reached for the telephone.

"Helen? It's Gina. Is Kessler on the floor?"

CHAPTER 16

Gary Bernstein paced back and forth in front of First Security's main entrance. He'd been there for ten minutes, feeling uncomfortably restricted in a business suit. His eyes were fixed on the large, Roman numeral clock in the window, the sweep of its second hand inching around with agonizing slowness. It now dragged past XII again. It was 8:59 a.m.

"Damn it!" he muttered. Then he resumed repeating the single word he'd used over and over since his arrival, like a rapid-fire mantra: Hurry, hurry, hurry—hurry, hurry, hurry.

A guard finally approached the door, unbolted it; the sound had a high-pitched screech, unnerving like a fingernail raked across a blackboard. The hairs on Gary's neck were still standing as he rushed inside, where he was immediately greeted by the bank's vice-president. Everything had been prearranged; the transaction itself took less than five minutes.

The banker, a friend, was in a chatty mood. Gary was polite, but firm about not having time to talk. Still, the banker probed, asking personal questions that Gary managed to avoid answering. Once again the banker tried to talk him out of carrying so much cash. He shrugged off the advice. Walking away, he sensed his friend's questioning eyes boring into his back, probably wondering what he really needed the money for.

Fifty thousand dollars. Jesus!

As he exited the bank, he studied the crowd before choosing the right moment to join the flow of foot traffic that would take him in the direction of his car. He was edgy, ready to bolt if anyone looked even remotely suspicious. Although he'd been involved in large money transactions many times in his life, he'd never before had that much actual cash in his hands.

He clutched the handle of the money-filled briefcase until his fingers started to cramp. Frightening possibilities sparked his imagination into an uncontrollable wildfire. Every situation, every encounter along the route to the parking garage blazed with danger. Scurrying pedestrians bumped into him, his fists automatically balled, ready for combat. A desperate street person touched his shoulder. He spun around, shoved viciously, and ignored the curses that followed him down the sidewalk. He focused on minorities, silently ascribing to them all the stereotypical, disparaging characteristics he'd ever heard. He hated himself for it, but everyone was a threat. Everyone!

It seemed to take forever to reach his car. As each second ticked away, he became more certain he was going to be robbed in broad daylight right in the middle of San Francisco's financial district.

When he reached the garage where his BMW was parked, he paid, scooted into the car and quickly locked the doors, shutting out the world. He closed his eyes for a moment and rested his head against the soft leather seat, breathing in the reassuring rich aroma. For that instant, in the locked car, the money secure at his side, he felt safe.

But he had to go. It was growing late, only twenty minutes to get to the drop. His stomach tightened as he turned the key in the ignition. He could still remember Tracy's trembling voice giving him detailed instructions, making him repeat the time and place several times before she'd been satisfied he understood everything perfectly.

Traffic seemed more congested than usual; he was so cautious he almost caused an accident, slamming on the brakes at a traffic light when the anticipated red remained green. Simultaneously there was the whooping of a siren. Blinking red lights challenged him in the rearview mirror. He tried to stuff the briefcase under the passenger seat but it was too bulky. If the cops pulled him over, how would he explain the money; explain that he didn't have time to stop; explain he was in a life-and-death situation; explain that he couldn't do anything right because he was scared shitless?

He felt his face flush, then burn as an ambulance zoomed around him. Fumbling, he loosened his tie, yanked at his collar button until it popped off, allowing a sudden rush of air to raise chills; goosebumps immediately broke out all over his flesh. His loud, labored breathing assaulted his ears; he almost didn't identify the ragged and frightened sounds as his own. Without warning, his stomach flip-flopped and he vomited bilious liquid all over the front of his shirt, tie, and suit.

"Shit!" he yelled, groping for a handkerchief. He daubed helplessly at his clothes as he drove, not daring to stop for even a moment.

In the midst of everything, it hit him like a sledge-hammer, pounded away at his brain in rhythm with the disappearing blinking lights of the ambulance: Tracy's going to die!

Not in the far, distant future; not twenty, not thirty years from now. Maybe next week. Maybe even tomorrow.

His eyes watered as he visualized her dead, her remains in an urn.

Dread surged through him like a viscous tar that wouldn't wash away no matter how much he scrubbed. He tried to stem the rush of tears, but his chest heaved with emotion. As he flipped away the salty drops from his face with a flick of his head, new ones quickly replaced them. He looked up and slammed on the brakes, barely seeing a red light in time.

"Oh, my God!" He draped his arms and chest over the steering wheel while the sound of his voice, his loud sobs echoed in the car. "Not Tracy!"

Blaring horns roused him; he looked around in a daze, trapped between the reality of the bustling Geary Street traffic and his searing pain. The truth was so simple, so stupidly apparent:

I love her, damn it! I still love her.

It was like entering a tomb, he thought, as he spiraled with loud squealing tires down into the bowels of the Ridgewood Hospital underground parking complex.

Down through Level B he reacted with tightness in his chest.

At Level C, he was breathing shallowly.

At D, his mouth was open, taking huge gulps of air.

At E, he was drowning in claustrophobia, mumbling syllables in guttural sounds while sparks of light flashed in front of his eyes.

He was near total exhaustion, lightheaded. All he wanted was to go home, leave behind the sour smells and wheezing chest noises that filled his car. The underground plunge assaulted his senses like a drug-induced surrealistic journey. He was diving into a large hole—an ugly, frightening gateway to nothingness. Soon he would be gone, sucked under the earth in this massive burial chamber.

Enough, already! Enough!

Only a few cars were parked at the bottom level of the complex.

Swallowing hard, he started his second circuit of Level E, as Tracy had instructed.

When he completed the second lap, he pulled into the designated slot. A row of light bulbs was out, leaving the space in shadow. He couldn't see his watch, but he knew he was five minutes late. He sat still for a moment, aware of his reeking, sodden clothing—clothing that was long beyond absorbing the sweat that continued to drip from under his arms, down his back, and in his crotch. In the suffocating silence, he gripped the wheel in an attempt to stop his hands from shaking.

I can do this! I can do it!

He mopped the sweat from his forehead with his coat sleeve, then wiped away the salty perspiration stinging his eyes.

He looked around the garage. It was deadly quiet.

He knew someone had to be waiting.

Do it!

He grabbed the briefcase, resisting the temptation to flick on the headlights.

I can't botch this.

Before hoisting the case, he rubbed his wet hands on his pants, opened the door, turned, and slid off the seat.

The money seemed to grow heavier as he wobbled toward the front of the car. Groping, he found the corner juncture and set the case down as instructed. He backed away from it—slowly back, back toward the car.

A forearm slid quickly across his throat, pulled harshly up and back. He struggled, tried to twist away. A knee smashed into his kidney. "Who—"

"One more word and the Mrs. will be nothing but a memory."

Gary's kidney was pounded again.

107

"You hear me, asshole?"

Stabbing pain radiated, followed by numbness; a spasm of coughing clawed at his chest.

"Answer me, or you're going to be responsible for one dead broad."

Gary nodded.

"Is it all in the case?" the voice rasped in his ear. The arm tightened against his neck.

He tried to nod again, but couldn't move against the stranglehold.

The arm crushed harder; he could barely suck air into his lungs.

Flashes of neon whipped before his eyes; his legs started to fold beneath him. He kicked back at his assailant without effect. As he collapsed, his arms reached out like a swimmer being strangled by a large, tentacled creature. Ripples of garbled words echoed in his head, words that ebbed and flowed in undulating particles of sound—louder, softer; louder, softer.

"You tell the Mrs. this little transaction better remain forgotten or I'll be back to see her. Maybe today, maybe to-morrow . . . maybe the day after. Whenever, she'll be sorry she ever fucked with me."

Gary could feel the throb of his heart, faster and faster. He tried to stay conscious. My name is Gary, my name is Gary, my name is Gary.

"Tell her that cute little stunt with the buzzer almost cost her, her life. Tell her . . ."

Gary could no longer grasp the meaning of the words; he tried to hear, but couldn't. Instead, he swam silently away from all his fear, all the ugliness.

The phone rang. Faye grabbed for it, knocking over a

rack of tubes filled with blood samples. "Cripes," she said, watching the viscous circle spread like a heavy handed Rorschach.

"Damn it, Lindstrom!" another lab tech yelled. "Are you trying for some world record in clumsiness?" There were other catcalls.

"I'm sorry," she said meekly, grabbing up the phone receiver. At the same time, she saw Gina waving at her from across the room.

"Sorry, hell! Get some absorbent on that blood," yelled another voice. "Haven't you heard of AIDS? Jesus, isn't it bad enough we're exposed to this shit without you constantly splattering it all over the place?"

"Lab. This is Faye," she said with a quivering voice into the receiver.

"Hi, baby!"

"Frankie," she whispered into the telephone. "Is everything all right?" She looked around and met the angry eyes of Bob Ghent.

"Oh, yes. Everything is perfect, darlin'."

CHAPTER 17

Faye hung up the phone and stared at the broken glass and sticky blood strewn across the counter. Silently, she cursed her clumsiness. The individual blood samples were oozing together to form a gelatinous blob, undercoating tube racks, over-coating lab reports, and finally dripping and splattering onto the floor—contaminating everything it touched.

Normally, the accident would have thrown her into a deep funk, but instead, she was merely impatient.

Talking to Frankie had made her feel deliciously happy, almost cocky. It wasn't the $50,000—the money was Frankie's thing. What really mattered was that she could make things happen; she could be as clever as anybody else in the whole damn hospital.

Everyone around the lab had made her feel clumsy and stupid, especially the lab chief—always bawling her out, embarrassing her in front of the others. He'd called her stupid; she knew she wasn't stupid. She glanced smugly at the cabinet under the sink. Tracy Bernstein's marrow was safe there, in its special insulated container—a small box that she had designed. Stupid people couldn't do that.

She started the tedious job of cleaning up, following hazardous material control procedures. Because she'd had to clean up so often, she no longer needed to refer to the detailed OSHA-mandated instructions. Her coworkers were right: she had splashed a lot of blood around in the Laboratory lately, endangering them all.

Now, the unexpected appearance of Gina, and their conversation, unsettled her. What was the nurse doing in the lab?

She gathered up the chemical blood absorbent she'd spread out on the counter and floor, scooped it into piles, and collected it in a red hazard bag. As soon as she removed all traces of the blood, she would return the marrow to its assigned place in the cold storage unit. It would be safe again; Mrs. Bernstein would be safe again.

I'll be safe again; no one will be the wiser.

As she cleaned, she looked around to see what had happened to Gina. When she saw the nurse pass the Blood Bank and head for the marrow processing area, her uneasiness turned to panic. Gina could only be going there for one reason—Bernstein's marrow.

Damn!

The whole scheme was supposed to be like a game, something to show Frankie how clever she could be. But he had taken her seriously, grabbed onto the idea, and turned it into something scary.

Why hadn't Chapman simply paid the money like the others? Why did he have to go and die without ever getting back his marrow? The marrow that she stole.

And now they were probably going to discover that Bernstein's cells were missing. Then they'd know for sure that the Chapman situation hadn't been just a screw-up.

They'll find out it was me.

Jail! She hadn't thought about that before. Frankie had said everything would be fine—no one would get hurt.

But that wasn't true; someone had died. She was a murderer. Would they execute her? Jesus!

Icy drops of perspiration slid from under her arms as she ripped off her protective visor and gloves—her hands were shaky as she held them under the faucet and scrubbed them

111

clean. Reaching for a towel, she saw the marrow tech racing down the aisle, headed toward the deep storage vats. Faye stood with her back to the sink, her calves pressed tightly against the double doors of the cabinet as her stomach did a somersault. Gina came running back down the aisle and dashed out through the lab exit.

Gina paced back and forth in front of the elevator. Each time the door opened she held her breath, hoping for Mark Kessler's arrival. But it was a long ten minutes before he finally came down to the basement, despite the urgency of her call.

When she started toward the Lab, he took her arm and held her back. "We have to wait for Vasquez," he said.

"Mark, I wanted you to see this for yourself. Why did you call the administrator?"

"Look, Gina, I had no choice. Vasquez has made it a priority issue. We're out the door if we don't notify administration of any problems concerning the autologous marrow project." He shrugged. "Besides, he'd have to be told sooner or later."

"But Vasquez will talk to Bob Ghent. What if he's in on it?"

He looked sharply at her. "What are you talking about, Gina? The lab chief? In on what?"

"Don't you understand? I mean, doesn't it seem strange to you that within just a few days of losing Chapman's marrow, another batch is missing?"

Kessler shook his head. "Maybe, maybe not."

"Come on, Mark. Don't fight me on this. Cells can't continue to keep vanishing and still be attributed to logistics errors."

"Why do you keep focusing on that aspect of the Chapman case?"

"Damn it, Mark, he died because he needed those cells."

"No! Chapman died because we let him down in some way I haven't been able to define . . . as yet." Kessler cocked his head at her. "You make it sound like there was some kind of plot. I don't buy that for a minute." He shook his head. "I did something wrong . . . Chapman died . . . I have to take full responsibility for his death."

"I disagree."

He stared at her with large, sad eyes ringed with dark circles. "Chapman was . . . you know . . . a warm person . . . upbeat about his recovery. I would have bet anything on his pulling through." He suddenly looked away. "That man's going to haunt me forever . . ."

"I miss him, too," Gina said.

Kessler ran a hand nervously through his hair and leaned against the wall. "You know that ranch I own up in Sonoma? I've been thinking a lot about it lately. It's the only place I go where I feel at peace with the world. Maybe that's where I should be . . . leave medicine and move on to other things."

"But, Mark, I thought you loved this work."

"I don't know, Gina. Sometimes I love it; sometimes I hate myself for loving it. Maybe I'm not thinking straight at the moment, you know?" He gave her a weak smile. "I haven't had a decent night's sleep since we lost Carl. Each night I wake up in a cold sweat, go over it step-by-step. For the life of me, I can't figure out where I went wrong. It's a dead end, Chapman's dead end."

"Let it go, Mark. You did the best you could."

He moved away from the wall and gave her a wry smile. With a sweep of his hand, he said, "Maybe all of this is . . . is you reacting to Carl's death. I think you need to follow your own advice and let it go, also."

She nodded slowly. "Maybe."

"Anyway, I'll know about what happened to Carl when the final autopsy report is available."

"When will Pathology have it ready?"

"I would have had it by now, but the family tried to block the autopsy."

"That surprises me. They must have known Carl signed a consent on admission; it's a standard condition for any marrow treatment at Ridgewood."

"His parents knew that, they . . ." Kessler paused, took a deep breath. ". . . it's harder when the actual time comes." His eyes clouded with tears. "What a mess."

"If he'd had the cells, his chances would have been good," she said, squeezing his arm.

The elevator door opened and Alan Vasquez stepped out. Gina ignored the nasty look he tossed her way before leading the procession down the corridor toward the lab. In the lab doorway, he stopped abruptly and confronted Gina.

"What were you doing in the laboratory this morning, Ms. Mazzio?"

She was stunned by the unexpected challenge. Avoiding a direct glance, she said, "I was here to pick up blood."

"I see. Then how did you get in the middle of this marrow business?"

"After what happened to Chapman . . . I was here . . . I was just checking—"

"Our marrow tech is sufficiently competent to keep track of the specimens we store," Vasquez interrupted.

"Apparently not," she snapped back.

His eyes narrowed and a small smile creased his mouth. "We're not paying you premium wages to be a courier."

"Tracy Bernstein is my patient, Mr. Vasquez. Everything about her is part of my job."

"Well, I suggest you return to the floor and direct your talents to the patient herself, then."

Gina's chin jutted out. "I will as soon as we're finished here."

Vasquez's eyes hardened. "I want to see you later in my office. I'll have my secretary call the unit to tell you the time."

Gina pushed ahead and led the way into the Lab where they were immediately greeted by the lab chief.

"Bob, if you can't run things any better than this, we're going to have to find someone who can," Vasquez announced.

The lab chief's face turned a pasty white. "Look, this is all a mistake. Seems the marrow was there all along . . . just deposited in the wrong slot."

"It's not missing?" Gina asked. "But the tech and I checked and double checked the entire cold storage unit. It wasn't there!"

"You mean Tracy Bernstein's marrow isn't missing after all?" Kessler said with obvious relief. "You do have it!"

"Yes, thank God," Bob Ghent said. "I don't think I could stand another Chapman mess."

"May we see it?" Gina asked, a look of distrust clouding her face.

"If Mr. Ghent says it's there, then that's where it is, Miss Mazzio," Vasquez said sharply.

"I want to see it anyway," Gina insisted.

"Oh, for God's sake, as long as we're here, let's take a look at it!" Kessler said.

The lab chief led the way back to the marrow processing section. Once there, they checked the CRT—it still displayed Tracy Bernstein's marrow and storage placement information.

Ghent walked to the refrigerator, donned a pair of protective gloves, and opened the unit. Icy clouds billowed into the room. From the midst of the haze he pulled out one of the marrow bags.

They all crowded in to read the identifying information:

Tracy Bernstein
#041589
Autologous Bone Marrow

"Miss Mazzio, I hope it's obvious to you now that you've unnecessarily alarmed everyone in the Lab, Oncology, Administration, and who knows where else in this hospital," Vasquez said. "I will see you later in my office, along with the Nursing Administrator, to discuss your unprofessional behavior."

Gina started to respond, but was waved silent by Vasquez, who turned to Kessler:

"Doctor, you have overstepped your bounds by involving yourself in Laboratory operations. You acted without consulting the lab chief, which is a serious breach of hospital protocol. Further, I intend to report this incident to the Chief-of-Staff, and recommend that you be censured for your inappropriate behavior today."

The administrator turned on one heel and hurried out of the lab without a backward glance.

Gina and Kessler stood in front of the elevator, silently awaiting a ride up to the Oncology floor. Neither had spoken since leaving the Laboratory.

"What the hell happened?" Kessler finally blurted out, his face creased in anger. "I thought I could trust you, Gina. I came down here to back you up, and now I'm looking right down the barrel of a loaded gun." He thrust his hands into his pockets. "Damn it, isn't my life complicated enough?"

"I'm sorry, Mark. What else can I say? When I called you, the cells were missing." She touched his arm. "I feel terrible having dragged you into this mess. But I swear, Tracy's marrow was missing!"

He refused to look at her. Instead, he slowly shook his head. "I'm worried about you, Gina."

"What do you mean, you're worried about me?"

"Your judgment's always been above reproach. But this time . . . well, I don't know." He jabbed nervously at the lighted UP button. "I don't think you've really heard what you've been saying."

"What are you talking about?"

"Well, for instance, all that stuff about Bob Ghent being involved with the missing marrow that isn't missing. That sort of thing is damn unnerving." He jabbed at the button again, his face turning a bright red. "Jesus, Gina, I'm beginning to think you need some professional help to cope with Chapman's death. The whole thing is making you paranoid."

The elevator arrived; they stepped into the empty car. Gina jammed the heel of her hand against the #3 button. When the door closed behind them, she said, "I never said Bob was involved . . . I said he could be."

"Kind of academic at this point, isn't it?"

Her shoulders slumped as she leaned against the back of the car. "The point is, I know something's wrong. Whether Bob's involved or not isn't the question. It's simply that Chapman's marrow didn't disappear into thin air. Where did it go?"

Kessler put his hands to his mouth and blew his breath

loudly between his fingers. "Damn it, that's not my primary concern. Right now I want to get my hands on that autopsy report and find out what the hell went wrong."

"Report or no report, I still think the missing marrow is connected to his death, one way or another."

He folded his arms tightly across his chest. "Gina, it's time you became more objective about this whole marrow business. As it stands, you've discredited not only yourself, but me right along with you."

"I did what I thought was necessary."

"I don't give a damn about what you thought was necessary," he said, his face an angry red. "Just keep your nose out of where it doesn't belong, and leave me alone."

Gina narrowed her eyes and fixed them on his. "Yes, Dr. Kessler. Anything you say, Dr. Kessler." She straightened, gave him a military salute, turned on her heel, and stomped out of the elevator.

CHAPTER 18

Gina avoided Helen's questioning eyes and stormed into the medication room.

Bastard! Who the hell does he think he is?

But it wasn't just Kessler's attitude and remarks that made her angry; not even Vasquez's nastiness. She'd acted too rashly. Maybe Harry was right: Why should she put her neck on the block with nothing more than a hunch to go on?

She tried to compose herself, but her mind kept flying off in erratic tangents—Chapman's death, Harry's lack of support, Tracy's rejection.

Bringing it down to the now, she focused on her upcoming meeting with Vasquez. Even if he didn't fire her on the spot, would she want to stay on at Ridgewood? If not, what then? Go back to New York?

She hiked herself up on the counter and let her legs swing rhythmically back and forth. This was the quietest place in the unit. Everything was so orderly, so predictable—so unlike her life. Her eyes jumped from the stock of syringes to the huge floor-to-ceiling storage cabinet, filled to overflowing. She idly examined a few of the familiar plastic IV bags with their major components of electrolyte solutions: Dextrose, Sodium Chloride, Lactated Ringer's. Opposite her, she could see through the double glass doors of the refrigerator, packed with an assortment of antibiotics, chemo-therapeutics, and curative solutions.

Here, she was surrounded by the things she knew and understood, things she dealt with day in, day out. Looking at them was comforting, an affirmation of her training and expertise.

So why am I sticking my nose into places it doesn't belong? Locking horns with Vasquez isn't very smart, either. But thinking about the hospital administrator only made her angry again.

Damn him!

After ten years in nursing, she still let people like Vasquez get to her. They made her feel small, by treating her like a recalcitrant child instead of a health professional.

And what if she did go back to New York, would the laboratory fiasco stay with her, continue to hurt—like a bone lodged in her throat?

She slid off the counter and rested her cheek against the refrigerator; the cold glass was soothing. If only there was some way she could crawl inside, curl up and hibernate until it was safe to come out.

No! I'm not running this time. I ran from my marriage; I'm not going to run from my career.

She reached with shaking hands for her patients' medication cards, stacked in a wooden slot next to Helen's. She shuffled them like a miniature deck of cards.

Tracy's marrow *was* missing!

She shuffled the cards a few more times, then stood up, stretched, and breathed deeply. Stretching her neck from side-to-side, she felt the tension lessen, her strength returning. Finally, she smiled and held out one hand, then the other. Steady as a rock.

Vinnie Capello had managed five jumping jacks and, after three pushups, was having trouble getting up.

As an enervating weariness suddenly overcame him, tears spilled from his eyes. He cradled his head on his knees and rocked back and forth on the cold floor.

After a minute or two, he looked up at the Greenpeace calendar he'd tacked to the wall—an African elephant, ears flared, trunk raised, stood ready to charge whoever was holding the camera. Each passing day in May was crossed off in red; the senior prom was only two days away.

Angie had given him the calendar as a Christmas present. That was when she was still his girlfriend.

Gina entered the room. He stayed where he was and watched her wash up before she extended a hand to help him up from the floor.

"I can get up by myself," he said, struggling to stand while holding onto the edge of the bed. Perspiration drenched his bare scalp, his face.

"Tough as nails, aren't you?"

"Yeah, well, I don't need your help, that's for sure."

"Just a macho kind of guy, huh?" Gina said, pulling out a fresh gown from the stack of linens she'd left earlier on the chair. "Trust me on this one, kid—the more you try to be a man who doesn't need anybody, the more lonely you're going to be . . . and it has nothing to do with your age."

"What makes you so smart? And stop calling me, kid!"

"Okay, Mr. Capello. Get your macho butt into the shower." Gina gave him a bright smile. "Mr. Capello, this is the time I've set aside to make your bed. Do me the courtesy of getting cleaned up while I take care of things out here."

Their eyes locked for few seconds until he finally looked away.

He started toward the bathroom, but mid-stride his legs refused to move any further. He saw a flash of bright lights, the room began to spin. Clawing at the empty air, he stumbled, started to drop. Gina's hands caught and held him upright.

"Are you okay, kid?" She wrapped an arm around his waist. "Let me help you to the bed."

"You called me kid again." He leaned heavily on her and walked haltingly by her side on rubbery legs. "I . . . I . . . don't know what happened . . ."

She got him into the bed, wrapped a cuff around his arm, took his blood pressure, and checked his pulse. "Why don't you back off this exercise thing for a while, Vinnie? You're overdoing it."

"If you think . . . I'm going to turn into . . . a vegetable . . . while I'm . . ." He gasped for breath. ". . . stuck in here . . . you're full of—"

"Vinnie! Spare me! I already know what I'm full of. You've told me on numerous memorable occasions."

There was a ringing in his ears, and his own words became muffled. He looked at the nurse's mouth as she talked; the hum grew deafening, blotting out all other sound. He clamped his hands over his ears. The ringing halted as abruptly as it started, leaving him with an instant sense of relief, then an overwhelming sadness. A voice he barely recognized as his own spoke from some far off place:

"I'm so tired, Gina . . . tired of feeling weak . . . tired of being sick . . . tired of every little . . . or big . . . thing . . . making my life so . . . difficult."

She pressed a cool cloth to his head. "You're just worn out, kid. For almost a month you've spent every day fighting with everyone, everything, including your own body. You've got to let yourself rest if you're going to heal."

"You keep forgetting," he said, slowly shaking his head, "it's not the first time you've pumped your poisons into me." Words caught in his throat, he croaked out the rest: "I know that if I let myself relax, let my guard down, even for a second . . . I'll die here."

Gina touched his cheek, then took his hand. "No one told you it would be easy. It's tough. I know that. But it takes a tough person like you to stand up to it."

"You call it tough. Well, maybe it's not tough . . . maybe it's just stupid . . . stupid to try to hang on."

"Vinnie," she said, squeezing his hand, "you're in the home stretch. Get through this one, and the odds are in your favor of beating this thing."

His chest constricted, and he had to force his muscles to breathe in, and then relax them to breathe out. "You call it a thing. Apples are things; oranges are things. This isn't just a *thing*—it's leukemia. Acute Myelogenus Leukemia."

"True, that's what it is. But does it really matter what you call it?"

"It matters to me."

"Whatever it's called, it doesn't change what you have to do to get rid of it."

He reached over and took his well-worn Giants baseball cap from the bed table and pulled it down over his head until his eyes were barely visible beneath the brim.

"Yeah, that's the way you see it. But you don't know what it's like lying in this bed." He paused, waiting for his heart to stop pounding.

"I do understand, Vinnie."

He shook his head from side to side. "When they make their rounds . . . all those people—students, doctors, nurses—they surround me, talk about me and my goddamn AML . . . like I'm not even here. Shit!"

"Vinnie, I think you're just tired."

He studied her, as he had on numerous occasions. She was pretty; the same kind of flashing eyes as Angie. Even had his girlfriend's—ex-girlfriend's—temper; explosive, then forgiving. It hurt every time he looked at the nurse because she reminded him so much of Angie. He glanced again at the calendar: only two days. He'd planned for so long to take Angie to the senior prom; now it wasn't going to happen.

Other bits and pieces, filaments of thoughts, meandered through his head; his eyelids grew heavy.

He tried to remember the last time he'd slept through an entire night; slept dreamlessly; slept without wondering if he'd ever wake up again.

Gina held his hand tightly. His thoughts began to drift away. "Just don't call me kid, anymore," he murmured.

"No promises, kid."

"You'll be sorry, Bronx," he mumbled, drifting off.

"I already am," she whispered with a smile.

Gina was in deep thought when she returned to the nurses' station. Helen was in the midst of taking off a patient gown she'd been wearing to protect her clothes during a procedure. Gina watched her flip off her gloves, wash her hands. Helen looked up. "How's Capello doing?"

"I'm worried about him."

"I'd be more worried about me if he were my patient."

Gina smiled distractedly as she pulled Vinnie Capello's chart from the rack. She turned directly to the Nursing Care Plan she'd written for him; studied it for a moment. "You know, this is his second admission. He's already completed one round of chemo."

"Nine months into remission when they harvested his marrow, wasn't he?" Helen asked.

Gina nodded. "He'll be all right when he gets his marrow back."

Helen rested a hand on her shoulder. "So who are you reassuring, me or yourself?"

Gina stared off into space.

"Earth to Gina, come in please," Helen taunted, waving a hand in front of Gina's eyes.

"Sorry! Can't help thinking about that kid. He's really depressed."

"Yeah, well I've been worried about him from the moment he arrived," Helen said. "What a terror! I hope he gets along better with his family than he does with us."

"They're very close. They would have sold everything they owned if Kessler hadn't gotten the Ulrick Foundation to cover the cost of Vinnie's treatment, particularly after their insurance refused to cover the autologous marrow procedure."

"He's very lucky."

Gina studied the notes on Vinnie, finally turned to the psycho-social evaluation, and then abruptly shut the chart. "He doesn't feel lucky. Besides, there's something else bothering that kid, and it hasn't anything to do with AML."

"Beats me what's going on in Capello's head at any time," Helen said.

Gina began gathering supplies for Tracy Bernstein's scheduled procedure. She'd only picked up a couple of items when Helen reached out and stopped her.

"You won't need any of that today," Helen said.

She looked at her watch. "But it's almost time for Tracy's engraftment."

"Huh, uh! Kessler was here while you were with the Capello kid."

"So?"

"He postponed Bernstein."

Gina snatched up Tracy's chart and quickly turned to

125

the pink physician's orders:

DC orders for engraftment
Withhold for 24 hrs.

"Did he say why?"

"Only muttered something about Chapman's preliminary autopsy report."

"That's it?"

"Believe me, I tried to pump him for details, but all he did was mumble, grumble, and moan."

"Does Tracy know yet?"

"I assume he told her."

"God, I hate to think what that did to her." Gina slumped down on one of the stools and leaned her elbows on the counter. "She was already in such an agitated state that I damn near ordered a sitter for her. I'm really worried about leaving her alone."

Helen walked up behind Gina and began to lightly massage her shoulders. "Listen, girl, maybe you ought to worry about yourself for a change, you know?" She found a couple of polarity points and applied pressure. "Everybody's talking about your disastrous trip to the lab—"

"What a grapevine this hospital has."

"Eh, in a couple of days they'll forget all about it. But I thought you ought to know the word is out." When Gina didn't respond, she added, "And I guess you also ought to know, Vasquez called. He wants to see you at two-thirty."

"Oh, shit!"

Gina was within a few feet of the elevator, headed for Tracy's room, when the satin-finish steel doors slid open. A man stepped out, glanced briefly at her, then turned away and limped down the corridor. He stopped, looked around, and made a helpless gesture, as if he were lost.

"May I help?" Gina called out to him.

He looked back over his shoulder and frowned at her. "I'm looking for Tracy Bernstein's room."

Gina walked up to him, then backed off a couple of steps—his clothes were torn and disheveled, a sour aroma filled the air around him, making her think for a moment that he might have been drinking, possibly even been in a drunken scuffle of some kind.

"Excuse me, visiting in this unit is limited to the immediate family."

"Oh, sorry. I'm not thinking too clearly. I'm Gary Bernstein, Tracy's, uh, ex-husband."

"I see." She wasn't sure how to handle the situation, particularly after all the negative things Tracy had told her about her ex. "I'm Gina Mazzio, Tracy's nurse. Is she expecting you?"

He stood there, arms limp at his sides, looking back and forth between her and the row of rooms. He had stains all over the front of his suit; his shirt collar was crumpled, the top button missing; dark circles outlined the armpits of his coat. His eyes were red, the surrounding flesh puffy. He reached out with one arm and rested against the wall.

"Are you all right, Mr. Bernstein? Can I get you something?" Closer now, she had no trouble identifying the reek of stale vomit.

"Got to see Tracy . . . it's getting late."

She took him gently by the arm. "She's okay; there's no need to rush."

"But you don't understand, he's . . ." Suddenly, he focused on her. He took a deep breath and looked up and down the corridor. "She's expecting me," he said.

Gina nodded, still uncertain whether she should allow this man to go to Tracy's room without checking first.

Maybe she should just call security to be on the safe side.

"Why don't you go down to the men's room and freshen up a bit," she suggested, tentatively turning him in that direction. "I'm going in to see Tracy myself. I'll tell her you're here and that you'll see her in a few minutes. Okay?"

He started to object, then glanced down at the front of his soiled suit. "Maybe you're right," he said, still using the wall for support. "Will you be long?"

"What?"

"With Tracy, will you be in there with her very long? I need to talk to her alone."

"No," Gina said with a shrug. "I only want to see how she's doing." And find out whether or not you're welcome.

"Good." He continued on down the hallway toward the restrooms.

Gina entered Tracy's room and found her sitting on the far edge of the bed, her back to the door, head tilted downward.

"Just checking in to see if I can get you anything," Gina said. "Also—"

"If you want to do something for me, get me my marrow!" She deliberately kept her back turned to Gina.

"I wish I could, Tracy, but when you get your marrow is not my decision to make."

"Then there's nothing you can do for me. Go see some other patient, one you can do something for."

"Tracy, I understand how you feel—"

"No, you have no idea how I feel," she said, looking back over her shoulder. "No idea at all."

"Well, anyway, I wanted to ask whether you're expecting anyone. There's a man out there who claims to be Gary Bernstein."

Tracy twisted fully around on the bed. "Gary's here? He's okay?"

"He had to stop off at the men's room," she said, relieved that she wouldn't have to call security. "He should be here any moment."

Tracy plumped her pillows, scooted up onto the bed, and leaned back. "What do you have to do to get me ready?" she asked, sticking the middle knuckle of an index finger between her teeth.

"Ready for what, Tracy?"

"My engraftment, of course. Gary's here . . . Dr. Kessler should be able to proceed now."

Gina scowled. "I'm not following you, Tracy. Mr. Bernstein had nothing to do with postponing your engraftment; it was a procedural problem."

"You have no idea what you're talking about!" She adjusted the drab ecru scarf she'd been wearing on and off. "You'll see what I mean when—"

She was interrupted by Gary coming into the room. Gina could see that he'd done a creditable job of cleaning himself up, but it was still obvious he'd been involved in some kind of physical scuffle.

"My God!" Tracy gasped. "What happened . . . he didn't—"

Gary stopped her with a cautiously raised palm. "Everything's all right," he said.

"The money—"

"Shh . . . it's all over."

"Then why can't I have my engraftment?"

"What?" He turned and questioned Gina with his eyes, his lips tightening with anger.

"It's an administrative thing," Gina repeated. "The engraftment hasn't been canceled, just postponed."

"We're entitled to a better explanation than that," he said. "Where's Dr. Kessler?"

"Do you want me to find him for you?"

"Yes, and the sooner the better!" He turned back to Tracy and took one of her hands in both of his.

Gina eased herself out of the room.

"Now what in hell was that all about?" she asked herself as she started back toward the nurses' station.

CHAPTER 19

It was almost 2:40 when Alan Vasquez' secretary finally told Gina and the Nursing Supervisor that the hospital administrator was ready to see them. Gina was both surprised and irritated that they'd had to wait so long. Yet, Rhoda Wu, who was sitting next to her, showed no sign of being impatient with the situation.

Still, Gina was inwardly amused that he had not come through the reception area to enter his office, but had used the private side entrance. Was he afraid they might attack him before he could reach his seat of power? She thought it wise not to share her thoughts with Rhoda.

As the two of them entered the pseudo Bauhaus-decorated office, Vasquez was in the process of removing his suit jacket. But when he saw them, he nodded toward the pair of Wassily chairs in front of his desk, and settled the jacket back onto his shoulders. There was the sheen of perspiration on his forehead and upper lip. Gina guessed he had just come from the parking garage.

"I'm sorry you had to wait," he said perfunctorily. "There was a Board luncheon that ran longer than usual."

Gina started to respond, but deferred to the Nursing Supervisor, who had already taken a chair and was settled in, hands folded in her lap. They both watched as Vasquez looked from them to the mounds of reports, correspondence, and publications that covered the top of his desk. There was an almost imperceptible negative movement of his head. He made a halfhearted attempt to create some semblance of order out of the chaos, gave up, and redirected his attention to Gina.

"I'm going to repeat what I told you this morning, Ms. Mazzio—Ridgewood is not paying you premium wages to act as a courier between Oncology and other departments in the hospital. Is that clear?"

"I was doing what I thought was in the best interests of my patient," she said. "We'd already had one problem with a patient's marrow—"

"Enough about the marrow!" He turned to Rhoda Wu: "What are Ms. Mazzio's qualifications?"

"She's a Registered Nurse, with a bachelor of science in nursing. She trained at—"

"No, no," he interrupted again. "All of that's a given, otherwise she wouldn't be here. I want to know the extent of her experience at Ridgewood."

"She started in Med/Surg when she joined us three years ago and later transferred to Oncology," the Nursing Administrator said.

"Has she received orientation for any other department or service?"

"No, although I'm certain she has the capability to fill any nursing position in the hospital."

He lifted his hand, palm facing them. "I'm not questioning her competency as a nurse, Mrs. Wu. I'm concerned about her judgment, about this proclivity of hers to be a patient-advocate gadfly." He shifted his gaze back to Gina. "The point is, you had no business sticking your nose into the Laboratory's systems or procedures."

"If you look at it that way, I suppose you're right. However, I—"

"Good! I'm glad we're in agreement." He leaned back in his chair and looked from one to the other. "Now, correct me if I'm wrong: There is an established job description for

Ms. Mazzio's position in Oncology."

"Yes," said Rhoda.

"And there are specific protocols for the nursing staff in general, and for the Oncology Department in particular."

Gina and Rhoda both nodded.

"Exactly!" He swept a hand over the clutter of his desk. "I have more than enough here to keep me busy without having to get involved in a speculative crisis . . . a situation created by some Staff Nurse whose assigned duties apparently aren't sufficient to keep her occupied."

"If you're suggesting we're overstaffed in Oncology," the Nursing Administrator interjected, "I can show you—"

He held up a staying hand again. "I'm glad my point wasn't lost on you." With the same hand, he leveled a finger at Gina. "As for you, not only have your actions been disruptive, your speculations—had they become public—could have caused this hospital's reputation considerable harm. Do you understand that?"

"As I said before, I thought I was acting in the best interests of my patient," Gina said, "which, as I see it, is in the best interests of the hospital."

He stared at her for a long beat. "I will decide, thank you, what is in the best interests of Ridgewood. Further, when you have concerns about any of our Oncology patients, or about any department within the hospital, you will take them to the ordering physician. Period!"

"Am I allowed to ask a question?" Gina said.

"Go ahead."

"Has anyone ever found Carl Chapman's marrow?"

Vasquez stood and looked down on them. "When you leave here," he said to the Nursing Administrator, "will you please explain to Ms. Mazzio that she is this close to losing her job." He held out a thumb and forefinger with less than an eighth of an inch separating them.

By shift's end, Gina, had forgotten she had offered Faye Lindstrom a ride home. When she saw the lab tech waiting for her at the far side of the plaza fountain, all she could think was: Me and my big mouth!

She wanted to rush home, stand under a pounding shower, and forget the embarrassing meeting with Vasquez and the Nursing Administrator. Instead, she was going to have to play big sister to the sad-faced lab tech.

As she approached the Brianna Fountain, the sounds from the rush and spill of the water did little to soothe or lift her spirits as it usually did.

"Hi," she said, walking up to Faye, who sat on the edge of the fountain, trailing her hand in the bubbling water.

Faye smiled shyly at her. "I thought I'd take you up on your offer. You know, the ride home? I mean, it was fun riding in your car the other day."

"The little red devil is a mess, just like its owner," Gina said, laughing for the first time that day. "But you're right: it is a kick to ride in."

"Maybe I'm imposing," Faye said. "You look tired . . . perhaps you'd rather be alone."

Gina studied Faye: her arms were folded defensively across a utilitarian blue blouse, in keeping with her plain white skirt and Rockport walking shoes. Her initial openness and obvious pleasure at seeing Gina was fading—she was apparently expecting rejection.

"Nah," Gina said, "let's get in the monster and get you home."

As they walked towards the car, Faye said, "I'm sorry you had to get involved in that mix-up with the marrow this morning."

Gina flipped her hand. "It wasn't your fault . . . why should you be sorry?" She unlocked the car door for Faye and walked around to the driver's side. "Besides, I don't want to talk about it. I'd rather forget the whole thing." She undid the convertible top and folded it back before climbing into the car next to Faye. Then, in an unexpected burst of enthusiasm, she said, "What say we get the hell out of here, head out to the beach, and let the salty air blow away all the day's bad vibrations?"

Faye's eyes lit up, then just as quickly lost their luster. "I . . . I don't know. Will we get back late?"

"We absolutely cannot get back late—my boyfriend's coming over for dinner." She looked into Faye's worried eyes, and then tapped her finger on the face of her watch. "Oh, come on, it's not even four o'clock yet. Plenty of time. Let's just go! To hell with everything!"

There wasn't much conversation for a while; Gina was lost in her own thoughts and Faye seemed happy just to be riding along. But as soon as they crossed the Golden Gate Bridge, Gina let out a whoop with such animal delight, a couple of people nearby reacted by tapping their horns and waving. The gusts of air that whipped through the open vehicle barely mussed Gina's short curly hair, but Faye's shoulder-length strands swirled around in every direction. At first, she tried to hold down the flying mop, but then gave up, closed her eyes, and lifted her face to the strong rush of air.

"Makes you want to tear off your clothes and expose your naked body to the wind, doesn't it?" Gina asked.

Faye turned a beet red. "Maybe if I had your body."

"Come on, Faye, that's not the point—just get with the moment."

"When you look like me, you don't just get with the moment."

"Hey, there's nothing wrong with the way you look."

Gina turned the radio up and sang both the English and Portuguese lyrics to the "The Girl from Ipanema." After that, the station played a whole segment of Brazilian music. Faye hummed and joined Gina in making up words to the songs they didn't know. It was pleasantly warm and the sun beat down on them as the Fiat raced through the tricky curves of Highway 1 toward Stinson Beach.

Once there, they jumped from the car and quickly rid themselves of their shoes and socks, tossing them haphazardly back into the car.

Gina rolled up her scrubs to mid-calf. "Come on," she shouted, "last one to the water is a frog." She took off, sprinting toward the ocean. After a few yards, not hearing anything from her companion, she slowed and looked back over her shoulder. Faye was trudging through the sand, the hem of her skirt held tightly in one hand. Gina was disappointed, but accepted that Faye marched to a different drummer. She raced ahead and waded in the cold, toe-cramping water before returning to the dry sand to wait for Faye.

When they were together again, they plopped down in the sand and silently watched the waves erase Gina's footprints. With contented sighs, they lay back, arms akimbo, taking in the cloud-dotted sky and surrounding shoreline.

Faye lifted up on one elbow: "Wouldn't that make a beautiful painting?" She pointed to a hillside that had tumbled into the sea at some unknown time, probably without a human audience. Waves crashed against the huge boulders, filling the air with ocean spray; seagulls dipped and soared over the scree, daring the sea to capture them.

Gina rolled her head around, looked, and nodded. "Beautiful," she said, rising up also. "You know, I've always loved the sensuality of color. It seems unfair that I can fix my own car, do almost anything with my hands, but I can't paint and I can't sculpt." Her fingers raked the sand as she spoke, leaving telltale ridges behind. "I could never paint a scene like that."

"Have you tried?"

"Oh, yes, but you can't believe the abominations I create with a paint brush. I'm sure all my Italian ancestors are very disappointed."

"I used to paint," Faye said shyly.

Gina cocked her head to one side. "What kind of painting . . . oil, watercolor?"

"Mostly watercolor."

"What happened? Why did you quit?"

"Oh, I wasn't very good," she said, pushing up a mound of sand, then flattening it, pushing it up, flattening it again. "But I did love it . . . it was fun."

"You don't have to be a Michelangelo to do something you love."

A stormy darkness flitted across Faye's eyes, but was gone before she spoke. "I suppose not, but, you know, Frankie made fun of my paintings . . . it stopped seeming so important. I threw away most of them."

Gina was silent for a beat, then asked, "You really love this guy, Frankie?"

Faye flipped onto her back. "I love him." She was quiet for a moment, then asked, "What does your boyfriend do?" The subject of Frankie obviously was closed.

"Harry works at the hospital," Gina said. "He's an ICU nurse—Harry Lucke."

"I've met him up on the unit. He's funny."

"He has his moments, but he can be a big pain in the ass, too."

"Are you going to marry him?"

Gina sat up, looked out to sea—it was a dark gray-blue. "I'm not sure I could ever marry anyone again."

"I wish Frankie would marry me."

Gina reached over and tossed some sand onto Faye's feet. "Be careful what you wish for," she said, leaping up and screaming in the wind, "you might just get it." She ran toward the water, leaving new footsteps scattered in the sand.

Gina felt a lot better as they started back to the city, glad she'd spent the time with Faye. The lab tech was shy, sweet, and sad. Even her laughter was bittersweet, as if her sorrow were barely contained. She liked her; they'd had a good time just hanging out together. Now, having crossed the bridge and dropped back down into San Francisco, Faye became remote again. No matter how hard Gina tried to pull her back into conversation, her only response was silence.

It was still light, just after 7:30. Gina slipped into a parking place in front of Faye's apartment house.

"Come up for a cup of coffee?" Faye asked, her eyes troubled and pleading.

"No, I don't think so, Faye. Harry's probably already at my place, no doubt thinking I'm dead."

Faye gathered her things together, looking as though she might burst into tears at any moment.

"Oh, what the heck," Gina said, relenting. "But just for a few minutes." Then she was immediately angry with herself for once again getting so caught up in someone else's problems.

As they waited for the elevator, Gina noticed for the first time the lab tech was carrying two purses. When they entered the elevator, she said lightly, "The hospital must be paying you a lot more than they're paying me if you have to carry two of those."

Faye's mouth went slack; her eyes darted toward the purses. Without looking up, she said, "I left one of them at work last week . . . finally remembered to bring it home today."

Gina, caught off guard by what was an obvious lie, said nothing. A woman simply doesn't forget her purse for a whole week.

As they walked into the apartment, Frank Nellis looked back over his bare shoulder at them from the couch and hit the remote control to click off the television. When he stood up to glare at them, he was stark naked.

"Maybe I'd better leave," Gina said, not knowing whether to run or just tough out the moment.

Faye wrung her hands. "I . . . I promised Gina a cup of coffee, Frankie . . . go put on some clothes."

Nellis' dark eyes bored unflinchingly into Gina's. She willed herself not to break eye contact. She had no intention of allowing this man to intimidate her in the same way he apparently intimidated Faye.

"Don't worry about it, darlin'. I'm sure it's not the first time she's seen a naked man."

"Frankie, please!"

"Okay, okay," he said, giving Gina a lewd wink. He turned away and headed for the bedroom.

"Please . . . have a seat, Gina," Faye said, her eyes begging her to stay. "I'll have the coffee ready in no time."

Gina sat down, flustered and tense, not only from Frank Nellis' blatant nudity, but his rank behavior. She was still debating whether to stay when a painting over the fireplace caught her attention. She studied it for a moment, then called out, "Is this one of your watercolors in here?"

"Not very good, is it?" Faye responded.

Gina mentally agreed. She didn't like the forest scene—too controlled, too empty, too flat. She preferred explosions of color, as though the artist had suddenly gone berserk. But before she could give a diplomatic reply, Nellis came back into the room, still nude.

"Damn awful, isn't it?" he declared, nodding toward the painting. He slipped into a pair of faded jeans as he stood in front of her, but remained shirtless and barefoot.

"I wouldn't say that." She angrily plunked her elbow down on the arm of the sofa. Only then did she notice a headscarf draped across the curve of the sofa arm. She lifted one corner of the wispy, soft material and stared at the abstract design. It was familiar, but she couldn't quite recall where she'd seen that free-form combination of colors before.

"What were you going to say, Nurse Mazzio?" Nellis asked, watching her closely.

Faye interrupted the encounter by bringing in a tray of coffee and cookies. She gingerly set it down on a redwood burl table, looking first at Frank, then at Gina, who was still fingering the silk scarf.

"Isn't that a gorgeous design? Frankie gave it to me."

CHAPTER 20

The apartment door clicked into place as it closed behind Gina Mazzio, but to Faye, it was a thunderbolt going off in her head. She wanted to scream for the nurse to come back, wanted to beg her to stay. Instead, she rested her forehead against the painted wood while her mind raced wildly.

I shouldn't have gone to the beach . . . should have come straight home.

She could hear him breathing. Soon, she would have to turn to face him, but for the moment her legs refused to budge.

And when she did turn, which Frankie would be waiting—the handsome, sexy man she'd fallen in love with, the one who filled the torturous emptiness that had plagued her since she was a child? Or would it be the other one, the mean, ugly man, who pushed her, beat her, belittled her?

She jumped as his arms wrapped viselike around her waist from behind.

"What's the matter, baby?" he cooed, kissing her neck.

Tears filled her eyes as she turned within his arms. "Oh, Frankie. I'm so sorry I was late, but I was having such a good time. I . . . we forgot the time."

He unbuttoned her blouse, her bra; ran his hands up and down over her breasts. "What kind of good time?"

There was a subtle shift in his tone of voice, but Faye felt her heart wrench. "We went to the beach, over in Marin. There was hardly anyone there, Frankie. Mostly just the seagulls and us."

"And maybe just a man or two, huh," he insisted,

reaching down to her buttocks, squeezing, relaxing, then squeezing until she winced.

"I . . . I don't know. I didn't pay any atten—"

He jammed her up against the door, pinning her with his pelvis. "Don't lie to me!"

"Frankie . . . I wouldn't . . . I couldn't! I love you."

"Yeah, sure and any other guy you can get your hooks into. Feed that love crap to some other sucker. All you bimbos do is take, take, take. That's what you do." His voice dropped to a murmur. "Grandpa knew. He taught me all about women. Couldn't fool him."

Faye was barely breathing, sandwiched between his body and the door. "I didn't do anything wrong, Frankie. Please! I really do love you, just you."

He pushed off her, the iciness in his eyes suddenly gone. Falling onto the sofa, he draped an arm over his face.

She first wanted to run, to protect herself. But she couldn't, she couldn't leave him. Instead, she slowly crossed the room and sat next to him, tentatively stroking his upraised arm.

"Are you all right?"

The arm slid away, falling to his side; he smiled crookedly at her. "What a stupid question. I made fifty grand today, darlin'. Fifty grand!"

"I know, Frankie . . . but you just seem so sad." She leaned over to kiss his cheek.

"There's one-hundred-and-fifty grand socked away now, and you think I'm sad?" He brushed her away. "There must be something wrong with you."

She grabbed his hand and squeezed it. "Frankie, I'm scared. They almost found out today; I almost got caught." She raised his hand to her lips and kissed each knuckle separately. "I don't think we should do this anymore."

His fingers uncurled and clamped around her jaw. "Listen to me, you stupid bimbo." He shook her head back and forth. "You do what I tell you, when I tell you. Understand?"

She forced a nod, tried to blank out the pain that knifed through her.

"Don't ever tell me what you think we should do," he said, shaking her head again, digging his nails into her skin.

She screamed, hunching into the pain. "I won't, Frankie. I won't!"

"Good, baby, that's what Frankie likes to hear." He eased the pressure on her jaw, but didn't let go. He reached into his hip pocket with his other hand and pulled out Gina's calling card. "And don't ever bring that bitch Mazzio around here again."

"But . . . but . . . Gina's my friend."

"Not anymore."

Gina rested her elbows on the roof ledge and looked down at the street traffic. "I'm certain that was Tracy's scarf I saw at Faye's."

"How can you be so sure?" Harry asked. "Tracy Bernstein can't be the only person in the world with a scarf like that."

"Harry, I realize that; I'm not a dolt. But I know what I saw—the coincidence is too great."

"A little sensitive tonight, maybe?" He wrapped his arms around her and kissed her on the cheek.

She shrugged him off. "Look, I know other people could buy that same scarf, but certainly not naked-butt Nellis."

"So you don't like the guy. That doesn't mean he doesn't have good taste."

"That's not the point. Tracy told me how she happened

to buy that scarf when she was in Italy. It's by a famous Italian designer, Michaelia, or something like that. His stuff has never been imported to the U.S. I remember, because we had a long discussion about my Italian ancestors. It's the same scarf! And I want to know how he got it."

Harry shook his head.

"Damn it, Lucke, I'm not in the mood for this. I've had one hell of a day, what with Kessler, Vasquez, and the Bernsteins. Then having to watch that jerk boyfriend of Faye's strut around like he's God's gift was just too damn much." She turned to face him. "I'm in no mood for any more crap . . . especially from a man who claims to love me."

"Gina, I know you've had a horrible day, but I think talking about it is going to make you feel a lot better." He ran his fingers gently through her hair, continuing until her eyes closed.

"Why do you always have to be right?"

"I can't help it if I'm perfect," he whispered in her ear. "So tell me what happened with Vasquez."

She opened her eyes and shrugged. "What's to tell? They caught me where I didn't belong."

"Come on, doll, what did Vasquez say to you?"

"Don't call me doll! Any respectable feminist would barf at that," she said, looking down on the street again. She liked being on the roof, always had. It was one of the few places where she could think.

"You always liked it before."

"Just because I didn't tell you I disliked it doesn't mean I liked it."

"Okay, Barbie, what did happen with Vasquez?"

She laughed in spite of herself and looked at the sky. Dusk was her favorite time of day—everything was silhouetted against the dying light. Off in the far distance, her wishing star was twinkling back at her.

"Mostly, I admitted I didn't belong in the Lab and that I'd only gone there to check on Tracy's marrow."

"Shoot! Couldn't you have thought of something better than that?"

"Harry Lucke! Now you really are pissing me off. The thing is, I first tried to lie about picking up some blood. And guess what? They wanted to know whose blood it was—for which I didn't have an answer. And you know why?"

He just stared at her.

"Because it was one of those rare moments when not one poor soul up there needed a transfusion, that's why." She shook her head. "There was nothing left but to tell them the truth—a sad commentary of its own, don't you think?"

"And they got that upset over your checking on a patient's marrow?"

"Not exactly. It was when I told them I was worried because of what happened to Chapman's marrow."

"You didn't!"

"Yes I did. And they told me that if I stuck my nose into other hospital affairs one more time, I was out the door."

Harry put an arm around her waist. "Hey, it'll work out."

She leaned heavily against him, and for the second time that day wondered if maybe she shouldn't tuck her tail between her legs and go back to New York. She looked at Harry speculatively, wondering if she could just walk away.

"What say we drown our sorrows in a pepperoni pizza?" he suggested. "My treat."

"Harry, I know you're trying to make me feel better, and I appreciate it, but this really is important to me—it's got me all tied up in knots. Would you mind if we didn't go out to eat? It's getting late and I'd rather hang out here for awhile."

Harry clapped his hands together. "So, we'll have them deliver the pizza to us up here under the stars."

"In that case, you may call me doll."

It was about ten when they finally finished eating. They were sprawled across a blanket after having eaten around sporadic conversation that dealt with bits and pieces of everything and nothing.

"Faye's a strange bird," Gina said.

"Hmmm. I was kind of surprised you were out with her. Didn't think you cared all that much for her."

"You know, it's not that I don't like her. There's just something . . . something—"

"What?"

"There's something wrong there."

"In what way?"

Gina shook her head, shrugged her shoulders. "Can't really put my finger on it." She reached over to twirl a swatch of his dark curls in her fingers and laughed. "It's funny, but once you get to know her, she's sort of an anxious-to-please kind of person. Today was the first time I'd seen her laugh. And I really did have a great time with her at the beach." She tousled his hair. "If you think I was a bear this evening, think how I would have been without all that sea air."

"Were you cranky? I never noticed."

She stuck her tongue out at him and stretched, then yawned. "It's that boyfriend of hers, I think. He gives me the creeps."

"Who, the exhibitionist with the classy taste in scarves?"

Her response was a shiver that caused her to wrap her

arms around herself. The fog had finally come in; puffs of it floated around them.

"What do you suppose that preliminary Pathology report said that caused Kessler to cancel Tracy Bernstein's engraftment today?"

"Gina, I think you'd better take Vasquez's advice to heart and forget about this whole business."

She propped herself on one elbow. "That doesn't sound like the tough street kid I know."

He shook his head. "The key word there is kid. I gave up that life a long time ago, just the way you did. All I want now is a jug of wine, a loaf of bread, and thou."

"Harry, I can't forget Chapman. Not yet. Not until I know what happened to him."

"What happened is, he died."

"You think that's what the Path report says, 'He died'?"

"Funny lady! Of course not. There'll be a bunch of medical mumbo jumbo, but not much more."

"Then why didn't Tracy get her marrow today?"

"I don't know . . . and I don't care. Nor should you at this point. Let Kessler worry about it."

She sat up and tried to see his expression in the semi-darkness. All she saw were twin gray pools of shadow where his blue eyes should have been.

"Is that why you work in ICU, Harry? No patient attachments, no long-term involvements?"

He reached for her hand. "No, it's not. I work there because there's hope, the same hope that exists for your patients. But there's no hope for Carl Chapman. He's dead." He squeezed her hand. "Let him go, Gina. Losing your job isn't going to bring him back."

She bowed her head. "You're right about one thing: I can't afford to lose my job." She stood up and stretched.

"Still, I want to know what's in that Path report." She started walking toward the stairwell.

"Where are you going?"

"If I'm ever going to get an answer, it's going to have to be after regular hours."

"For God's sake, Gina, you're not going to the hospital now, are you?"

"That's exactly where I'm going."

"You really are crazy. You're not only going to get canned, you're going to end up in jail."

"Oh, bull!"

"Gina, I don't want you to do this."

"Harry, I don't recall asking your permission."

"Then I'm going with you."

"No! I don't think that's a good idea. Two of us traipsing around down there would be too conspicuous."

"I still say it's a bad idea. Please don't go!"

CHAPTER 21

Frank Nellis eased his '82 Firebird into a parking place across the street from the apartment building and looked out to study the five-story structure. He sat there under the street lamp, running his hand back and forth across the new sheepskin seat covers—he liked the way the natural off-white contrasted with his dark pants. It was nice, but he couldn't help visualizing himself in a new set of wheels. A Caddie. Soon!

He glanced up to watch the digital clock blink over to 10:00 p.m.

The fog had dipped down into the Sunset area of the city, and he shivered as he opened the car door and got out. He hesitated, then crossed the street, watching for any foot traffic in the quiet residential neighborhood. All he could see was an old woman, half a block away, trudging along the sidewalk, pulling a wheeled cart stuffed with a large, overflowing shopping bag.

He stepped quickly through the outer glass door into the apartment house and scanned the row of occupant names until he found: **Mazzio, 3C**.

There you are, you little bitch!

His lips curled into a smile. He tried the locked handle of the building's inner door just as the elderly woman pushed her cart into the lobby.

"What do you want, mister?"

"Came to see a friend, but he's not home." He smiled pleasantly, edging past her to leave. As if having second thoughts, he paused and asked, "Need some help with your groceries?"

"Sure, sure! Do I look like I was born yesterday?"

He spread his hands and gave her a hurt look. "Just trying to help."

"Knock off the horseshit, buster. If your friend's not home, get your ass out of here before I start screaming my head off."

Nellis backed out of the door, giving her a mock bow as he turned away from her. Fuck you!

He could feel the old woman watching him, her eyes boring into his back as crossed the street and climbed into the Firebird. Only when he was inside with the door closed did he risk a glance back in her direction. She was there, staring out the door; then she turned and disappeared within the building.

"Old whore!" His palms were sweaty on the leather-covered custom steering wheel; a surge of malice made him feel disjointed. "Cool it, man," he muttered. "Don't do anything stupid. Not with all that cash waiting for you."

Fingering the ignition key, he watched the lights in a third-floor apartment flick on. All he could see was a shadowy outline, but he was certain who it was.

"Nosy witch!"

Firing up the car, he drove slowly down the street, then cruised around the block and parked once more, this time farther away from the apartment building entrance.

His fingers drummed a nervous rhythm on the steering wheel. "Gotta think, gotta think, gotta think!"

A vision of Gina staring at the Bernstein woman's scarf flashed through his head.

"That cunt knows who it belongs to." He balled his hand into a knotted fist. "Can't let her spoil this." He started to leave the car again, but a man and woman exited the apartment building, stopped for a moment on the stoop.

The entrance lights flooded over them.

It's that goddam Mazzio!

She and the guy were hassling each other about something. Nellis sat up straighter in the seat, his teeth clenched. The man suddenly walked away. The nurse stood there, watching him depart, then walked toward Nellis and got into a small foreign convertible parked two cars in front of his.

Her lights blinked on and she pulled out into the street. He waited until she was a half block away, then followed her. Even though she stayed within the speed limit, he had to run a red light to keep from losing her.

"You're not getting away from me," he said.

Ten minutes later, she cruised towards Faye's apartment. Was she going back to see Faye? But she continued on and finally slowed as she approached Ridgewood Hospital.

She circled the area, apparently looking for a parking place. He stayed on her bumper as she took turn after turn around the block. Suddenly, she darted into a just-vacated empty space; he quickly pulled in at the curb in front of a fire hydrant.

Stepping out of the Firebird, he paused as two screaming ambulances and a police car roared up onto the hospital emergency ramp. Four people were whisked away on stretchers as he watched. When he checked on Mazzio again, he found that she also had waited, standing off in the shadows of a walkway.

All the police milling around outside worried him. But one by one, they entered the building. Mazzio stepped out and hurried past Emergency Receiving and on down the block toward the main entrance.

What the hell is she up to?

151

★ ★ ★ ★ ★

Gina recognized several of the people hustling the stretchers through the hospital doors—bloody sheets were thrown over the victims, apparently from some kind of major catastrophe. The staff moved in a flurry of activity—running, shouting orders. Her first instinct was to rush inside and offer her help. But the presence of the police made her realize she couldn't risk being seen. Not if she was going to carry out her plan. Instead, she forced herself to stand helplessly in the shadows of the tree-lined street, hands clutching her sides as she waited for things to quiet down.

Soon the ambulances pulled out of the hospital driveway, their emergency lights extinguished. As the policemen entered the building, she edged cautiously past the bright lights of the receiving entrance.

She'd arrived about thirty minutes before the graveyard shift was due to come on duty, not really that unusual. Some of the staff liked to hit the cafeteria to exchange a little gossip; others were more than happy to get away from home and their mates that much earlier.

She strolled through the front door as if it were her regular shift. The guard paid little attention, barely lifting his head from his magazine.

Holding her breath until she stepped into the elevator, she hit the "B" button and closed her eyes. Harry was right. This was crazy. Her legs were rubbery as she moved from the elevator into the basement hallway. Was it her imagination or were the lights twice as dim as usual?

The eerie silence was broken only by the soft squeak of her running shoes, echoing in the maze of corridors.

Winding through the labyrinth, she glanced at each aluminum bubble mirror hanging from the ceiling. At one corner, her eye caught the flash of a dark shadow in the corridor behind her.

She spun around, clamping her teeth into her lower lip.

No one there! Her skin tingled with cold sweat. She stood stock-still.

Stop it! Damn imagination's going to do me in before I even get started.

She shook it off and hurried past "The Hole"—the hospital's sub-level auditorium—before looking over her shoulder again.

Something was wrong. She could almost smell another presence, sense a shift in the coolness of the air on her skin, feel the rush of fear rippling the base of her spine.

She stared at the exit sign and was tempted to bolt up the stairs; the intuition that had saved her ass many times on New York streets was talking to her, screaming at her.

No! I've got to finish this.

When she passed the Laboratory, she was power walking; she was in a full trot as she arrived at Pathology.

Pushing through the double swinging doors, she startled a morgue tech sitting behind a desk, checking off completed tissue reports.

He stood and confronted her: "Sorry, no visitors without an authorization slip."

Gina gave him her brightest smile and showed her hospital identification card. "I'm Gina Mazzio from Oncology, upstairs. I wondered if I could see the Post report on Carl Chapman?"

He looked carefully at her photograph, then back at her. His whole demeanor changed as he returned her ID card and eased back down into his swivel chair.

"Hey, you know I can't do that without some kind of authorization."

Gina studied him: twenty-five, lank, fair hair; the kind of pallor that comes from spending a lot of time indoors. He was furtively eyeing her breasts, trying to see them through the sweatshirt she had thrown on.

"Are you always alone at night? Must be pretty tough."

"It's not too bad." He ran his hands self-consciously through his hair, leaning back in the squeaking chair. "It's usually a lot busier than this."

She read his ID. "Listen Joey, I'd really be grateful if you'd let me see the Chapman file."

He started to shake his head.

"Please don't say no. It's very important." She looked at him with pleading eyes. "How could it hurt anything?"

He stared at her for a few moments before standing again. "Look, I can't let you do that. That's all there is to it." Walking toward the door he smiled at her and said, "Anyway, it's time for my break. You'd better be gone by the time I get back or I'll have to call security."

He turned, leaving only the scuffing of the swinging doors to break the silence. She wished she could have asked him where the files were kept, but she didn't dare push it.

She hurried down the hallway, darting from one room to another, peeking through the glass panels, entering only when she couldn't see the full expanse of the room. Pushing through one of the doorways, she paused for a moment and held her breath.

"Ugh."

She'd stumbled into the dissection area. The place was spotless, but she could still smell the sickly sweet odor of blood, laced with a tinge of formalin. Even in the diminished light, her eyes were drawn to the stainless steel tables where bodies were placed, splayed open, and probed in search of answers that often never came. Here, there would never be any of the frantic activity she'd just witnessed out-side emergency—no desperate lifesaving measures—only the cold, calculated assessments of death.

She eyed the scales where organs were weighed, then reached out toward the clean rubber aprons that were care-fully placed on each table, ready for use. She fingered the pliant rubber, then pulled back her hand as though burned.

Wrinkling her nose, she moved on toward another doorway at the back of the room. When she pushed through, she found herself in the Morgue. The walls were lined with latched, squared doors. She knew the corpses were neatly slotted in each of the shiny metal compartments.

Her stomach turned queasy as she backed out of the room, the rubber door seals swooshing against the floor. She stood still for a moment, leaning against the wall. Her throat was raw, as though it had been scratched by sand-paper.

Gina hurried down the corridor and found a large room filled with gunmetal gray filing cabinets. She yanked out the closest drawer and found detailed biopsy reports and other tissue studies—not what she was looking to find. She moved to another section and tried again: Histological slides. She mentally kicked herself for even bothering with the diminutive slide drawers. When she looked up, she saw a sign directly across the room, mounted above a row of file cabinets: **AUTOPSIES**.

It took only a moment to find the right cabinet. She yanked open the drawer marked **A–C,** then flipped through the files until she finally found what she was looking for.

******Preliminary Report******
Subject Name Submitted by Account Case Number
Carl Chapman Ridgewood M. Kessler 7776654

Although it was a preliminary report, the study of the organs, extremities, and systems of the human physiology was extensive.

As she studied the Pathology protocol that delineated the gross or visual descriptions of the body organs, it became apparent that Carl's vessels had been damaged, then destroyed by massive multiples of various enteric endotoxins.

The words jumped out at her. In her hand was a road map of Carl Chapman's destruction, his respiratory system reduced to bare essentials: *trachea, bronchi, pulmonary arterial tree, multiple lobes. Kidneys divided into capsules, tubules, cortical medulary, renal pyramids, conical masses.*

The report went on and on, covering all of Chapman's dissected systems.

Carl Chapman had become a non-thing, a cadaver.

A sudden rush of tears washed across her cheeks. Then she was sobbing, totally out of control. Every time she tried to stop, she cried even harder.

Finally, disgusted with herself, she yanked a tissue from her pocket, blew her nose, and turned her attention back to the report.

******Preliminary Diagnosis******

1. Pulmonary failure

2. Cardiac failure

3. Distributive shock secondary to gram negative bactermia. Specimens retained: Blood, urine, fixed tissue for microscopic examination.

On the last page, a yellow "Post-It" note was affixed at the bottom:

For Christ's sake, Mark, you should see the microbes in this guy. Someone must have covered his insides with shit!

CHAPTER 22

Gina skimmed through the autopsy report one more time, then stuffed the papers back into the filing cabinet.

The pathologist's cryptic note to Kessler made it very clear why Tracy Bernstein's engraftment had been cancelled—massive fecal contaminants had invaded Chapman's bloodstream. She shook her head. Where had it come from? Certainly not Chapman's marrow; he never received it. The same question must have crossed Kessler's mind, which meant he wouldn't risk exposing his other patients to the same contaminants.

She quickly exited the file room; Joey would be returning at any moment. She needed to get out of Pathology—he'd done her a favor. No sense screwing up that along with everything else.

She'd taken no more than a couple of steps when she heard the distinctive brush of a door seal on the polished tile floor. She froze, one hand braced against the wall.

"Joey?" she whispered, taking a couple of small steps forward.

"Joey?" she repeated, this time a little louder, trying to keep her voice from trembling. Fear held her immobile.

Finally, sniffing at the sour air permeating the hallway, she forced herself to place one foot in front of the other. She slid along the wall, listening, moving forward only a few inches at a time.

She heard the scuff of a shoe and picked up her pace. At the first doorway, she slipped through, holding onto the door, wincing as she tried to close it soundlessly.

"Damn!" She was back in the autopsy area where anyone could easily spot her. She rushed to the back of the room, entered the Morgue, and stood in front of the wall of stainless steel doors. She tried not to think of the cadavers resting inside.

Tentatively, she unlatched a door, pulled timidly on the handle. When it wouldn't budge, she had to tug with both hands. Suddenly it sprung open—a rush of chill, stale air slapped at her face. She peered into the black hole. Seeing nothing, she pulled the roller tray toward her. A stony blue-white face appeared, its protective sheet pushed to one side.

She slammed the drawer home, stood there, shivering, not sure what she should do. Then she heard the brushing sound of the autopsy room door being pushed open.

She pulled on the handle of the next cooler drawer. Lifting one shaking leg, she stretched it out on the tray—the chill penetrated her jeans. Flattening the rest of her body out horizontally, she reached forward and began to roll herself into the waiting box.

She reached out for the door, stopped. There had to be a way to jam the latch, keep her from being locked in.

Patting the pockets of her jeans, she found a couple of wadded up tissues. She quickly stuffed one into the latch opening, ripped off the leftover tissue, and pulled the door closed. She was blind and deaf to everything except her own panicky gasps. She pushed at the narrow confines of the chamber; shoved a hand to her mouth as the iciness of the cooler spread through her.

Stay. Stay. *You have to stay.*

She was suffocating, in the blackness; she knew that at any moment she would scream. Pushing frantically at the sides of the chamber, she banged the door open with her head.

As the tray raced outward, she scrambled off the pallet, a low hum of terror vibrating in her throat.

Gulping in the fresh air, she staggered around for a moment before she was able to press an ear to the door and listen.

She cracked open the door and peered into the autopsy room. Empty.

Sidling along the white tile wall, she edged around a row of sinks. One of the faucets dripped into the tub; the soft splashes boomed in her ears. Her stomach cramped from the smell of the formalin that permeated the air; but it was the smell of her own fear that forced burning bile up into her throat.

At the double doors, she looked through one of the glass panes, snapped back with a swallowed gasp. Someone was standing on the other side, and she'd seen enough to know it wasn't Joey.

Trapped.

She lowered a shoulder and rammed herself bodily against the occupied door. As she burst through the entry, half stumbling, half running, she caught only a fleeting glance of a figure sprawled on the floor.

She dashed away from Pathology and zigzagged her way through the corridors. But even before she reached "The Hole," she heard footsteps pounding behind her. She glanced quickly at the stairwell opposite the auditorium, but turned away, having no idea where it went.

Instead, she slipped into the auditorium. A single light on the stage created eerie shadows throughout the cavernous room. She hurried along one wall until she came to the first side exit. She jammed both hands down hard against the release bar; the door remained fixed, locked. She tried two more with the same result.

Spinning around, she surveyed the room, from the back row of its bolted down wooden seats, to the small, curtainless stage; nothing offered any hope of concealment.

Gina ran down the aisle and stepped onto the stage. This is where he would find her, corner her, unless she came up with something damn soon.

She moved center stage and circled the lectern, a box-like structure with a high-intensity reading lamp affixed to its slanted top. She crouched down, compressed herself into a ball, and squeezed into the narrow back opening of the structure. Her chin smashed against her knees, her calves immediately began to cramp. She swallowed down the pain as she heard the door to the auditorium swing open.

She clamped her eyes shut, trying to quiet her panting. The footsteps came closer and closer, up the steps, onto the stage.

Gina screamed as a hand reached in, grabbed her, and pulled her to her feet. She tried to twist away and struck out blindly with both fists.

"Hey! Hey! Gina! Cool it! It's okay. It's me!"

Her eyes snapped open. Harry!

"It's okay, doll. It's me."

Her legs gave way, and she collapsed in his arms. When she could finally speak, she asked, "Was that you in Pathology just now?"

"No. I was on my way there when I thought I saw you sneak in here like a scared rabbit." He rubbed his stomach and grimaced. "Next thing I knew, some guy punched me in the gut and took off up the stairs. I'd sure as hell like to get my hands on him."

"What'd he look like?" she asked, straightening.

"Can't say. It happened too fast. All I know is that he's a strong son-of-a-bitch."

160

Gina threw her arms around him. "Harry, I was so scared. I don't remember ever being that frightened. I hate to think what might have happened if you hadn't showed up when you did."

He hugged her tightly. "You're the most stubborn person I've ever known."

"I know, I know. Thank God you love me."

"Yeah, but it ain't easy."

CHAPTER 23

Frank Nellis' stomach cramped as waves of nausea swept through him. He clutched at his gut, rubbed it, tried to snuff out the searing pain. Nothing helped.

It wasn't fair: He'd kept himself together, solved every goddam new problem instead of losing his temper and messing up things like he'd done so many times in the past. He'd stayed in control, stashed the money, and was finally finding a way to escape. Then he'd screwed up by not nailing that goddam nurse.

Pulling the covers over his head, he slid down toward the foot of the bed and cursed Faye for the noise she was making getting ready for work.

He'd hardly slept; tossing and turning, he finally curled up, hugging himself smaller and smaller until he was no more than a tight little knot. Still, he couldn't hide from the images that plagued him: his mother's final haunting stare as she closed the door and left him behind forever; his grandpa crushing him to the floor with his heavy work boot so he couldn't run after her.

He'd tried to forget, to bury the visions, only to have them pulled out of the depths by some devilish force that refused to stop replaying his past. Today, it was the blurry, black-and-white film—the version that no longer brought despair, only anger.

"Frankie?" He felt her tug at the bed covers. "I have to leave soon. I need to talk to you."

He held perfectly still, trying to make her believe he was still asleep. He wasn't finished trying to drive away the demons.

"Frankie?"

He flipped the covers away and jumped from the bed, all in one huge, dramatic motion. Faye tried to get out of his way, but only managed to trip over her own feet and tumble to the floor.

Planting a foot on either side of her hips, he stared down at her. Breathing heavily, he smelled the rankness of his own body—he ran his palms over bunched muscles and tried to wipe away the sheen of sour sweat. Beneath him, Faye attempted to push herself away, but he forced her back down, pressing his foot harshly against her belly.

"Frankie, let me up," she said in that whiny voice he hated. "Please!"

He bent over, gave her a resounding slap across one cheek. "It's all your fault . . . YOUR FAULT!"

"What did I do?" she pleaded, holding a hand tightly against her reddened face.

"You brought that Mazzio bitch here. Started her nosing into our business."

"No, Frankie! She doesn't know anything. I swear." Faye tried to rise again, but he stomped harder into her gut. "Frankie, please. You're hurting me."

"I knew that bitch was nothing but trouble. Didn't I tell you that? Now she's up to something. Wish to hell I knew what it is."

"What are you talking about?"

"I followed her to the hospital last night; almost nailed her ass, sneaking around Pathology."

"Pathology?"

"Don't be so goddamn stupid, Faye. She's checking on that dead guy, Chapman."

Her forehead wrinkled in concentration. "But why?"

"Never mind why. I want her out of the picture. Get it?"

"Frankie, leave her alone. She can't hurt us."

He grabbed her by an arm, jerked her up from the floor, and threw her across the bed. "You big cow! Don't you ever tell me what to do!"

"Please, Frankie, listen to me," she said, lifting up on her elbows. "Let's get out of this mess now before we get caught."

She was like all the dumb bitches he'd ever known. Just looking at her face made him want to bash her. He took a deep breath, tried to swallow the anger; he knew he had to stop it right now. But he could feel it all blowing up, getting away from him again.

She grabbed for his hand, rubbed it against her cheek, kissed it several times. "We can put back the Capello marrow, take the money we have and go . . . go before it's too late."

"God, you're pathetic," he sneered, yanking his hand away. "You're not touching that stuff; it stays right here with me in the freezer. And we're not pulling out of this until we get the rest of the money, first Capello's, then the Oldham girl's. That was the deal, remember? Six of them! Three hundred big ones!" He held up a fist, pushed it under her chin. Oh, how he wanted to hit her; oh, how he wanted to smash a fist into her pouty, puffy face. Instead, he tapped her chin roughly with his knuckles. "Better not chicken out on me, baby." He ran a finger slowly down her forehead, along the bridge of her nose, and stopped with it pressed against her lips. "You're not going to, are you, darlin'?" he asked with a forced smile.

She shook her head rapidly back and forth.

"Good girl! And you planted the phony Capello marrow, like I told you?"

Her eyes glowed with fear, like mirrored pools. "Yes,"

she said, nodding at the same time.

He snorted. "That'll take care of your nosy nurse friend, or anyone else checking the inventories." A sudden thought made him roar with laughter: "Can you imagine what would happen if they tried to give that Capello kid the mess we made up. Jesus, I couldn't tell the difference between the real marrow and that water and vegetable mixture you concocted."

Faye bolted upright. "Frankie, please . . . Vinnie Capello's only seventeen. Can't we give him a break?"

His laughter disappeared as he clamped his mouth shut, lips tightly compressed. He stared at her for a long time before turning away and starting to pace back and forth.

"Let me take back his marrow, Frankie . . . please!"

He stopped abruptly, smiled sweetly at her just an instant before his hand folded into a tight fist. With a loud grunt, he punched her solidly in the abdomen. When she screamed, he covered her mouth with his hand. "Goddamn it!" he exploded. "Don't talk to me about some pampered, little pimply-faced shit. I was only ten when they blew my old man away. Did anybody care what happened to me?"

Faye twisted her face away from his hand. "FRANKIE . . . please . . . let me . . . put it back."

"Bitches!" he yelled, spittle flying from his mouth. "All of you . . . bitches. Supposed to help us, take care of us. But no, all you do is nag. My old man was gunned down robbing a dumb-ass liquor store. Shit! Never would have happened if my mother had stuck around and taken care of him. Not on your fucking life. Ten years old . . . ten fucking-years old and left alone with the meanest bastard who ever walked this earth. And I'm supposed to worry about some useless teen punk?"

Faye sobbed loudly; tears and saliva mingled and

drooled down her chin. "Frankie, just this once!"

Blue buttons flew in every direction as he ripped off her blouse, shredding the thin material. "Didn't you hear me? Didn't you hear what I said?" He grabbed her shoulders, shook her until her teeth rattled.

"Frankie . . . I love you; I'd do anything for you. But please, let me return Vinnie Capello's marrow. He's suffered enough; they all have. Let's stop the whole thing now. Please!" Then she started sobbing. "I can't do it anymore. What if another one dies?"

"There's no reason for any of those assholes to die. All they have to do is cough up the money."

"But Vinnie's just a boy!"

Frank felt a hot coal slosh around in his stomach, push its way into his chest before splashing into his throat. He fell on her, and with a grunt sank his teeth into her belly. Her piercing scream was choked off as he smashed the heel of one hand tightly up against her lower jaw.

Explosive snorts, flying mucus erupted from her nostrils as she arched her back, bucked up and down. The more she fought, the more the soft, yielding flesh shredded between his teeth, filling his mouth with the metallic taste of blood.

Only when she stopped struggling did he pull away, spitting small pieces of tissue back into the ugly wound. "I won't kill little Vinnie Capello . . . if I get my money, got that?" He got up from the bed. "Now get your ass out of here and do as you're told, or the next time I'll really hurt you."

"Frankie," she whispered, staring down at the oozing mess in her stomach. "Frankie . . ."

His eyes widened in mock alarm. "Darlin', I don't want to hurt you. If you'd just be my good little girl everything would be fine."

Faye covered her face with an arm. Her shoulders shook.

"Stop sniveling! This is nothing," he said, tapping her mutilated belly. "Nothing!"

"It hurts, Frankie," she whimpered. "It hurts so much."

"Good! Every time you think of taking that punk's marrow back before we get the money, I want you to remember this." He pushed his face down close to hers until their noses almost touched. "And remember, there're lots of other soft places I can nibble."

Faye stared at him with defeated eyes.

"Now don't get me wrong, darlin'. I do love you the way you are." He reached over and kissed her gently on the chest. "But a woman your size . . . well, there's just that much more to work with . . . places where . . . well, you know, where no one will ever see what it takes to keep you on the right path." He stared at her for several beats. "And if I were you, I'd think twice before mentioning any of this to that snotty nurse friend of yours. Understand?"

Faye nodded quickly, murmured, "All I've ever done . . . all I ever tried to do was make you happy, love you."

He trailed his fingers through her hair. "Now, darlin', when you do take care of me, I'm sweet as a newborn babe. Isn't that so?" He laughed harshly, wiping his bloody mouth on the back of his arm. "But you've got to take the good with the bad. You didn't think it was going to be just one long, continuous roll in the sack, did you?"

She shook her head, looked down at her abdomen and clamped a hand over the torn skin, hiding the ugliness of it.

"You'd better clean up that mess, darlin', and get ready for work. You've got a big day ahead of you."

As she limped out of the room, he smiled and stretched his hands high above his head. The pain in his gut was gone. He called out to her, "Oh, darlin'? Don't you forget to bring home the Oldham girl's marrow tonight."

The phone rang and rang. Frank counted to fifteen before it was finally picked up. The man at the other end sounded breathless, anxious.

"H-hello."

"Mister Capello?"

"This is Tony Capello."

"Yeah, well, this is the guy who wrote you the note. Did you get it?"

Silence.

"Pay attention, asshole: if you don't talk to me now, I'm hanging up and dumping your son's marrow down the john. You got that?"

"No! Don't hang up!" The voice choked, coughed several times before continuing. "I got your letter; I got it!"

"That's better, much better. And you have the money?"

"Listen, mister, please, listen to me. I don't have fifty thousand dollars. But I can give you twelve . . . twelve thousand. That's every cent we have."

"Then you're going to have to get more! Twelve thousand doesn't make it, asshole. It's fifty. Period!"

"Mister, if we could get it, I'd give it to you right now. I'd do that . . . anything to save my son." His voice cracked as he continued, "My wife and I are only teachers, we don't have that kind of money."

"Now isn't that a goddamn touching story."

"My God! He's just a boy!"

"You're still not paying attention, Mr. Schoolteacher: I don't care if he's King Kong in drag. You get me that money no later than ten tomorrow morning or you're going to watch him turn into just a dead boy."

CHAPTER 24

Vinnie Capello stepped out of the shower, felt his legs start to give way, and had to grab the bathroom sink to keep from falling. He stood there watching helplessly as the room spun around and around.

The nurses had warned him about taking hot showers, but he'd ignored them. He'd opened the hot water faucet all the way for just a moment, pleased with the way his skin immediately colored to a bright red instead of looking its usual pasty white.

His world hung strangely atilt in the steamy mist of the tiny bathroom; he clutched the sides of the small basin and gagged. As he hunched over, dry heaves wracking his body, he knew his insides were being squeezed through a knot-hole. He forced himself to face the truth.

The torturous exercises, the hot showers were nothing more than childish games, cover-up games. He might as well be playing hide-and-seek for all the good they were doing. The bottom line was that he was going to die. And he'd better accept that fact once and for all.

As he allowed the reality of that concept to take shape and grow, all his carefully constructed illusions were boxed up, stored away forever.

The disquieting topsy-turvy sensation lasted only a moment before everything settled into its proper place. A queasy stomach was all that remained of the episode. Then a coldness began to work its way up through his arms and legs, settling in his chest. He started to cough.

Cold air rushed in as he cracked the bathroom door,

chilling him further, yet, strangely, it made him feel better at the same time. He dried off thoroughly, deep breathing the last of the dissipating steam as he tried to catch his image in the fogged-over mirror.

Four weeks ago his parents had brought him back to the hospital, all but kicking and screaming. He hadn't wanted to come back, begged to wait until after the senior prom, his graduation. But Dr. Kessler had been adamant, insisted that they had already pushed the time factor to the limit. Said if he lost remission before further treatment, it would make a dramatic difference in his survival chances.

Vinnie was willing to risk it. Begged to risk it. No one else would.

His mind wandered as he shifted uncomfortably from foot to foot. A part of him had realized the truth all along, but he'd refused to acknowledge it. Instead, he'd adopted a tough-guy attitude, trying to bluff his way past the fact he really wasn't going to make it. Why hadn't he figured that out sooner so he could stop tormenting himself?

Several times he'd overheard hospital staff commenting about his behavior and how difficult he was to be around. They were right. He was obnoxious and childish, like some dumb high school freshman. Gina had been the only one who seemed to accept him, tried to understand. The others? How could he blame them for not liking him? He didn't like himself very much.

What difference did any of it make?

He would continue to strike back if anyone got too close, keep them all at bay, even if it meant acting hateful and stupid.

He dried himself carefully, examining his thin body. The bright pink skin had become mottled as it reverted back to fish-belly white.

Leukemia!

At first, it hadn't seemed that frightening, more surprising than anything else. The weakness, fainting spells, and bleeding gums were upsetting, but the real shock hadn't set in until they told him that he might not live to graduate from high school, especially if he didn't start treatment immediately. He'd never believed he would die, not for a minute . . . even though his doctor had always been straight with him. Kessler had given him all the possibilities, best and worst scenarios. He just hadn't listened.

He used his wet towel to clean the steamed mirror, then folded it neatly and hung it on the rack. Somewhere in the back of his mind he knew the towel would be whisked away to the dirty laundry, but he hung it up carefully anyway.

He saw his bald head in the mirror and remembered his first hospital admission; the chemo had almost finished him. At one point, he'd wanted to die, but in the end the treatments had saved him, put him into remission; and during that year, he'd become stronger both physically and mentally. They'd warned him, though, that this wasn't the end of it: He'd have to go back into the hospital, donate his marrow, and receive high-dose chemotherapy for the best possible cure rate. But those were just a lot of words, words he'd quickly brushed aside.

Those months of remission had been good ones, among the best he could remember. He'd met Angie and fallen in love.

Just thinking about her made his insides go soft, ache with an emptiness that had grown daily since he'd deliberately broken off with her two months ago, right after he found out he'd have to go back into the hospital. He hadn't wanted her to be tied to someone like him; miss all the excitement of her senior year—the parties, the ceremonies, the prom.

She'd fought him all the way; he'd almost weakened. But in the end, he'd been cruel: refused to see her, refused to talk to her on the phone. And from that experience, he'd learned how to isolate, how to keep himself from caring too much about anyone.

He shrugged at his own thoughts. Angie, his parents, maybe they were right—a dance is just a dance. What's the big deal?

But he couldn't lie to himself. It was a big deal. The senior prom was tonight, and he wasn't going to be there.

He stared back at the face in the bathroom mirror. Looked at the dull eyes, the ears that appeared so strange with no hair to soften their stark angles. He hated looking at himself, felt like a prisoner in his own diseased body. Angie hadn't seen him since he'd come back into the hospital. Could she stand to look at him like this? Would she even know him?

He left the bathroom and walked slowly to his bed, his hospital gown hanging limply around him. He sat down and stared at the floor, thought grimly about whether he should bother with his exercises. Before he could make a decision, Gina Mazzio popped into the room.

"How's it going this morning, kid?"

He gritted his teeth, forced a smile. "Great." He interrupted himself coughing. "Just great!"

"When did you start coughing?" She whipped the stethoscope from around her neck and listened to his back, then moved his gown aside and listened closely to his chest.

"There's nothing wrong," he insisted. "I just had something caught in my throat."

She shook her head. "Vinnie, don't give me that nonsense. You know I have to check anything unusual." She frowned as she retied his hospital gown and patted his shoulder. "It sounds okay to me, but let's see what Dr. Kessler says."

"I know what he'll say—let's give him a stat dose of krypton, or Preparation X, b-i-d, t-i-d, q-i-d, et cetera, et cetera."

Gina laughed. "Hey, not bad; sounds better than 'take two aspirins and call me in the morning.' Maybe you're ready to take up the profession."

"Don't think I have that much time," he said.

She gave him a long, hard stare before responding. "I really am going to have to talk to Dr. Kessler about checking you. We can't take chances with your coming down with something at this stage." She winked at him. "Besides, there's a rumor you're going to be getting your marrow in the next day or so."

"So what!"

He saw her stiffen, turn grim. She sat down next to him and released a long sigh. "Come on, kid, what's bothering you? I mean, something's been bugging you since the day you checked back in." When he didn't answer, she touched his hand. "This is what all those weeks of treatment were about, Vinnie: your marrow is going to make things all right again." She held up two crossed fingers.

"It'll be too late; it'll all be over by the time I get out of here, *if* I get out of here."

She tilted her head and scowled. "What will be over?"

"High school, graduation, the prom, everything! You don't understand—it's just not fair!"

"No, Vinnie, you're wrong. I do know how you feel, and it is a raw deal. But whoever said fair had anything to do with it?"

He shook his head and stared at the floor, unable to respond.

"Come on, Vinnie. You've been acting like a tough guy ever since you checked in here. So, okay, let's see you be a real tough guy."

"What do you mean?"

"This is the toughest fight you're ever going to have, kid, so why not put all of that anger and energy into winning it?"

He shook his head, tears smarting his eyes. "What's a senior prom like?"

He felt her shift on the bed. It was several seconds before she answered. "I don't know," she said softly. "I didn't get to go."

Vinnie looked up at her. "You didn't? Why not?"

She turned her head away for a moment, then back to look directly into his eyes. "I ran with a crowd who thought proms and things like that were kind of stupid." She paused. "Besides, nobody asked me."

"Give me a break, will you? I can't believe you didn't have a date. You're so . . . so beautiful." Suddenly he was embarrassed and felt himself flush. She smiled at him and for the first time he realized she had dark smudges under her eyes. She looked very tired.

"That was sweet, Vinnie," she said, touching his cheek. "But do you really think being beautiful makes everything okay?"

"No. But beautiful people seem to always get what they want."

He watched Gina close her eyes, tighten and relax her shoulders, stretch her neck. "And I suppose you think you're ugly?"

He sneered at her. "Hey, I checked the mirror again this

morning and the frog was still a frog . . . hadn't turned into a prince yet."

"How come a smart guy like you hasn't figured out some pretty basic things?" She stood and walked over to the window. He could see past her that the morning fog was starting to dissipate and wondered if the Golden Gate Bridge was visible yet. "You've been blasted with chemo for weeks," she continued, turning to look back at him. "Those aren't exactly beauty treatments, you know. But you're not ugly, Vinnie. Where did you ever get an idea like that? Why can't you try to see yourself as you truly are—important, wonderful?"

"What a bunch of crap!"

"Vinnie, you've really been hammering me with this crap business," she said, laughing out loud. "Trashing my ego."

"Yeah, well, thinking I'm wonderful would be just plain egotistical."

"So you say. But if you can't love or respect yourself, how can you even begin to love anyone else?"

He studied the lines of his palm, straightened his hospital gown, looked down at the floor again. "I don't care about myself anymore, Gina . . . but I don't want anyone I love to suffer because of me."

She walked up to him and rested her hand on his shoulder. "Trying to protect other people is usually a pretty thankless job."

"What do you mean?"

"People don't like you assuming that you know what's best for them."

"You always have some dumb answer for me, don't you?"

"That's right, kid—good questions, dumb answers."

Gina was jittery. It was the kind of uneasiness that

comes from thinking and rethinking every action you take—
something like how you feel if you concentrate on watching
your legs when running down the stairs. Since almost being
trapped last night, trying to focus on any one thing had
been near impossible. Her mind jumped from one thought
to another, even while caring for her patients.

What would have happened if Harry hadn't shown up?
She asked herself that over and over and over.

And why would anyone in the hospital want to hurt her?
The bigger question was, *who?*

She tried to clear her head as she walked into the nurses'
station, carrying Vinnie's throat culture. Helen was at the
computer terminal checking lab values, a frown on her face.

"Have you seen Kessler this morning?" Gina asked,
tossing the culture into a cylinder to be tubed to the lab.

"Not yet, but I had to beep him. Deana Oldham's
turning sour. He'll be here soon."

Gina rested a hand on Helen's shoulder. "I'm sorry. I
know how fond you are of Deana."

"Hey," Helen said, flicking away a tear. "They all love
us and leave us one way or another. Sometimes I wonder
what I'm doing here. Maybe I ought to write a book instead, let everyone know the kind of stress nurses—"

Gina put an arm around Helen and hugged her.

Helen sucked in her stomach and stood a little taller,
smiled at Gina. "Maybe sometimes I do wonder what I'm
doing here, but not today. Today, I'm all right . . . and
Deana will be all right, too. It's just a small setback."

"I'm worried about Vinnie, also." Gina took Helen's
place at the terminal and brought up Vinnie's blood values.
"The kid's neutropenic. The last thing he needs is an infection. He's going to need that marrow as soon as possible."

"Not until Kessler clears up the Chapman business."

Gina took Helen's hand and led her into the medication room, looked around quickly, and said, "I sneaked into Pathology last night and took a look at Chapman's autopsy report."

Helen's mouth dropped open. "Are you crazy, Gina? Vasquez is going to eviscerate you if he finds out."

"What our administrator doesn't know won't hurt him." She squeezed Helen's hand. "I really had to know."

"So, what did you find out?"

"Chapman had septicemia . . . overwhelmed by GI pathogens."

"Not too surprising," Helen said. "E. coli?"

"Yeah. That and the whole coliform spectrum. But in tremendous numbers, unbelievable numbers. He never stood a chance, poor guy."

Mark Kessler stuck his head through the door, interrupting their conversation. "Fill me in on Deana, will you, Helen?"

Helen started rattling off the patient's latest lab values as she left the room and started toward the computer terminal.

"Mark?" Gina said, following them into the nurses' station. "When you finish with Deana, I need to talk to you about Vinnie Capello."

Kessler's eyes rolled to the ceiling. "For Christ's sake, not him too?"

CHAPTER 25

"I don't understand," Gary Bernstein said, glaring at Alan Vasquez and Mark Kessler from the edge of Tracy's bed. He'd left her side only once since returning, and then just long enough to rush home for a shower and change of clothes. While now more comfortable in his customary corduroy jacket and faded denims, the nerve-wracking tension remained. "Yesterday," Gary continued, "you canceled Tracy's engraftment on some flimsy pretext. Now, you're saying it may be yet another twenty-four hours before you can proceed."

"I thought Dr. Kessler explained the situation to the both of you," Vasquez said. He looked expectantly from Gary to Kessler, then nervously stretched his neck inside his collar and adjusted his tie.

The doctor crimped his lower lip between thumb and forefinger, pulled at it, and said to Gary, "Whatever I said or didn't say, I'm doing what I think is best for Tracy."

"That's still not an explanation," Gary growled. "Before, we were merely informed that there was some kind of procedural delay. Now the two of you are giving us a bunch of double talk, trying to delay everything another twenty-four hours."

"I think you misunderstand, Mr. Bernstein—our primary concern is always the safety of the patient," Vasquez said, nodding toward Tracy. He looked to Kessler for help, but received only a noncommittal stare.

"Stop giving me this public relations mumbo-jumbo," Gary said, taking Tracy's hand. "Dr. Kessler has repeatedly emphasized that the timing of Tracy's engraftment is critical. Suddenly, you're playing games with us, apparently stalling for time." He shifted his weight from one foot to the other, still sore from being kneed in the kidney.

"I felt the delay was necessary and wouldn't significantly alter her prognosis," Kessler said.

"There seems to be a damn serious conflict of priorities working here, gentlemen."

Behind the anger, Gary was terrified. He wanted to confront Vasquez and Kessler—ask them point blank whether or not Tracy's marrow was where it was supposed to be. But he knew he couldn't risk that. What if they said no? In front of Tracy? It would destroy her. He looked down at her and was alarmed by her gauntness, her lack of vitality.

"I'm not sure what you are accusing us of," Vasquez said.

Instead of responding, Gary squeezed Tracy's hand, felt her return the pressure.

"Does this delay have anything to do with the man who died the other day?" Tracy asked, suddenly coming out of her silence.

Vasquez' eyebrows shot up; Kessler gave the barest nod, as if confirming something to himself.

"I'm sorry," Vasquez said, "it's against the hospital's confidentiality policy to publicly discuss—"

"I'm not the public." Tracy snapped. "I think I have a right to know."

Kessler started to say something, but was interrupted when Gina Mazzio entered the room, carrying a small tray of medications.

"Could you come back in a few minutes, nurse?" Vasquez said, more an order than a request.

"It's time for Tracy's meds," Gina said.

"Can't they wait a few minutes?" Vasquez asked irritably.

"The meds should be given as scheduled," Kessler interrupted, overruling Vasquez.

Gina looked from Vasquez to Kessler, and frowned. "Is there some kind of problem?"

"No," Tracy said. "And as long as you're here," she added, "I'd like you to stay." She gently touched her headscarf with her fingertips.

"I'm sure Miss Mazzio has other duties that require her attention," Vasquez said.

"I want her here," Tracy insisted, motioning for Gina to bring her medicine to her. "Gary and I need someone we can trust."

Vasquez opened his mouth, but Tracy impatiently waved him quiet. "Now, will one of you please tell me the specific reason for delaying my transfusion?"

"The delay," Kessler said, "resulted from a sudden and so far unexplainable bacterial infection in the patient you were concerned about." He moved around and sat down on the side of the bed opposite Gary.

"What does that have to do with me?" Tracy asked.

"Probably nothing, particularly since it occurred prior to his engraftment."

"Was there any problem with his marrow," Tracy continued, "any problem directly related to his death?"

"None whatsoever," Kessler said.

"So his transfusion was never delayed, for any reason?" Tracy asked Gina, ignoring Kessler.

"Absolutely not!" Vasquez said, intercepting the question.

Gary sat down on the other side of the bed and asked Kessler, "Is there any specific reason now why Tracy can't have her marrow?"

"Hospital policy—"

"We originally stopped all invasive procedures throughout the unit," Kessler said, cutting off the administrator's protest. "We then conducted a thorough investigation to make certain the bacterial infection wasn't something more than an isolated incident. We wanted to forestall any possibility of general bacterial contamination."

"And?" Tracy demanded.

"So far, we've found nothing. The final step in our investigation was to test your marrow."

"Do you know the results?" she asked nervously.

"It tested negative, I'm pleased to report."

"Then there's really no reason why you can't proceed, is there?" Gary said.

"No, it's all been a matter of taking the appropriate precautions," Kessler assured him, then said to Tracy, "I've rescheduled your engraftment for two o'clock this afternoon." He turned to the others. "Now, I think we should leave Tracy alone so she can get some rest."

"Other questions?" Vasquez asked.

When there was no other comment, the administrator took a moment to silently, but pointedly, reestablish his displeasure with Gina by scowling at her, then quickly preceded Kessler out of the room.

Gina lingered in Tracy's room after Kessler and Vasquez had departed, fussing with this and that. She knew Tracy's marrow had been missing, but she couldn't prove it unless one of the Bernsteins was willing to confirm it.

But they were only involved with each other. As she quietly left the room, they were holding hands, their foreheads touching.

"What's with all the high-level activity down in the Bernstein suite?" Helen asked when Gina returned to the station.

"All I know is that the engraftment is on again—two o'clock this afternoon."

"What was Vasquez doing there?"

"Who knows why administrators do anything."

"So Mark changed his mind about the engraftment?"

Gina nodded. "I think he finally realized he was over-protecting Tracy. In any case, I'm happy to say she seems to have gotten over her antagonism toward me."

"Speaking of antagonistic patients, I couldn't find your teenage terror while you were powwowing with the high and mighty in Bernstein's room."

"Vinnie?"

"Who else?"

"He should be in his room," Gina said. "He wasn't scheduled to be off the floor for any reason." She checked his chart, though, to make certain. "Are you sure he wasn't hiding out in his john? He does that sometimes."

"The door was wide open; no Vinnie."

Gina thought for a moment. "Let's check around the unit."

"I already did that," Helen said. "No one's seen him since morning rounds."

"Damn! I hope he hasn't gone off and done something stupid."

"Anything's possible with that brat."

"He's got to be here. He promised me he would stick with the program." She picked up the phone and called hospital security to request a facility-wide search, then took off on her own, checking every room, closet, and bathroom on the entire floor.

When she finally came back to the nurses' station there were tears in her eyes. Helen looked at her questioningly, but she merely shook her head and sank down onto one of the station chairs. She called security again, listened to their negative report, and put in a call to Kessler to tell him that their teenage patient apparently had gone AWOL.

CHAPTER 26

Alan Vasquez paced back and forth in front of the nurses' station, even though the nurses' sidelong glances made it clear they wanted him to return to the administrative wing where he belonged.

He moved away from the station to greet a middle-aged couple who stepped out of the elevator.

"Are you the Capellos?" When they nodded, he introduced himself. "I'm sorry I don't have anything new to report about your son." They eyed him suspiciously. "Perhaps it would be better if we went to my office so we can discuss this privately."

"Mr. Vasquez," the man said, "I have no intention of leaving this floor until I know where my son is."

"I certainly understand how you and your wife must feel, Mr. Capello; and I want you to know we're doing everything humanly possible to find Vinnie." He put a reassuring hand on the man's shoulder.

Capello took a half step back, allowing Vasquez' hand to drop heavily. "No!" he shouted. "You don't have any idea how we feel." He started to raise his fist, but his wife grasped his arm and held him back.

"We want to wait in Vinnie's room, where his things are," Mrs. Capello interjected, pulling on her husband's arm.

Capello planted his feet and refused to move. "If anything happens to my son, I'm going to hold you personally responsible—then we'll find out how much you understand."

Vasquez, chagrined, watched the couple disappear down the corridor.

Maria Capello was sitting on the edge of her son's bed, holding his well-worn Giants baseball cap in her hands when Gina entered. Tony Capello had his back to her, staring out the window, hands jammed into his pockets.

"Wouldn't you be more comfortable waiting at home?" Gina asked, needing to say something, anything. She looked from one to the other. Finally, Mrs. Capello looked up and said, "We'll wait here." She lowered her eyes and continued to work her fingers around the circumference of the baseball cap.

It was close to noon when Gina again entered Vinnie's room. This time she went to Maria Capello's side and gently placed a hand on the woman's shoulder. "You really would be more comfortable in the hospitality room. There's coffee, tea . . ."

Neither of the Capellos looked at her.

"Look, I'm sorry to intrude, but it could be a while before we hear anything. The police are looking for him, and the media hotline has agreed to help."

"And they'll bring him back here when they find him?" Mrs. Capello finally asked.

"Yes."

"Then we'll wait here." She still didn't look up.

"But what if he goes home before someone finds him? Shouldn't one of you be there?"

"My sister's at the house," Mrs. Capello said. "I feel closer to Vinnie here." She patted the bed lightly with the palm of one hand.

Tony Capello, for the first time, turned away from the window. His skin was sallow, his eyes sunk deep within their sockets. Absently, he ran the fingers of both hands through his salt-and-pepper hair. He shifted uneasily in his jacket, shirt, and tie—his teaching clothes. He opened his mouth to speak but instead chewed on his lower lip. Suddenly he blurted, "Why? What could have gotten into him to do such a stupid thing?" He shook his head, shoved his hands back into his pockets and rattled his loose change to the beat of each word. "How could he just walk away like that? Irresponsible! Irresponsible and selfish!" He looked across the room at his wife as if expecting a confirmation from her.

Maria Capello raised her head; her sorrowful eyes suddenly flashed in irritation. "Will you please stop jangling that money in your pocket, Anthony? Stop it! Please!" She glared fiercely at him; their eyes locked in battle for several seconds. Finally, she turned away and carefully put Vinnie's baseball cap on the pillow. She reached into her purse, withdrew a string of rosary beads, and began working them between thin, restless fingers.

"I also wish I knew why he left," Gina said to the father.

Capello continued as though neither his wife nor Gina had spoken: "He knows how dangerous it is for him to be out there in his condition. Dr. Kessler told us even a minor infection could kill him . . ." His voice trailed away as he turned his back on both women and again stared out the window.

"Did anything unusual happen today, something that would make Vinnie run away?" Mrs. Capello asked, looking up at Gina with widened eyes. "I know I'm asking the same questions over and over, but it's so unlike him to act this way."

"Vinnie's been upset ever since he checked in," Gina said. "He didn't want to come back again, and every day has been an emotional roller coaster. But under the circumstances, it's not too surprising."

"Then explain it to me!" Tony Capello roared, turning away from the window, his hands extended, palms up. "I certainly don't understand any of it."

"Try to see it from his point of view—he thought he was cured the first time he came to the hospital. Having to come back while he was still feeling physically okay was hard to take. And what happens? We make him sick all over again. That's hard for anyone."

"But he's always been such a sensible boy," Mrs. Capello said.

"I don't think being sensible has anything to do with it," Gina said. "He was angry when he got here, and he stayed that way right through this morning." Gina reached over and gently touched the back of the woman's hand. "I tried to get him into counseling several times, but he wouldn't have any part of it."

"Yes, I know. We tried also," Mrs. Capello said. "He wouldn't even discuss it."

Gina looked across the room and studied the calendar Vinnie had pinned to the wall, trying to find some message in the red Xs he'd drawn through each day. After a moment, she said, "I keep trying to think of what might have set him off, made him leave the hospital. He seemed pretty much himself this morning . . ." She hesitated. "Well, maybe a little sadder. He's usually pretty feisty, but today, it was more like . . . resignation."

"And you didn't call us?" Capello accused, pointing a finger at her.

"What would I have said? Vinnie's having a bad day? I'd be on the phone every day . . . no . . . two or three times a day. Besides, it didn't seem that unusual at the time."

Maria Capello slipped her hand from beneath Gina's and resumed working her rosary beads. "I feel like I'm responsible in some way. Maybe . . . maybe it was our fault." She looked up at her husband. "We should have waited for him to finish his senior year . . . like he wanted. He pleaded with us. Now, it seems like such a small request."

"How dare you say that," Capello said, glaring at his wife. "How dare you!" he repeated louder. "My God, we didn't send him back to the hospital on a whim. Damn it, we brought him here for treatment . . . so he would have the best chance to live. Isn't that important enough?" He covered one eye, as though a sudden stabbing pain had pierced his skull. He leaned heavily against the wall. "For Christ's sake, we don't have to apologize for wanting him to live, do we? Doesn't that take priority over everything else?"

The Capellos were exhausted. Even Gina's head was throbbing from trying to solve Vinnie's disappearance. But she couldn't let it go. "Maybe just being alive wasn't enough for Vinnie, Mr. Capello."

"That's ludicrous and you know it. What could be more important than his life?"

Gina stood up. "Mr. Capello, I know you're upset and worried, but you still need to believe in your son, believe that Vinnie had a good reason for doing what he did. Something was on his mind, and I don't think it had anything to do with his treatment for leukemia. Otherwise, why would he just walk out?"

"That's another thing that's been gnawing at me," he said, jabbing a finger forcibly against his palm. "How did our son walk out of here without anyone stopping him? Don't you watch—"

"Tony! Stop it! It's no one's fault!"

"Our patients are not prisoners, Mr. Capello. We don't

force them to stay. Vinnie's no exception."

Anthony Capello's face flushed a bright red; he turned, held out a clenched fist that vibrated with passion for several seconds before opening it in supplication. For a moment, he could barely speak. Then he said, "I know I must sound like a complete fool . . . and I'm sorry. Maria, Gina, please forgive me."

Capello looked into his wife's eyes, moved toward the bed, and sat down heavily next to her. Leaning over, he cradled his head in his hands. His shoulders shook.

"Maria, what are we going to do? Vinnie's gone . . . even if we find him . . . bring him back . . . I still may not be able to save him."

Gina was bewildered. "What are you saying?"

Before either of the Capellos could respond, Mark Kessler eased into the room, his face pale, his eyes flitting from the chart he held to each of the three people in the room.

"Has there been any word from your house?" he asked the Capellos. When they shook their heads in unison, he looked uneasily at Gina before continuing. "I know you're worried about Vinnie. We all are." He tapped the chart with a forefinger. "Unfortunately, his situation has become critical."

"What does that mean . . . exactly?" Capello demanded.

"Vinnie left the hospital at a time when he's most susceptible to infection. If we don't get him back here immediately, God only knows what diseases he may come in contact with outside."

The hope that had briefly brightened Mrs. Capello's eyes when Kessler arrived now faded. "He's going to die, isn't he . . . our Vinnie?"

"We need to complete his treatment now."

"Suppose we did find him right away? How long before you could give him back his marrow?" Capello asked.

"Provided his physical condition hasn't deteriorated, we could infuse him immediately."

"And without the marrow?"

Kessler seemed unwilling to answer.

"Without the marrow, what?" Capello insisted.

"I think you know the answer to that."

Maria Capello emitted a long, pain-filled wail. The sound grew, expanded, filling every corner. Her husband pulled her to him, rocked her back and forth in his arms.

"My baby's going to die . . . my baby's going to die," she sobbed.

Gina was wired from the caffeine she'd consumed since Vinnie's disappearance. Regardless, she headed straight for the coffee pot after she and Mark Kessler had temporarily quieted the Capellos.

She was uneasy with Kessler—things had continued to be strained between them since the incident in the Laboratory. And even though their professional interaction hadn't changed, their personal relationship had cooled.

"We've got to get Vinnie back here right away," Kessler said.

Gina nodded. "I feel like I've let the kid down in some way, like he was trying to tell me something and I wasn't listening closely enough."

"Vinnie has a way of making us all feel insecure. Every time I talk to him, I wonder: is this going to set him off; is that going to set him off, or worse yet, set him back. I never know which way he's headed." Kessler looked down the hall in the direction of Vinnie's room. "A tough nut right from the start, from his very first admission."

"I didn't know him then."

"He was a Pedi patient, refused to go back there this time."

"Not surprising."

Kessler shook his head. "From the moment he walked into my office, I knew it was going to be an uphill battle. And I'm not talking about his disease, either."

"No one knows that better than me."

"His parents think he's a loner, but I think he's just lonely."

"Vinnie's many things," Gina said. "Lonely, alone, and most definitely deep into denial."

"It's made a fighter out of him, a realist."

Gina forced a laugh. "Yeah, well, who needs reality if it not only steals your life, but who you are?"

"Maybe," Kessler said.

Gina took a sip of coffee and sighed. "You know, it really bothers me that I didn't key into his change of mood today. I guess I was too tired, what with Chapman and everything else that's been going on."

"Was he really that different this morning?" Kessler asked, laughing. "It's hard to imagine him being anything but a brat. That would have been too much to ask."

"No, you're right. Instead of giving me his usual lip, he was almost too cooperative. Alarms should have been going off in my head."

"It's not like you to let anything slip by," he said with an ironic grunt.

Gina turned away; Kessler's penetrating stare made her edgy. "Truthfully, things have been all out of kilter since Chapman died. Maybe . . . maybe I feel the way you did then—time to think about moving on to a different field."

He rested a hand on her shoulder. "And the same reasons you gave me for staying are valid for you. Aren't we at our best right here? Stay with it, Gina."

She lowered her head. "But it's so painful, like banging your head against a stone wall."

"So where else would you like to bang your head?"

Gina's face softened, and she laughed. "Maybe you're right."

Kessler nodded, hesitated. "Listen, I'm sorry for the way I behaved about the marrow down in the Lab. Truth of the matter, I haven't been the same since Chapman died either. Now I'm worried about Tracy Bernstein."

"Why?"

"You know, the usual—when one thing goes wrong, everything goes wrong. Probably why I held off with her engraftment in the first place. Not very fair to her, I suppose, especially since her marrow is free of contaminants." He held out a hand. "Anyway, I did want to apologize for acting like an idiot the other day. We've both been under a lot of stress lately, so why don't we just forget it?"

"Done!"

"Friends?"

"Friends," she said, taking his hand.

CHAPTER 27

Gina was still filled with questions about Vinnie as she helped Helen bathe Deana Oldham. No matter how hard she worked to push him from her mind, he remained a constant worry. Where on earth could a skinny, baldheaded, sickly looking kid go without being noticed? Her stomach churned loudly as she imagined him collapsed in some back alley.

She watched Helen tenderly hold the frail hand of Deana, who was only a couple of years older than Vinnie, but in much worse condition. Try as she might, she couldn't banish the negative thoughts about Vinnie, and although she knew it was stupid, she was afraid they might somehow sway future events.

After leaving Deana's room, she quickly headed down the hall, anxious to see how the Capellos were doing. She winced at the soreness in her back and legs, a souvenir of crawling under the auditorium dais the night before.

"I feel like I'm dangling from the end of a Goddamned rope," Tony Capello shouted at his wife. "I've tried everything I can think of . . . can't raise a penny on our house, we're mortgaged to the hilt."

"I thought the bank—"

"Damn it, I'm telling you, they practically laughed in my face when I suggested a personal loan. That's what being an educator gets you—little thanks, little money, little future."

"But we're not broke, Tony. What about the twelve thousand in your IRA? Wouldn't that at least help?"

"It's not good enough! Haven't you heard anything I've said? We need fifty thousand."

"There must be something we can do."

"Then you tell me what."

"Tony, please . . . I feel just as helpless as you do."

"I know that," he said gruffly. "Just because I can't raise any money doesn't mean I've suddenly turned stupid."

"No one said you're stupid. But you have to stop taking your frustrations out on me. We're in this together, remember?"

He stared at the wall for several seconds. "I'm sorry, Maria. I'm not rational anymore. Half the time I don't even know what's going to come out of my mouth; the rest of the time, I'm scared to death."

"Tony, we only have until ten tomorrow morning to get the money." Her voice quavered. "If we don't, that man may destroy Vinnie's marrow."

"May destroy it? Oh, no! There was nothing conditional about it. That bastard *will* destroy it."

"What kind of person could do that?"

"What difference does it make? He said he'll do it, and I believe him."

"He's a very sick man."

He looked at his empty palms. "I feel like such a fool, like I've wasted my life. I never should have gone into teaching, never should have let you talk me out of taking that job at Apple. All that idealism about helping young people doesn't amount to shit if I can't raise the money to save my own son's life."

"Tony, please!"

"I'm . . . helpless." He held the sides of his head with his palms. "What can I do to get Vinnie's marrow from that bastard?"

They both turned as Gina whisked into the room.

"Who has Vinnie's marrow?" Gina said, looking from one to the other.

"Unless you've brought news about Vinnie, you're intruding on a private conversation," Capello said, dropping his hands to his sides.

"If someone has stolen Vinnie's marrow, it's not just about him," Gina said.

"I asked you, do you have any news about Vinnie?"

"There's nothing new."

"Then there's nothing to talk about."

"But if there's a problem, maybe I can help."

"There's a man," Maria blurted out. "He says he has Vinnie's marrow—"

"Maria!" Tony shouted.

"No! I want to save my son."

"Telling her isn't going to change anything."

"Mr. Capello, I think we need to call the police."

"I have nothing to say to you or the police," Capello snapped.

"Please, let me help."

Maria covered her mouth and refused to speak again.

"You must go to the police!"

"Do you think I haven't thought about that?" Capello said. "That won't help Vinnie."

"If they could catch—"

"Oh, yeah, they'll probably catch the bastard somewhere, sometime. But by then, my son will be dead. I'm not taking that kind of a chance with his life."

Maria's eyes were vacant. "It'll all be fine . . . it'll be fine. We just need a little time to get the money."

Capello turned away, shaking his head.

"You must go to the police," Gina repeated. "If you

won't go, I will!"

Capello stood eye-to-eye with Gina. "I want you to listen very carefully to me, Miss Mazzio, because right now I'm running on fumes." He turned away and paced back and forth between her and the door.

"You will not go to the police!" He stopped and glared at her. "If you do, this maniac will not only destroy Vinnie's marrow, he'll destroy all the marrow he's stolen. He made that very clear. So you see, it's not only Vinnie's life on the line, there are others. How many, we don't know." He moved until his nose almost touched hers. "Am I making myself clear?"

Gina looked into his steely eyes for a long time before nodding.

Only then did he take a step back. "Don't you think I want my son to live? I'll do anything but go to the police. He swore he would act if we said anything to anyone."

"He could be bluffing," Gina said. "How can you be sure he even has Vinnie's marrow?"

"Because he mailed us a bag of the cells, and I had them lab-tested by a friend." Tears ran haphazardly down his cheeks. He shook a fist at Gina and said, "The bastard didn't even have the decency to send it refrigerated. He wasted them, just wasted them."

"But you don't know for sure they were Vinnie's, do you?"

"Can I risk thinking otherwise?"

Gina touched his shoulder as he shook his head. "I'm so sorry."

"Jesus! It's disgusting to think people like him are breathing the same air we are."

"I agree, but we can't handle this ourselves; we need help," Gina said.

Capello pointed a finger at her. "If you go to the police, I'll deny everything you've heard here."

"Please, Mr. Capello, at least let me check with the Lab. See if Vinnie's marrow is there."

"Aren't you listening? This maniac will destroy all the marrow if there's any inquiry. I have no choice but to believe that. I can't risk doing anything else."

"But if you don't have the money, what is there left for you to do?"

Capello shook his head, then looked at his wife. When their eyes met, he said, "I wish I knew."

Alan Vasquez stepped into the elevator and hit the #3 button as the door slid shut. He was dyspeptic, irritable; he couldn't remember having had a single decent night's sleep since everything hit the fan in the Oncology unit. He closed his eyes in the momentary solitude, but his mind continued to race ahead.

An image of Gina Mazzio popped into his mind. Somehow, she had been at the core of all his recent problems. First, the whole mess with that poor bastard, Carl Chapman. Then, the uproar over Tracy Bernstein and her marrow. He pulled at the collar of his shirt and swallowed hard, remembering the embarrassing scene in the lab—all the personnel drawn in by Mazzio's craziness and her obvious disdain for his authority.

Arrogant bitch!

When had he had so much trouble with a nurse? Most of the time he was barely aware of the nursing staff's existence, except as a monumental budgetary problem. Now this one nurse had become the nucleus of everything that was going wrong. He clenched his hands so tightly the nails carved half moons into his palms. Chapman,

Bernstein, Capello. All Gina Mazzio's patients. If he didn't know better, he'd think it was some kind of conspiracy.

Damn! He should have overridden the Nursing Administrator and fired the woman. To hell with the union. At this point, he'd rather deal with them than Mazzio.

Now, the supreme insult of this obviously irrational teenager running away from the hospital. He could already see the research grants drying up. Just thinking about Vinnie Capello brought back the scene with the boy's father. One calamity after another.

Vasquez stepped out of the elevator and blended with the corridor traffic on the way to Capello's room. He hated this, hated facing the parents again, but he couldn't have them thinking the hospital wasn't on top of the situation, or worse, that Ridgewood didn't care.

He looked up and saw Gina Mazzio coming out of Capello's room. There seemed to be no way to avoid her, like continually bumping a sore thumb.

"Ms. Mazzio," he said, blocking her path.

"Yes?"

"How are the Capellos?"

"Not very well. Have you heard anything from the police? Have they found Vinnie?"

"None of that really concerns you at this juncture." He placed a restraining hand on her arm. "I hope you haven't alarmed these people with more of your harebrained ideas."

She removed his hand as though she'd encountered something particularly unsavory. "Well, since it doesn't concern me, I'd better attend to things that do."

She stepped around him; he watched her walk purposefully down the hall.

As soon as this business is over, she's out of here!

Gina banished Alan Vasquez from her mind. At the station, she grabbed a telephone and dialed Harry's ICU extension. As she waited, she checked her watch—it was already lunchtime, and still no Vinnie.

When Harry picked up the phone, he was out of breath. She could tell he was rushing around, in the midst of something; obviously not a good time for her to call, if there ever was one in that ICU.

"Harry! I'm sorry to bug you, but I've got to talk to you right away! Can you take your lunch break now?"

"I don't know. I've got a lot of sickies here."

"Please, Harry. It's urgent."

There was a long pause. "Okay, I'll try, but only because it's you." His voice became muffled; he'd obviously covered the mouthpiece. Then he was back again. "Meet you at the cafeteria in ten minutes."

Gina immediately dialed the lab.

"Hi, may I speak to Faye?"

There was a grumbled response she didn't quite understand, and then she was put on hold. She listened impatiently to the canned baroque music.

"This is Faye."

"Hi, Faye, Gina! Could you do me a favor? I mean, I really need some information from the Lab, but I'm sort of *persona non grata* down there after that to-do over Bernstein's marrow."

There was a pause before Faye responded. "Uh, what do you need?"

"Could you check the repository for me, make sure one of our patient's marrow is there?" She read off Vinnie Capello's hospital number.

198

"I guess . . ." There was a longer pause. "Maybe we shouldn't—"

"Listen, Faye, I don't want you to get into any trouble over this. If you can't do it, say so. I'll understand."

"Why do you need to know?"

"I can't answer that right now." She held her breath as she waited for Faye's answer.

"Hold on for a moment."

"No, wait!" But Faye was gone and the infuriating music was back again.

Gina stood there self-consciously twisting the telephone cord, afraid someone might enter the nurses' station and over-hear her conversation. Within a short time, Faye was back.

"It's there, Gina."

She needed time to think; there were so many questions. Gina tapped her fingers on the cafeteria table while she waited for Harry. She'd just taken a sip of iced tea when he came striding across the room; she smiled to see his hair flying in every direction. He saw her, waved, and smiled back. His eyes were so bright, so warm; she wondered again why she continued to avoid commitment.

"Hi, beautiful," he said, slipping into the chair next to her and reaching for her hand.

"Thanks for coming." Gina squeezed his hand. "You're the only one I can trust."

"Any news about the kid?"

"Nothing." She told him about the Capellos. "I don't know what to do," she said. "I don't want to make things worse, but I can't stand by and let the kid die, provided we even find him."

"But you said the marrow was in the repository."

"No, I said Faye said it was there. I want to believe her,

but I haven't checked it out myself. I don't dare."

"So you're suddenly not so certain about this new friend of yours?"

"Harry, I don't know what to think. I keep seeing that scarf, Tracy's scarf. I don't understand how Faye could have gotten it unless she stole it."

"So? Even if she does have Tracy's scarf, that doesn't mean she's also involved in this business with the marrow."

"Perhaps you're right. I hope so. But there's still something strange going on with that woman and her creepy boyfriend."

"All right, supposing the marrow is where it's supposed to be? Then what did this guy send to the Capellos? I mean, you said they had it checked, but checked for what? That it was marrow, or that it was their kid's marrow? Maybe the guy's bluffing."

"How can we be sure? I mean, Chapman, Bernstein, Capello, there must be a connection. Yet, the pattern keeps changing—no one's ever found Chapman's marrow; Tracy's was missing, then suddenly turned up; and with Vinnie, some of it was supposedly destroyed, but now I'm told it's all in the deep freeze."

"Maybe they're not connected."

"I don't believe that, but there doesn't seem to be much I can do about it. While Kessler and I have reached a tenuous truce, the lab people turn the other way when they see me, and Vasquez pretty much has everyone convinced I'm a neurotic idiot. So if I go to the police without the Capellos, I'm nowhere."

Harry laughed. "Come on, let's not make it worse than it is."

"Oh? If you remember, up until last night, you didn't believe me, either."

"I know, and we still don't have any solid proof."

"That wasn't my imagination chasing me last night."

"I can testify to that," he said, rubbing his stomach. "But it isn't proof of anything."

She sighed. "And wouldn't Vasquez have a heyday making me appear an even worse fool after all the trouble I've caused him? And this time he'd have the backing of the Capellos."

"Are you positive you can't get them to change their minds and go to the police with you?"

"Absolutely!" She thought for a moment. "Do you think Vinnie ran away because he knows about his marrow being held for ransom?"

"No, I don't think so. At least if I were his parent, I wouldn't have told him."

Gina swirled the ice in the bottom of her glass, sucking up the last of her tea with the straw. "I've got to do something, Harry. I'm not going to back away from this . . . or anything else, for that matter . . . not again, not ever!"

"What are you talking about?"

Gina ran her fingers through her hair, then kneaded her brow. "I've told you before, I ran away from Dominick because he abused me. I've let that hang over me all these years—running away from confrontation, not standing up for myself."

"If you're trying to convince me you're a wimp, forget it. I know better."

She reached across the table for his hand. "Thanks, but I still have trouble facing things head-on. It's about time I changed that, don't you think?" She leaned across the table and gave him a lingering kiss, which quickly drew applause from nearby tables.

Harry squeezed her hand, smiled warmly at her. "I think

this may be the luckiest day of my life."

"Okay, Lucky Lucke, help me work this out before I go nuts."

Harry thought for a moment. "There's nothing here for you to work out—"

"Can't you see there has to be a connection between Faye and Tracy's scarf—"

"Don't hit me with that scarf business again. As I said before, what if she did steal it? It's a long stretch between that and stealing someone's marrow."

"I know. I know. But the connection must be there."

CHAPTER 28

Tracy was limp with exhaustion.

It was evident that her future was out of her hands; she had no control over what was going to happen to her. If she was destined to die, so be it.

No!

An inner force rejected that; recognized it for what it was: a lie!

Gary was suddenly back in her life and she wanted to live, wanted her life to continue.

She closed her eyes, immediately receding into a frightening nothingness. She fought to escape the emptiness, only to be confronted by a single, terrifying question: *What if they were lying about her getting the marrow?*

She forced her eyes open, found Gina standing next to her bed, adjusting the tree of IVs. She focused on the nurse, vaguely aware that Gary was holding her hand. Why was Gina so serious, so seemingly preoccupied with the IV setup? Had Gary lied, had the creep taken the money and kept her marrow?

No, no, no! She couldn't allow herself to think that way.

She fingered her headscarf with trembling fingers, tucked in the ends while Gina continued to read and reread the label on each bag of solution, acting as if it was the first time she'd ever seen them.

Something's gone wrong! I know it!

Gary squeezed her hand; she turned to him, tried to smile. He looked tired. No, not tired. Something else. It was something she hadn't seen in his face in a long, long time—a deep inner expression of love. It infused her with warmth, then confusion.

It's because I'm ill. If I live, he'll be gone again.

She glanced back at Gina and watched as the nurse rolled, slid, and adjusted the IV tubing's blue release valves; read and rechecked the solutions all over again. *Why does she keep fussing with everything?*

"It won't be much longer before we start," Gina said, pushing the unit of IVs off to one side, then quickly glancing at her watch.

"Is . . . is everything all right?" Tracy asked.

"Couldn't be better. We're right on schedule."

Tracy wanted to ask more but a woman in a lab coat, pushing a metal cart, interrupted them. On top was a Styrofoam cooler, not much different from the kind she used to take on picnics; on the bottom was a large plastic basin, filled with an assortment of medical supplies.

After the woman had washed her hands, Gina said, "Eva, I want you to meet Tracy Bernstein. Tracy, Eva's the one who has worked with your marrow from the very beginning, from the moment it was harvested."

Eva came to the side of the bed and took her hand. "Big day for you," she said, pointing at the cart. "Don't let any of this stuff frighten you."

"There isn't very much there," Gary said. "I mean, I thought it would be a large complicated machine of some kind."

"Most people are surprised at how simple this part of the procedure is. It's not much different than any blood transfusion. The most complicated part is getting the right marrow. When it's your own, even that part's simple."

Tracy couldn't wait any longer. "You do have my marrow," she blurted. "I *am* going to have it today, aren't I?"

"You bet!" Eva said firmly. She walked back to the cart and placed the cooler on the floor and patted the top of the box. "It's right in here."

Tracy released an audible sigh and smiled widely. Gary leaned down to kiss her cheek and whispered in her ear, "That's a relief."

Tracy nodded, squeezed his hand against her hip and asked Eva, "Is it thawed and ready?"

Gina and Eva both laughed. "Actually, it's still hard as a rock," Eva said. She reached for the square plastic basin from the bottom of the cart and filled it with water, then set the basin on top of the cart on a special warming unit that she plugged into the wall. "We'll thaw it, bring it to body temperature as we use it, one bag at a time."

Gina opened the cooler, releasing a foggy mist. She pulled out one of the packages of marrow and quickly showed it to Tracy—a small, bright-burgundy, almost square plastic package with two valves protruding from the top. Gina juggled it for a second, then returned it to the cooler. "It's icy cold," she said shaking her fingers.

"Such a small package, so flat," Gary said. "Not at all what I visualized."

"That's so the preservative comes in contact with all of the cells," Eva said. "The DSMO gives them that bright color and keeps them from bursting when they're frozen." As she spoke, she began setting out the equipment, naming each item for Tracy's and Gary's benefit: "Ten 50cc syringes . . . three-way stopcock . . . Kelly clamp." She pulled some plastic tubes from her pocket and explained how they would be used to culture the remains of each cell package. Studying the temperature reading of the water, she nodded almost imperceptibly. "The protocols are very rigid. Either do it right or the cells are useless."

"Not as simple as it looks," Gary said.

"We harvest it, filter it, remove the bone chips and fat. Then it all goes through a cell separator. That's when we get the white cells."

"What do you do with the other cells . . . the red ones?" Tracy asked.

"We gave those back to you a long time ago."

"Everything seems so . . . diminutive," Tracy said. Her throat constricted, cutting off anything else she might have said. All she could do was wonder when would they start? Get it over with?

Mark Kessler rushed into the room. "I know, I'm late. I'm sorry." He smiled at Tracy and Gary, gave an I-couldn't-help-it shrug to Gina and Eva, and bent over the sink to wash his hands. "I overheard your last comment, Tracy. I want you to know there's nothing diminutive about the number of cells we collected. We have 1000ccs of your marrow, and we'll probably only use half of that." He pulled several paper towels out of the dispenser and carefully dried his hands. "The rest we'll stash in liquid nitrogen and keep it in frozen storage for at least ten years."

Tracy's insides seemed to turn as frigid as the nitrogen freeze Kessler was talking about; she swallowed hard against a suffocating sensation that crushed down on her chest. This was what she'd thought she was waiting for, but all she could visualize now was an hourglass being flipped over, her life force rushing away.

Kessler placed a hand on Tracy's shoulder. "Well, we finally made it."

Tracy could just barely nod.

Eva pressed a button on the heating unit and the basin began rocking. She called out the temperature: 37 degrees centigrade. Tracy watched the tech clamp onto one of the marrow packages with a metal instrument, apparently so she could retrieve it easily, then let it float alongside another package. The basin gently rocked back and forth, heating and agitating the water.

"It'll just be a few more minutes," Gina said, moving the IV unit closer to the bed, then giving her a thumbs-up sign.

Tracy was lightheaded and forced herself to slow her breathing. At the same time she clutched frantically at Gary's hand.

He leaned over and whispered in her ear, "I'm right here, Trace. I'm not leaving . . . ever." She turned to him. Tears filled his eyes. He mouthed, "I love you."

Kessler pulled a stand alongside the bed and adjusted the height, while Gina swabbed off the access port to one branch of the central line, just as it had been explained to her when she'd initially agreed to do the autologous marrow procedure. Kessler immediately plunged the needle from the IV tubing into the rubber port; Gina taped it into place and loosened the IV lock. Sodium chloride ran slowly into one leg of the "Y" tubing, backing down and filling the other leg of the access device. She realized everything was now ready for the infusion of her bone marrow.

Tracy's heart pounded in her ears as Kessler took the first burgundy-colored syringe from the lab tech and attached it to the tubing. A three-way stopcock allowed him to remove any air bubbles in the line before injecting the marrow, yet continued to control the flow of the sodium chloride.

As a metallic smell spread throughout the room, Gina reached over and pulled up the wick in a bottle of mint deodorizer.

"What smells so horrible?" Tracy asked, alarmed.

"That's the DSMO," Eva said. "Probably the worst

thing about the whole procedure."

Tracy began to relax. "I'm sure it's my imagination, but my mouth tastes like . . . like wild onions, with a tinge of garlic . . . kind of nice."

Kessler, Eva, and Gina laughed together. "Not only that," Gina said, "by the time we're finished, you'll feel like you've had the humongous meal that went with it."

Tracy closed her eyes; a soft, calm grayness greeted her. She felt different, she *was* different: larger, potent, more connected.

Opening her eyes, she looked around the room: Kessler was infusing syringe after syringe of marrow into her body; Eva was lifting the packages of her cells from the cooler, warming them, drawing them up into the syringes; Gina was checking the IVs, reassuring her; Gary was solid, supportive, squeezing her hand.

A strange feeling of detachment overcame her—and with it came an unexpected sense of serenity—

—no more painful feelings about Gary's betrayal;

—no more driving ambition;

—no more hopes;

—no more fears.

What remained was surrender; total surrender to each and every moment left of her life.

Gina had carefully watched Tracy and Gary throughout the engraftment. She knew that they'd paid to get Tracy's marrow back.

Tracy Bernstein had paid to live while Carl Chapman had chosen to die. And Vinnie? What was his fate? Would he die as Chapman had?

She scribbled more sign-off notes in one of the charts and put it back into the rack.

Why wasn't Vinnie's marrow missing? Faye said it was safe in the lab. Was it or wasn't it?

It was almost time to leave. Harry had called—they were to meet outside the hospital.

But she kept stalling, knew what she had to do. Instead, she kept working at her nurse's notes—putting off the moment. Twice she started down the hallway toward Tracy's room, but each time she returned to the safety of the nurses' station.

She had to know. Talking to the Bernsteins was the only way she was going to find out.

They were still holding hands when she walked into the room. Tracy looked tired, but at the same time there was a contradicting calmness and radiance about her—certainly not what you would expect of someone who had just spent six weeks undergoing grueling chemotherapy.

"How do you feel, Tracy?" Gina knew the engraftment had gone well. Hopefully, the purged cells would now return to their home ground and regenerate, creating the embryonic network of healthy cells Tracy needed to survive.

She smiled brightly at Gina. "Human, for the first time in ages."

"She's even starting to get feisty," Gary said, laughing.

Was there some diplomatic way to question them? Probably not. "How much did you have to pay?" she blurted.

Both looked at her.

"What was it, fifty thousand?"

Tracy looked at her with pleading eyes—pleading for her to stop. Gary was stone faced.

"You've got to tell me," Gina said, feeling the first twinges of desperation tighten the muscles of her neck. "Other people's lives are at stake."

"That's exactly why we can't say anything," Tracy whispered.

"Please! One person has died already. If you don't help, there may be more."

"I'm not sure what to do," Gary said.

"Sure? You want a sure thing?" Gina shook her head and looked directly at Tracy. "You, of all people, know that's not possible."

"Gina, we're not trying to be difficult, we want to help—"

"What happened to your scarf, Tracy?" Gina interrupted.

Tracy automatically touched the beige silk covering her head. "What are you talking about? It's right here. I'm wearing it."

"Not that one. The one you bought in Italy, the Michaelia original." She moved toward the closet. "Where is it? I'll get it for you; it's so much more attractive than the one you're wearing."

Tracy looked at Gary; he shrugged weakly.

"Someone stole it," she said flatly.

CHAPTER 29

Vinnie huddled in a corner of the garage, a hand pressed against his mouth to stifle the sound of his labored breathing. It had taken him almost three hours to cover the five miles from the hospital to home, a distance he could have jogged in about 40 minutes in the past.

Despite the warm spring day, he shivered from the cold sweat that continued to accumulate and saturate his clothing. What he needed was a shower, something dry to change into.

He wasn't going to get either—his aunt's car was parked in the driveway.

He decided to sneak around the side of the house and enter the garage from the back door, hoping she wasn't planning to stay until his mother came home—that would ruin everything. He shivered and moved closer to the hot water heater, but the heavily insulated tank offered no comfort.

Until this moment, everything had gone as planned. Getting out of the hospital had been a snap, less of a problem than he'd ever dreamed possible.

He'd worked out the details during the past couple of days, deciding the best time would be after they picked up his breakfast tray, but before lunch. At first he'd thought about leaving during either the 7 a.m. or 3 p.m. shift change, but then realized there might be too many people in the hallways who could recognize him, wonder why he was wandering around in street clothes. The late afternoon to early evening hours also were no good since by then either

211

one or both of his parents would have arrived. And if he waited until they went home, it would be too late.

As soon as the candy-striper had picked up his tray around 9:00 a.m., trying her best to be cheerful, yet unable to keep her eyes off his bald head, Vinnie had gotten out of bed and dressed. He'd automatically pulled on his grungy Giants baseball cap, which had been at his bedside ever since he'd checked in. But he quickly returned it to its assigned spot. Gina and most of the other Oncology staff not only knew the cap, but also often teased him about it when the Giants lost a game. If they saw it was missing, they might become suspicious.

Instead, he put on the new Giants cap his father had brought a couple of days earlier, the stiff fabric scratching the exposed skin of his head. He'd turned the cap front to rear and scowled at himself in the mirror: the style was an affectation he hated, but the long bill better hid the fact there was no hair growing down the back of his head. He wanted to blend as much as possible with the non-patient visitors to the hospital.

No one had given him a second glance as he'd walked out of his room, taken the elevator to the main floor, and strolled out of Ridgewood. With no money for bus fare, he'd initially thought he would try to hitch a ride, but not one person slowed down for him, let alone stopped. After several minutes, he became worried someone would sooner or later spot him standing on the corner.

Toward the end of the long hike, stumbling along the sidewalk, he'd become less certain that he'd done the right thing. Now, he was barely able to stand. He needed rest and something to eat, if he could keep food down.

He eased open the door between the garage and laundry room and turned one ear to the interior of the house, trying to determine where his aunt might be hanging out. He almost panicked when he heard mumbled conversation drifting through the rooms.

He held his breath and strained to hear what was being said, and by whom, then cursed himself for being so naive and stupid—his aunt would almost rather die than miss an episode of the afternoon soaps. When he finally heard the start of a commercial, he took a deep breath and slumped against the doorway. If she stayed in the den with the TV, he could make it to his room without being seen.

He slipped off his shoes and waited for the string of commercials to end, then made his way through the kitchen, grabbing a carton of milk from the refrigerator on the way. He hugged the hallway wall to keep from falling and concentrated on holding onto the milk. Once inside his room, he wasn't sure whether or not to close the door—if he left it open, she might come down the carpeted hallway without his hearing her; if he closed it, she might notice the change and look inside, out of curiosity.

He compromised: left the door open just enough so he could continue to hear the audio from the television, yet move about his room in relative safety.

He dug out his savings account statement—he wasn't going to be able to do anything unless he got some money. And even the cash wouldn't do him any good if he didn't get some rest—he could barely lift an arm to pull open the dresser drawer.

He shoved his ATM card into a hip pocket of his jeans and checked his watch—almost noon. He still had plenty of time.

After struggling to change into dry clothes, he opened the bedroom door all the way before going around to the far side of the room and stretching out on the floor between his

bed and the wall. He set the alarm on his wristwatch, posi-
tioned it beneath his ear, and fell into an exhausted sleep.

Frankie, no!

The moment Faye Lindstrom heard that Oncology was
looking for Vinnie Capello, she was certain Frankie had
something to do with it. She bent forward and rested on the
top of the lab counter, trying to ease the searing in her
stomach where her flesh was torn. Some of the staff, noticing her discomfort, had asked if she'd been in an accident.

She'd made up her mind: no matter what Frankie said or
did, she wasn't going to steal any more marrow. Not only
was the deceit overwhelming, she was in constant fear of
being caught and going to jail. Besides, no matter what she
did or didn't do, Frankie would continue to hurt her.

And now, Vinnie Capello was missing. She tried to find
out what had happened, but all she could pick up from hospital scuttlebutt was that he was missing from his room,
hadn't been seen since morning.

Had Frankie gone off the deep end and snatched him in
broad daylight? She took a deep breath, gasped at the stabbing pain in her kidney.

Why does he always have to hurt me?

"Faye!"

She grabbed the edge of the counter, trembled, and pretended she didn't hear.

"Faye! Phone for you. Pick up on three, please."

She walked over to the nearest desk and put her hand on
the receiver. If it were Frankie, she would hang up. She
couldn't talk to him, didn't want to know what he'd been
doing.

And what if he asked about Deana Oldham's marrow?

She stared at the blinking light. She had to pick up the phone. Everyone was watching her, she was sure of it; everyone's eyes were on her. Slowly, she lifted her eyes to look around the lab; no one was paying any attention to her at all.

Cautiously, she lifted the receiver. "This is Faye."

"Hi, this is Gina . . . in Oncology. I know it's an imposition, but could you do me a favor?"

Gina Mazzio's words stung her like a swarm of attacking bees. She held the receiver away from her ear, tried to absorb what was being said. Look in the freezer? No, I can't!

But she had no choice but to respond to Gina's request. She punched Hold and stood there for moment, staring down at the telephone. Finally, she forced herself away from the desk, circled the lab as if looking for something, then went back to the phone. She took a deep breath, raised her eyes to the ceiling, and let the air slowly escape through pursed lips before releasing the hold button.

"It's there, Gina," she lied.

After she hung up, she rushed out of the lab and entered one of the patient toilets, locked the door, and collapsed on the floor. Uncontrollable sobs shook her body. Somehow, she had to sneak Vinnie Capello's real marrow back into the hospital; she'd have to find some way to deal with Frankie.

Deal with Frankie? How? Oh, God, how?

It was almost a half hour before she returned to the lab and a thorough chewing out by Bob Ghent.

Vinnie was startled by a noise and wasn't sure where it came from. It took several seconds to remember where he was and what he'd done. He fumbled with the wristwatch controls until he found the button that shut off the alarm. Three o'clock! Just as he'd planned.

He lay still, listening from behind his bed, his legs throbbing from the five-mile walk home. The television was still on, but by now he knew the soaps would have ended. It probably wouldn't make any difference: his aunt was equally hooked on the late afternoon talk shows.

When he was certain she hadn't heard the buzz of the alarm, he slowly pushed himself up from the floor and peered over the top of the mattress. He was still exhausted; every muscle and joint ached and throbbed. Twice he had to stop and sit on the edge of the bed before he could gather together clean underwear, his best black socks, a fresh white handkerchief, his least dorky wig, and a set of silver cufflinks and studs he'd inherited from his grandfather. He put everything into a small blue and gold University of California athletic bag, along with a couple of bottles of Mylanta.

After checking to make certain he had his wallet and ATM card, he started to leave, and then remembered the tickets. He stuck them in the side pocket of the bag and escaped from the house as silently as he'd entered it some three hours earlier.

First stop was the local florist, where he bought a wrist corsage and boutonniere. He paid to have the corsage, one of the prom tickets, and a note delivered to Angie's house. The note alone had taken him almost twenty minutes to compose since he didn't know whether she planned to go to the prom, or whether she had a date. Finally, he simply wrote:

If you go to the prom tonight, I hope you'll wear this for me. I miss you.

Vinnie

Faye watched the hands of the clock approach quitting

time, but couldn't move when the hour actually arrived. She sat planted on her stool, rehearsing over and over in her mind what she could say to Frankie when he asked for the Oldham girl's marrow.

She wasn't going to take it, that she knew. But could she stand another of his beatings? The pain was horrible every time she took a deep breath, and there was still blood in her urine.

She finally slid off the stool and left the building, but once outside she got no farther than the fountain, where she sat down heavily and dangled her fingers in the water. A couple of curious goldfish nibbled at her fingertips, but she was too distracted to respond as she usually did. Perhaps if she sat there long enough, she might see Gina. If she could only talk to her, tell her . . . tell someone . . .

When Gina did come pushing through the hospital double doors, Faye didn't see her until she was almost halfway out to the street. She started to rise, then saw that Gina was with someone, a man. For a moment, she felt betrayed, deserted. Then she recognized Harry Lucke, Gina's boyfriend. Maybe . . .

But before Faye could hurry after them, they started trotting down the street. She sat back down and started to cry.

"You really should have placed your order much earlier," the salesman told Vinnie, his manner more patronizing than informative.

"I didn't know I could go until this morning," Vinnie said, looking in the three-way mirror. The jacket wasn't a bad fit, but there was about four inches too much material drooping over the tops of the rental patent leather shoes.

"Can you shorten them?" he asked, pointing to the legs of the pants.

"Young man, this is a very busy time of the year for us. I don't know how we could possibly . . . our tailors are simply—"

"Look, just mark them the right length, okay? I'll take care of it myself."

"We can't have you cutting our—"

"Don't worry about it; I won't cut them. I'll pin them . . . or staple them . . . or something. I have to have this tux tonight, do you understand?" He couldn't bring himself to tell the man this might be the only time he'd ever get to wear a tuxedo. He continued to stare at himself in the mirrors, certain that he looked the dumbest he'd ever looked, with his Christian Slater wig, drooping pants, and a shawl-collared jacket over a white T-shirt.

"So?" he insisted. "Do we have a deal or don't we? I got to know now because it's getting late and there's this other place across town, but I'm not sure whether I can make it there in time . . . they'll probably be out of things because they charge a lot less than you guys . . . so I need to know now, okay?" He staggered a little and had to grab the back of a nearby chair to steady himself.

"Are you all right?" the salesman asked. "You look a bit . . . peaked."

Vinnie held up one hand. "I'm okay. Really, I am. It's just that I've been so worried about whether or not I was going to be able to get this tux."

The salesman pressed the fingers of one hand against his lips. "Stay right here," he said and disappeared through a door behind the three-way mirror.

Vinnie slumped into the chair and waited. He knew if he didn't get out of the rental store soon, he was going to pass out.

Should have started sooner.

218

The room was doing a slow spin.

No! Not now!

He leaned over and put his head between his knees.

"I really shouldn't be doing this," the salesman said as he came back into the room.

"What?" Vinnie sat up quickly.

"Young man, are you sure you're all right?"

"Yes, just a little tired."

"Well, one of our tailors said he wouldn't mind staying over fifteen minutes or so to fix the pants." He motioned for Vinnie to stand up in front of the mirrors again. "I'll mark the pants myself and he'll baste them for you. They won't be ready until about six-fifteen."

"I thought you closed at six."

"Exactly!" He knelt down on one knee and marked the bottom of one pant leg, then the other. "You'll have to go around to the alley door when you come back. The tailor will give you everything then." He stood up, looked at himself and Vinnie in the mirror, and tilted his head. "Slip out of the coat, pants, and shoes and get dressed. Then come up to the counter; I'll have your bill ready for you."

"You sure there'll be someone here when I come back?"

"In for a penny, in for a pound."

"What?"

"Never mind. Trust me. The tailor will be here."

Vinnie hid out in a back booth at McDonald's until almost eight o'clock, trying to consume a Big Mac, fries, and a chocolate milkshake. He hoped they wouldn't ask him to leave, since he had to keep running back and forth between his booth and the men's room—none of the food stayed down for more than a few minutes.

But no one paid any attention to him. He felt safe in the

restaurant, surrounded by a crowd of other teenagers, even though he panicked a couple of times when he saw a Plymouth Voyager like his parents' pull into the parking lot.

A little after eight, he used the restaurant's restroom one last time to change into his tuxedo.

"One dance," he told the cracked mirror as he turned to leave. "Just one dance!"

CHAPTER 30

"I think we're spinning our wheels," Harry said, hurrying to keep up with Gina. She pushed through the hospital doors and out into the plaza without answering. "The police are looking in all the usual places," he said, running to catch up with her. "There's family at his house . . . his parents are out scouting around . . . everything's being done that can be done, Gina. I don't know what you think we can accomplish driving aimlessly around the city."

"I can't sit around and do nothing." She stopped abruptly when they reached his pickup truck. "If you don't want to come with me, that's okay. I'll understand. But don't try to keep me from going. That kid's out there roaming around on his own; he needs help."

Harry unlocked the passenger-side door for her. "I didn't say I wouldn't go," he said, taking her hand. "I just don't think it's going to do any good."

"Harry," she said, leaning her forehead against his shoulder, "I don't know if it's going to do any good, either. But I have to give it a try." She took a deep breath and lifted her head. "I'm not going to lose another patient without a fight, without so much as following up on a hunch—no matter how stupid or wrong it may sound."

Harry kissed her on each cheek. "Why didn't you say it was a hunch? I'd follow you to hell and back on one of your hunches."

Gina glared at him. "This isn't funny, Harry Lucke. I'm very serious about this." She handed him a small senior class photo of Vinnie. "I got a couple of these from the

Capellos," she said. "We can show them around."

"Good idea," he said, closing the cab door. "Just remember," he added as he started the truck, "I wouldn't
make an offer like that if I didn't mean it."

Vinnie knew the taxi driver thought he was nuts. But he
planned to keep circling Angie's block until one of three
things happened: he saw her come out, dressed for the
dance; it got so late he was sure she wasn't going; or, he ran
out of money.

It was almost 8:30 when he saw a car pull up in front of
her house. She must have a date, he thought.

"Slow down," he told the driver as they approached
Angie's house for the umpteenth time. He saw her coming
down the steps, dressed in an ankle-length ball gown, a
shawl draped around her shoulders. She was beautiful. He
wondered who the jerk was who didn't have the smarts to
get out of his car and go up to the house for her.

"Wouldn't it have been easier if you'd just asked her for
a date?" the taxi driver said over his shoulder.

"Keep going!" Vinnie ordered. As they passed the other
car, he doubled up both fists, and shouted, *"Yes!"*

"What, yes?"

"You wouldn't understand."

"That's for sure."

Vinnie watched Angie as she approached the sedan,
waving at its occupants. She had his flowers on her wrist.
There were two other girls in the car, all obviously going to
the prom stag.

"I suppose you want me to follow them," the driver said.

"What?"

"Do you want me to follow their car?"

"Why would I want you to do that?"

"I don't know, just a wild guess."

"Yeah, well, you guessed wrong." He gave the driver directions for an intersection a block away from his high school. On the way, he took the boutonniere from the athletic bag, pinned it to his lapel, and sat back in the seat, satisfied with himself.

"What say we stop at the next 7-11 and get a cup of coffee?" Harry said.

"You must be exhausted," Gina said, looking at her watch. "I didn't realize we'd been at this for more than four hours."

"I really could use some coffee."

"Might as well stop," she agreed. "I can't think anymore and I don't know where else to look."

"I must have hit every street in town, at least once," Harry said, yawning. "Plus you've gone to the bus station, library, rec center, and every movie theater in the area." He slowed and pointed to a convenience store sign a block up the street.

"I can't quit until we find out what's happened to Vinnie."

Harry pulled into the parking lot, waited for another car to back out, and parked in front of the store. "Coffee for you, too?"

"Herbal tea," she said, then shook her head. "No, maybe the caffeine will wake up my brain. I keep thinking there's some clue I'm missing."

"Like what?"

"Like something Vinnie may have told me, like there being something special about today."

"It's the third Friday in May," he said. "Never been anything special about that that I can recall."

"Me neither. It's still more than a week to Memorial Day, but I can't see that having any special meaning for Vinnie."

"Not unless he's trying to make it back to Indiana for the Indianapolis 500." He saw her lips tighten, jaw go rigid. "Sorry! I'm getting a little punchy."

She took a deep breath, let it out slowly, and reached over to take Harry's hand. "You've been great. I really appreciate it." She gave him a quick kiss on the cheek. "Tell you what: why don't you get the coffee and a munchie of some kind and I'll call the hospital to see if they've heard anything."

Using her cell phone, Gina watched the foot traffic in and out of the 7-11 while she waited for someone to pick up the phone in Oncology. The charge nurse finally came on the line just as Harry came out of the store, trying to balance two hot coffees and a bag that probably contained something chock full of calories and cholesterol. Right now she didn't care.

After hearing there was still no news of Vinnie, she clicked off and again wondered where the kid could have gone. Harry drew her attention as he tried to fend off two teenagers in tuxedos. She watched him backpedal away from them, shaking his head slowly. But when one of them gave him a digital salute, she caught a look in his eye that told her she'd better intervene.

"Harry!" she called. "What'd you get us?"

Harry looked at her, looked back at the two teens, gave a shrug, and met her at the truck.

"What was that all about?" she asked.

"Wanted me to buy them a pint of vodka and didn't seem to want to take no for an answer. Then they started ragging me about being too old to remember my own senior prom."

"Oh, shit!" Gina cried out.

"What?"

"That's it! The senior prom!"

Vinnie had less than $2.00 left after he paid the cab driver, but he didn't care. He knew that after tonight he probably wouldn't need money, or anything else.

He stood at the corner and looked down the street at the entrance to the school gymnasium. The parking lot across the street was already full, causing late arrivers to drop off their dates and drive on to find distant parking. A few limousines pulled in, let out three or four couples at a time, and drove away.

Too early . . . should have waited another hour or so.

The question was, where to wait? He didn't want to just stand around on the street corner in his tuxedo, with a flower in his lapel. He considered going for a long walk, but he knew that was out—he would never make it back. The nap at home had helped, but that had been too long ago. He was drained, his stomach in spasm from the junk food; cold sweat kept forming on his brow, trickling down his face.

Vinnie uselessly patted his jacket pocket for the third or fourth time, but he knew he'd taken the last of the Mylanta almost an hour earlier.

He started toward the gym entrance, but turned off onto the path that led to the school athletic field. Holding onto the wooden edges of the stadium bleachers, he moved out onto the red cinder track and followed it around to where it almost merged with the close-cropped grass of the baseball outfield. He walked directly toward home plate, pausing for a moment at the pitcher's mound. He tossed an imaginary game-winning pitch, and doffed his cap to the cheering crowd.

His goal was the small, four-level bleacher section behind the batter's box, but by the time he made it to the backstop, he was panting and had to lace his fingers through the wire mesh of the screen to keep from falling. He lowered himself onto the scarred bottom plank and sat there, eyes closed, trying to slow his breathing. When he finally opened his eyes, he was staring down at the tops of his shoes.

"Shit!"

He reached down and began to wipe away the wet blades of grass that covered the rented patent leather shoes.

"Are you supposed to be chaperones?" the teacher-ticket-taker asked Gina and Harry, giving their rumpled hospital clothes a disapproving glance.

Gina shook her head as she strained to look inside where the graduating class was dancing to the music of a live band. "We're looking for someone. Vinnie Capello."

"I don't think you're going to find Vinnie here. He's seriously ill . . . in the hospital."

"Yes and no," Harry said, stepping up to the table. "He's supposed to be in the hospital, but he took off this morning without telling anyone where he was going."

"You think he might come to the dance?"

"He had it circled on his calendar," Gina said. "And I know he's been terribly upset about a girl. Angie Norris, I think."

"Well, Angie's here," the teacher said, pivoting around in her chair to gaze into the gym. "She came with a couple of other girls, but Vinnie wasn't with them." She turned back and consulted a list of names on the table in front of her. "Wait a minute," she said, turning the roster so Gina and Harry could see it: "Vinnie bought two tickets, numbers 211 and 212. Angie came in on number 212, but 211 is still unaccounted for."

"Could we please talk to Angie?" Gina asked.

"I don't know—"

"Look, I'm his nurse and this is an emergency. If we don't find Vinnie soon . . . well, let's say we have to find him. Angie might be able to help."

"Norm!" the teacher called to a man standing near the entrance. "Go find Angie Norris and bring her here. It's urgent!" She turned back to Gina and Harry. "Norm's one of our counselors; he should be able to find her quicker than anyone else."

Within a couple of minutes the counselor returned with a very worried-looking teenager.

"Hi, I'm Angie Norris," she said. "What's wrong? Has something happened to my parents?"

"No, not your parents," Gina said. "It's Vinnie Capello; we're looking for him."

"Oh, Vinnie!" She looked from the counselor to the ticket-taker. "I thought he was going to be here, too. I've been waiting . . ."

"What made you think he would be here?"

"He sent me these flowers today," Angie said, holding up her arm, "along with a ticket and a note asking me to save him a dance."

"But you haven't seen him?" Harry asked.

Angie shook her head, tears welled in her eyes. "Is he in trouble?"

"I'm afraid so," Gina said. "Did he say what time he would be at the prom?"

"No."

"Is there anything . . . anything else you haven't told us?"

"No. I mean, I was really surprised to get the gardenias and the ticket. Vinnie has refused to even talk to me since he went back in the hospital. I thought I'd done something to make him angry. I thought he hated me."

Gina took her hand. "It isn't you. He's just angry about everything. Besides, he's a very stubborn kind of guy."

"Boy, you can say that again," Angie said. "Whenever he has a problem, he just shuts you out and goes off by himself until he's solved it. Most of the time I'd find him out at the baseball field, sitting behind the backstop with that cruddy old Giants cap pulled down over his eyes. If he waved when I called his name, then I knew it was okay to go to him. Otherwise—"

"Where's the baseball field?" Gina asked.

"Over by the gym," she said, pointing. "Why?"

Gina grabbed Harry's hand and started pulling him toward the door. "Never mind why. Just keep Vinnie here if he shows up before we get back." She and Harry started running.

"I'm coming, too," Angie called out, kicking off her pumps.

The music drifted in and out of Vinnie's head. Every so often he tried to push himself up off of the ground, regain his seat on the wooden bench. So cold. So cold!

"Vinnie!" The syllables came in counterpoint to the beat of the music.

"Vinnie!"

Angie? He raised his head as blurry figures floated toward him. He pulled himself up into a sitting position and tried to clear his vision.

"Angie?" He pushed one arm up with his other hand and managed a small wave before the arm flopped down across the bench. The next thing he knew, Angie had her arms wrapped around him.

"I waited for you, Vinnie, waited so long," she whispered. "You never came; I didn't know what to do." She started crying. "I thought you didn't want me anymore."

"All I thought of was you . . . missed you so much."

"Vinnie," Gina said softly, "we need to get you back to the hospital."

He looked up, saw Gina standing nearby; some guy had his arm around her waist. "Hey, Bronx, how'd you find me?"

"It hasn't been easy, kid."

"Almost made it," he said, nodding in the direction of the music.

"Here, let me help you up, buddy," the man said, offering a hand. "I'm Harry, and I've heard one hell of a lot about you."

Vinnie managed a weak grin. Then, supported by Angie and Harry, with Gina walking backward in front of him, he managed to keep his legs moving until they got near the gym. There, he stopped, and turned away from Harry. He took Angie into his arms and haltingly danced her around in a small circle, his face buried in her hair, the fragrance of her corsage drifting around them.

CHAPTER 31

They stood at the entrance to her apartment building, Gina leaning heavily into Harry's arms, her head resting against his.

"I can't believe how lucky we were to find Vinnie," she said. "He looked so small and forlorn, curled up on the ground behind the backstop."

"At least Kessler thinks his chances are good," Harry said. "But only because of you and your damned hunch."

"Can you imagine the hell he must have gone through to get as far as he did?" She sighed. "He just wanted to make it to the dance."

"Yeah, but it's that kind of spunk that's going to save his life."

"I hope you're right," she said, holding up crossed fingers and realizing it was something she was doing a lot lately. "It's about time something good happened to that Vinnie."

"Are you game for a cup of coffee?"

"No way. I'm totally exhausted, Harry; nothing but one big ache from head to toe . . . got to get to bed."

"You do look tired; you've been pushing yourself to the max through this whole business." He caressed her forehead. "I'm really concerned about you."

"Thanks. It's just that so many things have happened today. My head is still spinning." She took in a deep breath. "I think this has been the longest day of my life. Truthfully, all I can think about right now is crawling into a hot tub and soaking until I turn into a wrinkled olive."

Harry laughed. "Prune. A wrinkled prune."

She stuck her tongue out at him. "Who wants to be a wrinkled prune?"

He kissed her cheek and buried his face in her neck. "Sure you don't want company?"

It was so comfortable in his arms, she wanted to stay there, but forced herself to pull away. "And after my bath, I'm crawling right into bed and not moving until morning."

"Tell you a secret: I'm looking forward to a steaming shower myself. You know, water pounding on my manly shoulders with hot thoughts of you in my head."

She chuckled. "See, we'd run out of hot water if we didn't have two apartments."

"A minor detail."

Gina studied him for a long moment, searched for the right words, and finally said, "I've been doing a lot of serious thinking this past week . . . about us." She tugged nervously at her hair, bit her lip, then looked downward. "But maybe this isn't the time to talk about it."

His eyebrows pinched into a worried look. "Talk about what?" He tipped her chin until she was forced to look in his eyes. "You haven't suddenly changed your mind about us, have you?"

The light from the entryway reflected on Harry's distressed face. "No!" she said. "As a matter of fact, just the opposite." She caressed and kissed his cheek. "Mr. Lucke, not only do I love you, I intend to hold onto you for dear life."

His face transformed into one huge smile. He squeezed her tightly as their lips met in a long, lingering kiss. When they finally separated, they were both breathless.

"Then you meant what you said at lunch?" he asked.

"Have I ever lied to you?" She flashed a smile, then

moved toward the entrance. "Later, for you." Her fingers fanned a good-bye as she entered the vestibule. She turned and peered out the glass door—Harry was still there, throwing kisses at her. She waved him away and watched as he trotted out to his double-parked pickup.

Gina trudged down the hallway, sighing when she saw the elevator still had the "Out-of-order" sign posted. Disgusted, she turned around and used the stairway. The three floors dragged by as she climbed, trying not to think about anything. She leaned heavily on the handrail, counting the steps by fives. Still, it seemed like an eternity before she stood motionless in front of her apartment.

She fumbled in her purse, searching for her keys. "Where the hell are the dumb things?" As she dug into a zippered compartment, someone grabbed her arm from behind.

"Hey!" She whirled around, swinging out with one fist.

Faye jumped back out of range. They stood there speechless, staring at one another.

"Jesus, Faye!" Gina finally said, hand to her chest. "You scared me to death. What's the matter with you, sneaking up on me like that?"

"I'm sorry," Faye said, backing up to the wall. "I . . . I didn't mean to scare you."

Gina looked at the lab tech's pasty face, then tugged on her arm. "Let's get inside."

As they entered the living room, Gina said, "Look, Faye, I might as well tell you I'm going to the police tomorrow."

"What do you mean?"

"I mean, you're the one who's been stealing the marrow. Who else could it be?"

Faye blinked, stepped back, her face a mask of astonishment.

"Oh, for God's sake! I know you must be involved in this mess." Gina threw her purse onto the sofa—lipstick, comb, keys, and Tums spilled out onto the floor.

"It just has to be you," Gina insisted. "You and that . . . that creep you're living with. When I finally realized it was Tracy Bernstein's scarf at your house, I was able to put it all together."

"I don't know what you're talking about. I never took anything from Mrs. Bernstein's. Frankie gave me that scarf."

"You didn't steal it from Tracy's room?"

"No, of course not! I wouldn't do that."

"I see," Gina said, trying to fight off the rage that kept welling up inside of her. "Of course not." Her eyes bored into Faye's. "How insensitive of me to think you would steal someone's scarf. Oh, it's perfectly all right to steal someone's bone marrow, but my goodness, steal a scarf?" Gina held the back of her hand to her forehead. "I do apologize, Miss Lindstrom, for daring to question your ethics."

Faye turned a bright red, stammered two or three times before she could speak coherently: "It can't be Mrs. Bernstein's scarf. It can't be!" Faye moved further back until she was flat against the wall. "Frankie gave it to me. If it's hers, how did he get it?"

"What a good question, Miss Lindstrom. If you didn't give it to him, where did he get it?"

Faye burst into tears. "I don't know. All I know is, I didn't take it!"

"I don't believe you."

"I know I've lied to you in the past, Gina," she said, "but not this time."

"Wow! Big surprise. True confession time."

"I didn't want to . . . but—"

"But what?"

"I couldn't tell you the truth; I didn't want you to . . . to hate me."

"What the hell's the matter with you, anyway?" Gina asked. "I mean, what are you doing in the middle of all this?"

"I . . . I couldn't help it."

Gina wanted to grab her, shake her, hit her, do something. Instead, she bent over, picked up everything that had fallen from her purse, and tossed the accumulation helter-skelter onto the sofa. When she straightened, she was still angry.

"Couldn't help it?" she snarled. "What kind of crap is that?"

"He beat me, Gina. Frankie . . . every time . . . every time I refused."

"You didn't have to stay with the bastard," she said, feeling her throat turn dry from shouting. She stomped into the kitchen, shoved a glass under the faucet, and drank the water in a single gulp. "Other women leave assholes like him; you could have left any time."

"It's so easy for you to tell me what to do," she said, jutting her chin out defiantly. "You've got a great guy; everything is happy-go-lucky for you."

"That's the way my life looks?"

Faye nodded.

Gina downed another glass of water. "So, just because things aren't hunky-dory and your life isn't a storybook fantasy, you hook up with some sleaze bag and start stealing people's marrow to make money. That's supposed to make everything all right?"

"It sounds horrible, I know . . . but . . . but . . ." She looked wildly up at the ceiling. "You don't understand. I need him; I need Frankie. I had to find some way to keep him from leaving."

"You're sick, Faye." Gina shook her head back and forth. "Very sick!"

Faye looked at Gina imploringly. "I can't help it if I need someone to love me. I deserve a life, too."

"Oh, yeah? Well, so do those people in the hospital . . . those poor souls who'll die without the cells you stole."

"They got their marrow back . . . almost all of them."

"Almost? You mean Carl Chapman, don't you? What happened with him?"

Faye's eyes grew large and frightened. "He wouldn't pay!"

The pulse in Gina's temple pounded, her eye twitched erratically. She slammed the water glass down on the counter, shattering it—splinters of glass flew everywhere. Gina clamped her eyes shut, shoved her hands into her pockets to bury their tremors.

"What happened to Carl's marrow, Faye?" she demanded.

"I tried to stop Frankie. I told him as long as the man was still alive, he might change his mind and pay. I begged him—"

Gina stepped forward, her face only inches from Faye's. "What happened to the marrow?" she demanded.

"Go ahead, hit me!" Faye screamed. "Why not you, too!" She moaned and crumpled to the floor, covering her eyes, sobbing loudly.

"Tell me what he did with the marrow!" Gina stared down at her, wanting to stomp Faye like some noxious insect.

Faye's eyes opened, flitted like those of a trapped doe. "He dumped it . . . washed it down the kitchen sink." She rubbed at her cheek, but wouldn't look directly at Gina. "I pleaded with him not to. Told him I should return it . . . at

235

least put it in the repository in the wrong slot or something
. . . help cover our tracks."

"Are you telling me you simply watched while that maniac washed Carl Chapman's life down the drain?"

"Frankie would have hurt me . . . hurt me badly if I'd
tried to stop him. I was scared."

"So, you not only allowed yourself to live with a murderer, you helped him." Gina started pacing in front of
Faye. Suddenly, she was outside herself, hating what she
saw herself doing. Was she any better than Frank Nellis, or
her ex-husband if she could continue to intimidate Faye like
this?

"I'm taking you to the police," she announced. "Now! I
can't even look at you anymore without feeling sick to my
stomach."

Faye brought her knees up to her chin, rested her head
on them. "You can't do that."

"The hell I can't!"

"No, you can't! Frankie has Vinnie's marrow . . . he'll
destroy it."

"What?" She stared at Faye, who wouldn't meet her
eyes.

"You miserable bitch! You miserable, lying bitch! You
told me his marrow was in the lab; made me think Vinnie
was going to be all right." She pounded her hips with the
heels of her hands. "I wanted to believe you. How could I
have been so stupid? I should have looked for myself. To
hell with Vasquez . . . to hell with Bob Ghent!"

"It wouldn't have done you any good," Faye whispered.
"I put phony packets in the repository. Frankie still has
Vinnie's cells."

"You mean the rest of his cells, don't you? He wasted
one packet sending it to the Capellos."

"But it was only one packet."

"You don't hear yourself, do you; don't hear the despicable things you're saying."

"Yes, I do. I do, I do! That's why I'm here . . . I want Frankie and me out of this, once and for all."

"Well, isn't that great. What the hell finally woke you up?"

"Vinnie Capello," Faye whispered. "He's so young . . . just a boy."

CHAPTER 32

Faye wept during the entire drive to her apartment, then once they were parked, pleaded with Gina once again. "Please don't get Frankie into trouble; he's all I have."

"Fuck Frankie! All I want right now is Vinnie Capello's bone marrow."

"Please, Gina, please!" She clutched at her arm. "Let me do it; let me get the marrow out of the apartment. I'll bring it out to you; then give us time to get away." She tugged desperately at Gina's sweater, wringing it in her hands. "Can't you at least do that? Is that too much to ask?"

"Faye, listen! I told you, I'm going to the police as soon as the marrow is safely back in Ridgewood. That's it. Period!"

Faye wiped haphazardly at her face, dug in her purse for a tissue and blew her nose. "I'll go get it . . . bring it out to you."

"No, that's not going to make it. I'm going in with you."

"You can't. He hates you, Gina. He told me never to bring you around again. If he even sees you, he'll destroy the marrow. You have to believe me!"

Gina shivered. Faye's panic was infectious, seeping into nooks and crannies, bringing her own private hells to the surface. She needed to talk to Harry, had tried to call him from her apartment but there'd been no answer. Now, there was no way to reach him.

Gina cracked open the car door, looked across at Faye. The lab tech's face was wet and splotchy; the fading bruise around her eye added to her expression of fear and desperation.

238

As she continued to stare at Faye, her breath caught with an anguish that was loud and ragged to her own ears. She gripped the steering wheel to still her shaking hands. There'd been a similar time, when she'd sat outside her Bronx apartment, trying to work up the courage to tell Dominick that she was getting a divorce.

Two years! Two years and she still lived in fear of her ex-husband—Dominick the handsome, devil-may-care scamp, whom the act of marriage had turned into a brutal, fist-swinging adversary. She remembered his meaty fists, remembered how they had smashed into her face and any other part of her he could strike when life didn't click just right.

She fought with the moment, overrode the nearly irresistible temptation to touch her own face as she relived the pain. Instead, she chewed on a fingernail and swore under her breath at the lapse—she hadn't bitten her nails since . . .

Maybe she should lie, just a little bit. Something to reassure Faye, give her hope; something to quiet her down, make her feel more secure.

No! Suddenly she could see what was happening. She was being sucked through an all-too-familiar trapdoor, falling down, down into Faye's quagmire of helplessness, self-hatred, and pain.

Gina pushed away the debilitating memories, sat up taller. No lies! Faye had to face the truth. She would have to pay for her relationship with Frank Nellis, pay for her part in this whole mess.

"I can't trust you, Faye," she said, pushing open the car door. "If I let you go in there by yourself, you won't come back, I know it. You'll run, both of you."

"Gina, I could have done that in the first place. I didn't; I came to you. I want to help Vinnie, too."

"I'm still going in with you."

"He's already going to be suspicious, Gina . . . you know, because . . . because I'm so late . . . angry, even." She held out an imploring hand. "He's going to know something's wrong the second he sees you . . . us."

Gina refused to hear anymore, slid out of the car, trudged around to the passenger side, and opened Faye's door. "Okay, I'll wait outside your apartment in the hallway. He won't see me."

Faye reluctantly exited the car, refusing to lift her eyes as they went inside and waited for the elevator. Only when they were outside the apartment door did she lift her chin and look at Gina, then only to place a fingertip to her lips for silence.

Gina nodded and stood off to the side. She watched as Faye pulled a huge, jangling key ring from her purse.

Before Faye could insert the key, the door swung open and banged against the inside wall. Nellis filled the doorway, reached out and yanked Faye into the apartment.

Gina yelped, slapping a hand over her mouth. She inched away from the door, but Nellis lunged into the hallway, grabbed her around the neck, and dragged her into the apartment. She stumbled over Faye and sprawled across the floor.

"What the fuck are you doing here?" Nellis roared as he slammed the door shut. Before she could answer, he kicked at Faye. "As for you, didn't I tell you to stay away from this bimbo nurse?"

Gina edged up on one elbow, still shaken. "You bastard!"

"Shut up," he growled. "I haven't even begun to think about what to do about you."

Frankie reached down, grabbed Faye's arm, and yanked

her upright. "Didn't I tell you what would happen if you brought her here again?" He raised a hand threateningly; she cowered against him.

"Please, Frankie. Don't—"

He backhanded her hard enough to knock her off balance, caught her before she could fall, and pushed her up against the wall. "I warned you, and you didn't listen, so this should come as no big surprise, you stupid bitch!"

Frankie held her in place with a hand against her chest, lifting each arm in turn. With exaggerated curiosity, he examined a hand, shook it, slammed it back against her body; repeated the sequence with the other hand.

"I don't see them, Faye," he said, as if talking to a school child. "I don't see those little packages you were supposed to bring me tonight." He moved his hand up and pinched her cheek, then twisted her head back and forth.

"Where are they, goddamnit?"

"Leave . . . her . . . alone," Gina stammered. She struggled to her feet, aware of an old familiar whine coloring her words.

Frankie ignored her. "I asked you a question, bitch! Answer me!" When Faye remained silent, he pounded at her stomach with both fists. She clutched at him to stay erect, but eventually slid to the floor, her hands raking down the length of his body.

"Frankie, I didn't do anything bad," she cried.

"I don't believe you, you fucking whore. Where's the packages? And what did you tell her?"

"I couldn't . . . didn't . . . anything," she gasped, huddling against his legs. She turned to look up at him, her face a mottled red and purple. "Please don't . . . please don't hurt me anymore."

"Stop it!" Gina screamed. She tried to stay on her feet,

but Nellis kicked out sideways and knocked her back to the floor. "Don't you dare—" A shoe caught her hard in the mouth.

"Leave her alone," Faye yelled, pulling away from him.

"You son-of-a-bitch!" Gina shouted. She scrambled to her feet again, fists swinging. "Keep your goddamn hands to yourself, asshole! All I want from you is the fucking bone marrow you stole."

Fending her off with one arm, Frankie rubbed at a spot on his chin where her fist had connected. At the same time, he glared down at Faye.

"I didn't tell her anything, Frankie . . . I didn't tell her . . . she already knew—"

Nellis kicked Faye's face, once, twice, a third time. With each blow, she screamed; blood spurted in wide arcs from her nose, splattering on her arms, clothes, and the floor. He growled as he grabbed one of Gina's arms and dragged her down the hallway.

"Fucking women! Fucking women!"

Gina tried to dig her heels in, then snag a doorway, but he pulled her along effortlessly. Flinging open a hallway closet, he grabbed her around the neck and shoved her head forward into the opening.

"You wanted the marrow, bitch! There it is! Take it out of the freezer!" When she didn't move, he yanked her up with a choke hold. "Do you know how easy it would be to break your skinny, chicken neck? Now open the goddamn door."

Gasping, she opened the small refrigerator. Puffs of icy air surrounded her face. When the mist dissipated, she saw a pile of frozen marrow packets inside.

"If that's what you came for, bitch . . . take it!"

She planted her feet, pushed at the doorway, trying to

back out. He lifted her off the ground by her neck. Everything went dark, her mind drifted into blackness; then, as her feet touched the floor again, she floated back. She reached out, her hand a detached thing moving through thick molasses, trying to touch the nearest packet.

By allowing her to reach into the freezer, he'd loosened his grasp just enough to allow her to suck in a large gulp of air. When her head cleared, she knew he wasn't going to let her go. Vinnie! No! She couldn't allow Vinnie to become another Chapman.

"Let her go, Frankie," Faye cried out hoarsely, crawling down the hallway toward them. "Just give her the marrow and let's get out of here. We'll take our money and hide."

"Our money?" Scorn etched itself in every line of his face. "You know, you really are a stupid slut!" He held up a finger and waggled it at her. "Do you know that?"

He suddenly released Gina. She fell to the floor, still clutching one of the frozen marrow packets.

"You still don't get it, do you, you cow?"

"I . . . I don't . . . understand, Frankie," Faye said, using the wall to inch herself up, one bloody handprint after another.

Nellis sauntered up to her, jabbed a rigid finger into her chest. "Of course you don't. You don't understand because you're nothing but a dumb cunt." He grabbed her hair and yanked her up against him. "Isn't that so?"

"I . . . don't . . . what do you mean, Frankie?"

He rested a free hand on his hip. "What do you mean, Frankie?" he mimicked. "Look at you, you big fat tub of lard. Why would I take you anywhere?"

Tears flooded over Faye's face, rivulets in the dark mask of blood. "Frankie, that's not funny. You don't mean it."

Her voice rose to a high pitch as she threw her arms around his neck.

"Oh, I mean it all right. I'm not taking you anywhere, Faye."

He shoved her with both hands, knocking her against the wall. She slid down onto the floor in a heap.

"Do you get it now!"

He stepped forward and began kicking at her face again. Her wails diminished to tiny whimpers when he stepped away; there was only silence.

Gina wanted to evaporate, will herself into nothingness. She stared at Faye, a motionless broken doll covered with tears and blood. She could barely breathe, the air was so heavy with Frankie's vileness, the reek of his animal excitement, the stink of his oily sweat.

She clung to Vinnie's marrow, petrified. Nellis slowly shifted his focus from Faye back to her. She stared into his tar-black eyes, numb beyond comprehension; she finally curled into a tight ball, exposing as little of her body as possible to the fists she knew would soon hammer her.

No! Not again. Never again!

She straightened, slammed the freezer closed, and sprang to her feet. "You rotten son-of-a-bitch!" she screamed. "I don't know what sewer you crawled out of, but you're not going to get away with this. People at the hospital know where I am. If I'm not back—"

"Take your clothes off!"

"What?"

"I said, take your goddamn clothes off!"

"Fuck you!"

He reached down and grabbed Faye by the hair with one hand; with the other, he pulled a long, silver-and-black switchblade from his pocket, snapped the blade open, and rested the tip against Faye's jugular. A trickle of blood oozed from the sharp point, ran down her fleshy neck and flowed into the spattered gunk on her blouse.

"Now, take off your goddamn clothes or I'll pig-stick her right now."

Gina hesitated, then slipped out of her sweater, blouse, and white pants. "You'll pay for this, you—"

"Maybe, but not in this lifetime."

"Listen, Nellis, you haven't actually killed anyone yet. Don't make this worse than it already is."

He released Faye, allowing her to drop to the floor like a sack of flour. In two steps he was at Gina, clutching her arm. "Another stupid bimbo heard from." He smirked until her skin crawled. "Lady, you don't know shit. How do you think that asshole Chapman got it?"

"Frankie . . ." Faye's voice carried down the hallway as a muffled, squished sound. ". . . you said there would be no . . . killing . . . promised me."

"See what I mean about being dumb?" he said to Gina.

She tried to pull away, but her arm was clamped in his viselike grip. She hit at him with the bag of frozen marrow, knocking the switchblade from his hand. He grabbed the bag, threw it behind them. He flung an arm around her neck, choking her as he dragged her into the bedroom.

She struggled to breathe, felt herself losing the moment, drifting from one thought to another: Vinnie . . . poor kid . . . Nellis, Carl? Murder? Faye . . . hurting . . . dying . . . Harry . . .

She pulled weakly at the arm crushing against her throat. ". . . me go, you bastard." She reached up over her head and yanked his hair, clawed at his face.

"Got me!" he laughed. "Now whatcha going to do, beat me to death one hair at a time?" He tossed her like a rag doll across the bed, a few of his black curly hairs caught between her fingers. Up and down, up and down, she bounced, forcing rushes of air back into her lungs. She stared at the ceiling, which had become a maze of swirling, flashing lights, then scrambled for the side of the bed.

Nellis met her there, holding a fist-full of leather belts. Before she could retreat, he grabbed one wrist and lashed it to the headboard; rolling across her, he did the same with her other arm. She bucked up and down, kicking out at him, trying to keep her legs out of his reach. But within seconds they, too, were tied down.

"Let me go!" she screamed, twisting and turning, trying to free herself.

"Silly little weak things . . . never can get it together . . . just don't know how to mind . . . keep a man happy."

"Aren't you the tough stud, having to tie me down."

"Don't try that smart-ass psych stuff on me, bitch. It won't work."

"You didn't really kill Chapman, Nellis. Just more of your bullshit . . . trying to show off. God, you're pathetic." She tried to stare him down, but his eyes were unflinching, empty.

He turned his back on her and walked over to a chest of drawers. She struggled against the bindings, squeezed her eyes shut, and imagined slipping her hands through the leather. When she opened her eyes again, he was standing over her. He held a syringe and a small bottle of murky fluid.

"I don't have to tell you anything, slut. But it was no fun doing that cheap bastard, Chapman. Fast asleep . . . never knew I was even there."

He unscrewed the top of the bottle and placed it on the night stand. A vile odor floated down to her.

"It was easy," he said. "Hospital types are so smug, so stupid. Think they're in some kind of fortress. Don't you people know everything's reachable, and anyone is get-able?"

She yanked again at her bindings, stretching, turning. "Chapman was in reverse isolation."

"Big, fucking sweat," he said, sneering at her. "I used to clean those rooms. Special to you . . . nothing to me. Just another place to get in and out of. Popped a little of this stuff into his IV and no one ever knew I'd been there."

"It was you in Pathology chasing me, wasn't it?"

"Almost had you, too." He turned to look at her and smiled sweetly. "But what matters is, I got you now, darlin'."

She felt one of the belts loosen slightly. "What's in that bottle?"

He threw his head back and roared with laughter. "Why, darlin', this here's my own special mixture." He winked at her. "Got to admit, though, it sure don't smell too good." He dipped the needle into the bottle and pulled back on the plunger, filling the syringe with the dark, viscous fluid.

Gina turned her head from the stench. "What is it?"

"Well, now, you people might call it a coliform special," he said, setting the syringe down and putting the cap back on the bottle. "But truthfully, it ain't nothing but plain old shit 'n water. Not sweet, but pretty damn simple." He gave her a mock solemn nod. "And you gotta admit, there ain't no shortage of it, either."

He put the syringe on the bedside table and removed the belt from one wrist. She pulled and twisted her arm once more. It came free and she punched wildly at him. He caught her fist in one hand, trapped it under his arm, and held it there while he looped the belt around her biceps.

She watched her vein rise and bulge beneath the skin. He sat there smirking at her, looking from her breasts to the crotch of her panties as he retrieved the syringe and held it in front of her face.

"After this, we should have some time for an intimate moment or two. I'll bet Faye's already told you how well I can use a woman."

Gina watched the needle inch toward her arm. She yanked violently at her bound wrist, but the leather only cut deeper into the abraded skin.

"Help me!" she screamed. "Somebody, help me!"

Nellis laughed. She looked at his twisted features, blinked, and saw a second head floating above him. She blinked again—Faye's broken face hovered there, one side of her skull caved in, mashed almost beyond recognition; the lower half of her face had become a gelatinous mass of fibers, flesh, and displaced teeth.

Gina strained harder to free herself, yanked relentlessly at taut leather as she saw the switchblade poised in the air.

Faye plunged the knife into Nellis' neck; the tainted needle fell from his hand. He howled, releasing Gina's arm to claw at the wound.

"What the fuck?" He jerked the knife from his neck, flung it down onto the bed, and fingered the oozing blood. "How could you, darlin'? All I've done for you?"

Gina quickly freed her other hand and released the tourniquet.

"Bitch!" Nellis snarled, grabbing Faye by the neck and pulling her down onto the bed across Gina's legs.

"Frankie!" Faye moaned. "Sorry . . . my fault . . . all I wanted . . . was . . . to love . . . you. Take care of . . ."

Nellis drove his fist into her throat, crushing her larynx. He paused, fist raised, ready to strike again, but there was only deadly silence. His anger shifted back to Gina.

"Get off me, you bastard!" she screamed, scooping up the switchblade. She held it point-first out in front of her with both hands.

Nellis lunged forward, hands extended toward her throat.

Gina drove the knife between his ribs and up into his heart. He stared at her, hands falling limp on her shoulders. She shoved him aside, struggled to pull her legs from under him and Faye.

The eerie silence was broken by a mournful, animal cry of pain. Then another and another. It was several seconds before she realized the sounds were coming from her. She sat there, on the edge of the bed, rocking to and fro, her arms wrapped tightly across her chest.

Nellis' breathing was loud, stertorous. He stared at her; a smoldering anger sparked for a moment, then diminished to bewilderment as his eyes glazed over with the defeated look of a beaten child.

She looked back at Faye and quivered. Poor Faye. Poor broken, dead, Faye.

Gina covered her mouth with both hands and cried.

EPILOGUE

Gina and Harry lay sprawled across a ratty blanket she'd taken from the trunk of the Fiat. As they watched wave after wave curl lazily onto Muir Beach, a summer fog started building above the chilly offshore waters. The warmth of the day was rapidly dissipating, yet neither made a move to leave.

"Poor, misguided Faye," Gina said. "I still feel sorry for her." She swiped at a tear that escaped from behind her sunglasses. "People do such incredible things in the name of love."

The fog grew thicker, creating white puffs across the surrounding hills. Gina and Harry huddled closer, watched others gather their families, leash their dogs, and disappear from the beach.

Harry gently touched the large, ugly bruise on Gina's cheek, then carefully lifted the dark glasses that not only masked her tears, but also hid her bloodshot eyes—a souvenir from Frank Nellis trying to strangle her.

"How easy it is to point a finger at the other guy from a comfy seat on the sidelines," Harry said, his voice lowering to a whisper. "But she could have walked away at any time."

"Not Faye. To her it was a simple equation—she'd found someone to love and she was going to hang on to him no matter what." She took Harry's hand and pressed it tightly to her chest. "It's so horrible—all she could think about was pleasing Nellis."

"And in return, he beat her to death," Harry said. He

poured a cup of steaming coffee from a Thermos and handed it to Gina.

She took a sip and set the cup down next to her. "It was my fault. I blame myself for what happened to her."

"That's not fair. She went with you because she really wanted to save Vinnie."

"Detective Mulzini wasn't convinced of that," Gina said. "He insisted that without Faye, Nellis' whole scheme would never have gotten off the ground."

"Nellis needed an inside person," Harry said. He reached for Gina's cup and gulped down the rest of her coffee. "He found Faye, seduced her, and turned her into his slave."

"I wish the police hadn't made me sign a formal statement. Faye thought I was her friend. It felt like a betrayal."

"Yeah, well, the police operate like any good business— all the t's have to be crossed; all the i's have to be dotted." He rested his head against her shoulder and sighed. "Mulzini said it was a really ugly scene at Nellis' apartment. I'm just grateful you're alive."

Gina rested a hand on his head and ran her fingers through his hair. The only sound was the lapping of the waves and a whistling breeze moving through the shrubs.

"I killed a man, Harry," she whispered. "How will I live with that?"

He pulled back, lifted her chin, and stared into her eyes. "He would have killed you."

"I know," she said softly. "But it still hurts. I can't explain it. I only know it hurts like hell."

"And that feeling probably won't ever totally go away." He pulled her into his arms and whispered, "Give it some time, Gina."

"Mulzini said pretty much the same thing."

"At least there's a bright side to all of this," he said. "You saved Vinnie's marrow. That's a big plus."

She nodded. "I was sure the cells had been trashed, then Kessler gave me a thumbs-up. It looks like things are going to work out okay for the kid."

"So when do we set the date?"

She smiled, a spark returning to her eyes. "What date are you talking about, big boy?"

"Don't play innocent with me, lady. You damn well know what date I'm talking about—our wedding."

Gina struggled to her feet, held onto her sore side as she grabbed for her shoes, and limped toward the parking lot. She glanced over her shoulder and saw Harry shuffling through the sand, dragging the blanket behind him.

She eased herself into the driver's seat and waited while Harry tossed the blanket into the trunk and plopped down beside her.

"I didn't get an answer," he said.

"What was the question again?"

"Has anyone besides me called you a terror?"

"Almost everyone, and at least a zillion times." She pushed the key into the ignition. "How about this weekend?"

"What about this weekend?"

"Do you want to get married or not, Harry Lucke?"

He covered his eyes and shook his head, a big grin spreading across his face. "You are too much."

"Yeah, yeah," Gina said, adjusting the side mirror. "Let's get out of here."

The Fiat's engine gronk-gronked, sputtered, and fell silent.

"I'll be damned," she said and struggled out of the car. She flung open the hood and started tugging and pushing at every wire and hose she could reach, all the time swearing in Italian.

"Never, never, never, never will I ever buy another one of these spaghetti burners," she yelled.

Harry vaulted over the closed door of the convertible and walked around the car, laughing and pointing a finger at Gina. "Is everyone from the Bronx as cuckoo as you are?"

Gina's glare melted into an evil grin. She tried to move with a vampish strut, but tripped on her own feet and tumbled into Harry's arms. She held on tightly, snuggled into his neck, and whispered, "You bet your sweet ass."

AUTHORS' NOTE

Oncology is a fast-changing field of medicine, with ongoing research finding new treatments and techniques on an almost daily basis. As a result, an autologous bone marrow transplant (ABMT) may no longer be a leading form of treatment for some of the types of cancer described in this book.

ABOUT THE AUTHORS

Bette Golden Lamb, a registered nurse, has developed a parallel career as a painter, sculptor, and ceramist. Her art works have been shown and sold in California through galleries, stores, asssociations, and art festivals.

As a writer, her first published short story, "Slip Up," appeared in *Dark Star*, written in collaboration with her husband J.J. She has also written nonfiction pieces and is a member of Sisters in Crime. *Bone Dry* is her first published novel.

J. J. Lamb is a career writer: newspapers, Associated Press, Lloyd's of London Press, consumer and trade magazines, advertising and public relations, and fiction. He is the author of three private-eye novels (Ballantine & Carlyle), with German reprint (Wilhelm Goldmann Verlag), and several pubisihed short stories, the most recent in "New Mystery" and "Over My Dead Body."

A full-time freelance writer, he also has written two business-history books, and his byline has appeared in such publications as *Holiday*, *Modern Bride*, *Travel*, *Air Destinations*, *New York Times Magazine*, *California Living*, *Road & Track*, *International Business*, *Civil War*, and *San Francisco Magazine*.

He is a member of Mystery Writers of America (three years as MWA Northern California vice president), and a past member Private Eye Writers of America (PWA) and the Society of Professional Journalists. He has also served on annual awards committees for MWA and PWA.

The Lambs live in Northern California and are currently concentrating on writing medical suspense and husband/wife amateur sleuth novels, along with being involved in a number of other creative projects.